THE
HAUNTING
Quilter's OF Square

Copper Crow Publishing

Published by Copper Crow Publishing
Bella Vista, AR

First printing: July 2023

ISBN: 978-1-960985-02-6 (paperback) |ISBN: 978-1-960985-03-3 (ebook)

The Jenny Doan name and the Missouri Star Quilt Company names are trademarks of
and property of the Missouri Star Quilt Company, used with permission.
This is a work of fiction. Names, characters, business, events and incidents are the
products of the author's imagination.
Any resemblance to actual persons, living or dead, is purely coincidental.

More from the
Missouri Star Mystery Series

———————

The Haunting of Quilter's Square
Chain Piecing a Mystery
A Body in Redwork

Serial novellas published in
Missouri Star Quilt Co.- BLOCK magazine

———————

Mystery in the Old Quilt
Bound in Secrets and Lies
The Stolen Stitches
Clue of the Broken Template

Dedicated to my father —

Your love of beauty and creativity has shaped my passion.
Your strength of character has shaped my world.
Your desire to love, serve, and always stand up
for what's right has shaped my heart.

Thank you for your confidence and
your unwavering belief in me.
I love you, Daddy.

Hillary Doan Sperry
THE
HAUNTING
OF
Quilter's Square

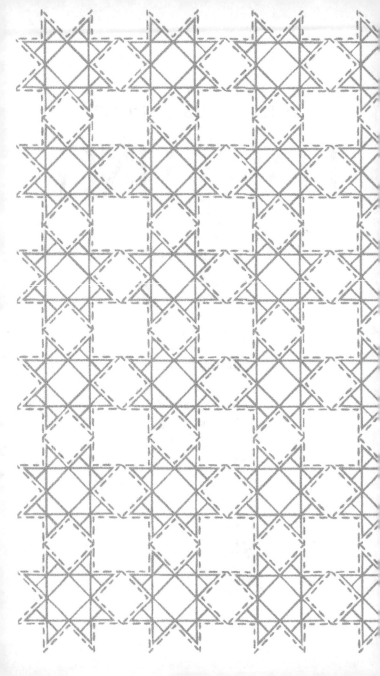

1

CLOUDS HUNG LOW in the gray afternoon sky as the camera crew huddled close on the crowded platform. The movie premiere had concluded an hour ago and the station had quickly flooded with boom mics, and excited fans. A large train engine, pulling more than a dozen cars stood strong behind them. A sentinel of days long past, it made a dramatic backdrop of black steel and history for the actors, actresses, and TV personalities doing interviews.

Then there was Jenny. Still not certain how she'd ended up working on a summer blockbuster, she smiled into the camera aimed at her and addressed her fans. "Thanks for joining me here at Quilter's Square, for the movie debut of Quilted Battle Stars." She was excited, of course. Jenny had been called in to help establish the authenticity of the quilting aspects of the film set in the 1940's. Across from Jenny, Cherry smiled widely, encouraging her to keep the energy up as she finished the live video. "The patterns and tutorials for our featured quilts will be online soon. I'm Jenny Doan—"

A train whistle blew as Jenny finished and the crowd applauded. The movie had been an unexpected surprise. Six months ago, she'd gotten the unbelievable call to consult on a World War II thriller using the quilters in an old mining community as one of the decoys.

Working with big name actors and their egos had been a unique challenge, but the crews behind the scenes were dedicated and hard working. In the end, and the movie had worked the art of quilting into the action of smuggling information and soldiers in a way that both entertained and informed. She'd been impressed and happy to be a part of it.

And tonight, she'd been invited to enjoy the fruits of their hard work at the premiere.

"Good job, everyone!" Cherry called out, wrapping an arm around Jenny. The younger woman walked Jenny back into the crowd, her red hair contrasting brilliantly with Jenny's short dark curls. With an age gap of several decades, and stark differences in fashion and tone, the two women were apparent opposites. But appearances aside, Jenny and Cherry had been fast friends for years now. Whether quilting, shopping, or getting into dangerous situations, the two could often be found side by side. "I still can't believe you got to consult on a Thomas Quinn movie. You are so lucky."

"Lucky is right," Jenny said, scanning the platform for her husband. Ron stood near the rails, admiring the trains. They were beautiful, but in Jenny's opinion, they were nothing compared to the vintage train station where they'd filmed. "I can't believe I'd never heard of this place before."

Glamorous swirls of cream and gold stone arched over the walls in tiled patterns of traditional quilt blocks. From half-square triangle stars to fence rails, the floors and arches were worked in large and small blocks of monochromatic patterns, giving the building its name.

The Haunting of Quilter's Square

Quilter's Square had been a grand train station in its day, renovated only a few years before for use as the corporate headquarters of the Summit Group. The owner of the Summit Group was a train aficionado and had kept a few trains active on a small loop for recreational rides, and apparently for the filming of blockbuster movies.

"I'm just glad Mr. Quinn invited you to consult." The moment the words had left her mouth, Cherry froze, gripping Jenny's arm and stopping their progress. "Oh, my gosh." Her voice had lowered to a hiss. "There he is."

Jenny followed her friend's gaze to find a salt-and-pepper-haired man in the next group over. His formal suit gave him the physique of a twenty-year-old and the jawline of a firefighter-turned-model.

"You mean Thomas?" Jenny asked.

"*Thomas?*" Cherry nodded. "Yeah, Mr. Quinn. *He's beautiful.*"

Her breathing grew shallow as she watched reverently, and Jenny chuckled. The interview with Thomas' group finished, and the cast members looked for directions to their next camera.

Jenny waved at the producer. She'd met him a few times—enough to make an introduction, anyway. "Do you want to meet him?"

"Yes! No." Cherry shook her head before ending with a very slow nod. The only thing she seemed sure of was that she couldn't look away from the handsome producer.

"Come on," Jenny said. "You can get an autograph."

"No!" Cherry insisted as Jenny caught Thomas' eye and started forward. "Don't. Jenny, he'll think I'm ridiculous. I need to check my makeup. Jenny—"

"Thomas." Jenny smiled at the producer who'd asked her to lend her expertise to his film. "This is my friend, Cherry Carmine. She's quite a fan of your work."

Despite his fame and busy schedule, he'd always treated her with respect. Whenever there'd been a question on quilting, he'd deferred to her knowledge. It had felt good to be appreciated by a man who could change the world in which he worked with a snap of his fingers. He greeted Jenny pleasantly as she held her hand out to Cherry. your work."

The admission sent Cherry's eyes wide, and she gave an awkward laugh. She stepped forward and held out her hand. "Hi. I'm Cherry. You have such a gift for visual storytelling and emotion. I really enjoyed your film."

Laughter would be inappropriate, so Jenny simply smiled as Thomas shook Cherry's hand.

"Thank you," he said. "That's high praise, but it's kind of you to say so." He glanced at Jenny and quickly changed his tune, leaning into Cherry. "I had a lot of plans that had to be changed, but thanks to Jenny's work, it really came together in the end. She put the heart back into this project."

"Well, I thought it was wonderful." Admiration oozed from Cherry's words. Stepping closer, Cherry kept her eyes trained on Thomas, her hand still in his. "This was your second attempt at making the movie, wasn't it? That's quite a triumph to resurrect a canceled film and make it such an acclaimed success."

Jenny cringed. She'd never specifically been told not to mention the previous cancellation of the film, but bringing it up to Thomas' face felt callous.

"I didn't know we'd already been classified as a success." He hesitated, but Cherry barely noticed.

"It's unofficial."

Cherry's rapt attention fed the producer's ego, and his next words came with a grin.

"It's untrue. I'm pretty sure that has yet to be determined." He took a step closer to Cherry, and she released a longing breath, hanging from his gaze. The space between the two intensified like a vacuum, sucking away life and sound as he focused on her. "The first production was canceled after my wife passed away. She would have made it shine."

"Your wife was Eleanor Grace, is that right? You dedicated this version of the film to her." Cherry asked, innocently.

The skin tightened around Thomas' eyes, confidence battling with emotion. "Yes. My wife and my lead actress. We wanted to honor her by finishing the film the way Elle would have wanted us to."

Jenny cleared her throat. Thomas had gotten overly emotional about his wife a couple of times now, and she didn't think he'd appreciate that happening here. "You did a wonderful job, Mr. Quinn."

"Thank you, again." Thomas removed his hand from Cherry's, tipping his head politely. "Your praise is a tribute to her."

He excused himself. Cherry's eyes locked on his retreating form.

"You forgot to get an autograph," Jenny whispered.

"Shoot." Cherry looked away, digging through her purse for a paper and pen. "Does it make me look desperate if I give him my number?"

"He's not ready. Besides, he's too old for you." Jenny immediately second-guessed herself as she heard Thomas' jovial laugh. "Isn't he?"

"I don't know." Cherry sounded slightly offended, but her lips still turned up at the corners before she looked away. "The man is ageless. Anyway, I'm not asking for a date. Just a signature . . . and maybe a drink . . . and to carry his children." Deep pink splotches bloomed on Cherry's cheeks as she casually shrugged.

"Cherry!" Jenny turned to her friend. "Tell me you did not just say that."

"What?" Cherry said. "You saw him, right? He's precious and kind . . . he's gorgeous. Thomas Quinn is officially the new definition of my type."

"Should we tell Officer Wilkins?" Jenny asked, teasing Cherry about her on-again, off-again relationship with the local police officer.

"Jenny? Oh, come join us, Mrs. Doan." A woman in a purple wrap dress cut Jenny's admonishment off, beckoning her into the circle of light cast by the interviewer's camera. "You have to meet this woman. All the quilting scenes were overseen by Mrs. Jenny Doan. She's amazing."

With all the cameras and lights, it took a moment to recognize the woman as Stella Grace, Eleanor's sister and the new lead actress in the movie. Stella turned to Jenny, glowing with genuine pleasure. It was the same expression she'd gotten when Jenny showed her how to do a whip stitch for her closeup. The girl had seemed excited just knowing how to hold the needle. "I'm so glad she agreed to be a part of our little project."

"It was an honor," Jenny said. "Everyone's been so kind—"

"Of course we were." Bonnie, one of the supporting actresses, stepped in front of Jenny and flipped a golden swoop of hair over her shoulder. "We're professionals. We know how and when to take instructions, even if it's not essential. Mrs. Doan contributed some very valuable slivers of experience."

Bonnie's harsh laughter shoved needles into her nerves. Bonnie's presence felt very much like an overused pincushion. Attractive, somewhat useful, and even occasionally essential, but always carrying the risk of sharp objects drawing blood from an unsuspecting hand.

Bonnie was the source of every complaint Thomas had brought to Jenny. No one had expected Bonnie's sewing skill to be perfect, just believable. Still, Bonnie had managed to mess up every scene requiring a needle and thread, before Thomas forced them into private quilting lessons.

Bonnie blinked at Jenny and turned to the camera with a simpering smile. "Even if Jenny didn't have much to contribute, Thomas wanted to make sure we were accurate, and we would never dismiss her work. I mean, she's sewing, but we're the ones making a movie, right?"

"So, you already knew how to quilt before the film, uh, Mrs. Beale, Bonnie?" The interviewer's lack of recognition got under the actress' skin in record time.

"Of course I did." Bonnie shot a venomous look through the woman and sighed dramatically. "You must be new. You haven't gotten a good shot of my dress yet. Most people know I'm the only one wearing a quality designer in this cast. Well, except for Warren Cole, the lead. But we recently broke up so we can hardly stand next to each other."

"Of course, but what we'd really like to know is: what was it like to work with Stella? Everything we've seen has been so incredible. And her sister was always flawless— such a talented family. We were devastated when Eleanor died."

Both Stella and Bonnie stared, speechless, at the expectant reporter before Jenny stepped forward. "Everyone in the cast did a wonderful job. The level of talent here is unrivaled —"

"It's true," Bonnie sneered, pushing herself in front of the group again. "I feel so blessed to work with them. We didn't know what Thomas would do when he had to recast after Eleanor, you know . . . died. A lot of people assumed I'd get the lead since it was between Eleanor and me before. But I was thrilled to let Eleanor's sister have it." Twisting slightly, Bonnie struck a dramatic pose like she was standing for a portrait. "It's just *so sweet* that Thomas chose her, even though she's new to the industry. Giving her this role, it's a great way to honor Eleanor."

Bonnie clicked her tongue, looking over to Stella, whose mouth hung open with barely contained shock.

"Stella, what's it like trying to step into your sister's shoes?" The microphone was thrust in the young woman's face, past Bonnie, who let out a squeak of surprise and stepped backward.

Jenny's involuntary laugh drew a glare from Bonnie. She stifled it quickly, but the crew had endless questions for all three of the women. By the time the interview was over, their smiles had melted into a flattened endearment. The three women stole glances at each other as they walked away from the cameras.

Outside of the set's lights, Jenny spoke up. "Ladies, thank you so much for inviting me and including me. I'm going to get back to my team before they have to go."

Cherry stepped forward to take Jenny back to their group. A whistle blew, and they all turned at the sound. A faded train pulled away from the platform.

"That's weird. Where's the whistle coming from?" Cherry checked her watch. "There shouldn't be any trains coming through until the whole cast leaves for the celebration trip."

Jenny stared at the specter of a train, its wheels turning in a slow mournful groan. "I don't think that's a normal train."

"Please, they're all just trains." Bonnie rolled her eyes and walked into the next circle of lights. Her greeting rolled out before the microphone got close enough to hear it.

"You don't see that?" Jenny asked.

Cherry gave Jenny a funny look. "Not to side with Bonnie, but all the trains look pretty normal to me."

Even as Cherry spoke, Jenny watched a young woman jumped onto the steps of the faded train as it picked up speed. Her deep purple suit and ruffled collar matched the felt cap she held on her head. She could've stepped right off the screen of Thomas' film premiere.

"What's she doing?" Jenny gasped.

"Who?" Stella scanned the edge of the platform.

"There." Jenny raised a hand and pointed at the woman. "She's on the train." Even at this distance, Jenny felt their gaze's link.

The woman's red lips parted, hanging open in silence before she released a scream that unraveled Jenny's confidence into brittle strands of fear.

"I don't know who you mean." Stella shook her head, smiling as if nothing had happened.

The whispers of the crowd died off as the shriek continued. It rattled inside her like someone had spilled a box of buttons in her throat, and she was simultaneously scrambling to keep them all together and not fall.

Then it stopped.

The woman, the train, the heart-wrenching scream. It all just vanished.

Jenny's pulse vibrated deep and fast, scattering in sharp rhythm against the cage of her body. She couldn't be the only one who'd heard the woman's terror. "Who was that?"

Stella had started to turn away, and Jenny grabbed her arm, as much for strength as to get her attention.

"She screamed—like she was dying." Jenny couldn't move as she stared at the train tracks where the woman had been.

"Who's dying?" Stella asked. "Are you all right?"

"I don't know." Questions threaded their way through Jenny's mind, piecing facts together into an unbelievable possibility. "You didn't see her? The woman . . . she screamed and then she was gone."

Stella's arm went stiff under Jenny's fingers. "Gone, like, she left?" Stella whispered. "Or gone like—?"

"Gone." Jenny had always believed in spirits. That people existed outside of their physical form, but she never assumed she'd see something supernatural. She tore her gaze from the platform and looked at Stella. "It was like she was from a different era, with golden hair and dark piercing eyes. Then she screamed, but the train didn't stop moving, and it all vanished, like she was—"

Nothing came out. She couldn't say it.

"A ghost," Stella finished for her, "With golden hair and dark piercing eyes." The young starlet trembled as she took Jenny's hand. "You saw my sister."

2

"I<small>T'S GOT BRASS</small> fittings on everything, even the door latches." Ron stumbled after Jenny as she dragged him through the historically restored train. "Even the fire extinguishers are vintage. I can't believe it's so authentic."

Stella stopped several steps ahead of the couple to check Jenny's ticket. "It's just a covering," she muttered. "You pull off the old cannisters and they're the same as every other fire extinguisher you've seen."

Ron didn't look disappointed. He leaned in closer examining the illusion, just as excited as before.

They'd been invited to join the cast on a three-day train ride around the mountains where Thomas Quinn had set and filmed his big movie. Three days on a train, and Ron couldn't be happier. He'd always loved trains. At one point he'd dreamed up an entire system of model trains to run throughout the house and tell time or deliver messages.

With a sigh, Stella looked up from the ticket and beckoned for them to follow. "Sorry, we got on a couple cars too early."

"You don't have to do this." Jenny held Ron's hand as they followed Stella down the dimly lit hallway of the train. "I'm sure we can find our room."

The gray sky outside reflected dimly off the polished cherry wood trim around the windows and doors. Portraits and framed news articles lined the outer wall of the train car. A printed map was posted at the end of the corridor over the embossed wallpaper. As far as Jenny could tell, they were about halfway through the sleeper cars.

Stella slid the door open at the end of the corridor. "Maybe," she said, glancing at Ron. "But I need to talk to you, somewhere private."

They passed through the vestibule that connected the train cars, Jenny pulling her still gawking husband along. They repeated the process twice more before Stella paused in the middle of the corridor.

"This is your compartment. Can we go inside?"

Ron dug in his pocket for the large key and stepped in front of Jenny, his hand hovering over the lock on the sliding door. "I can't believe we're here."

Stella looked up at the ceiling impatiently as the door to the vestibule they'd just left opened at the end of the corridor and two young women entered behind them.

Jenny patted Ron's arm. "We'll go exploring later. Can you let us in?"

He slid the key into the lock and held the door open. "Look!" His hushed excitement tickled Jenny's lips into a smile. "They've already brought our luggage, just like real porters."

Ron touched every trim board, corner, and prebuilt accessory as he worked his way into the room, from the tiny bookshelf to the button positioned at the end of the entry. It lit up when he pressed it, buzzing an unknown source for no reason. He settled on the leatherbound bench, moving a welcome basket of prepackaged snacks, and pulled out an information packet.

As Ron settled in to read, Stella slid the door closed behind them.

"Jenny," she whispered, hooking Jenny's elbow she pulled them back into the room's entry hall. "I need your help."

"My help?" Stunned at the request, Jenny took a step back. "I thought—what do you mean? I thought you were going to ask about the ghost."

"I am, I mean, it's kind of the same thing. I've been unsure about what to do, but now that Eleanor has shown herself to you, I'm sure you're meant to help me."

Jenny turned to see Ron looking over his paper at them. She shook her head at Stella. "I still don't know what you mean. Did you see her? The ghost—er, your sister? It didn't seem like you saw her."

"No." Stella drooped against the wall. "My brother is the only other person that I knew of who had seen her. I'm sure you've heard the rumors of the ghost train before now."

"Train?" Ron spoke up, fully ignoring his art-deco-trimmed information packet. "Who said anything about a ghost train?"

"It's a legend. That's all." Jenny waved her hand, dismissing the idea. "People claim to have seen a ghost train coming through Quilter's Square."

"You sound like you don't believe." Stella furrowed her brow at Jenny. "But you've seen it."

The irony of Jenny's unwillingness to claim the experience dragged over her mind. The haunting was supposed to have been a game of the crew, to tease and scare people. It meant nothing . . . until today.

"I didn't believe it before today," Jenny said.

"What happened today?" Ron looked confused. "You saw a ghost train? What do you have to do with this ghost train?" Ron turned his attention to Stella. "What does she have to do with a ghost?"

Stella paused, taking a breath before she answered. "The ghost train is a legend of Quilter's Square, but I think Jenny saw my sister's ghost. She died here while filming the movie about a year ago."

"Like here, here?" Ron asked, looking around the room.

"I'm sorry for your loss." Jenny struggled between sympathy for Stella and concern for his wife. "I remember hearing about that at the time. How did she die? Do they know what happened to her?" Jenny asked.

"No, not really. We only know what the police told us and they just stopped investigating after a couple of weeks. How could a case go cold that quickly. I've seen the file—" Stella's face crumbled as tears welled in her eyes. "Please, I need help. Eleanor and I didn't always get along, but her death wasn't an accident. I know it wasn't."

"How can you be sure?" Jenny's curiosity defied the concern in Ron's eyes.

"They said she hit her head and fell, accidentally shooting herself." Stella looked away with a sharp breath. "I was the one who found her, and there was no gun anywhere around her. Someone took it. You don't accidentally get shot and then hide the gun."

"Did they ever find the weapon?" Jenny bit her tongue as Ron put his arm around her.

"No." Stella looked at the floor, rubbing her toe over the carpet. "After the police ran out of leads Thomas just let it drop."

"That was a year ago." Ron's brusque tone was quite different than it had been moments earlier. "I'm sure they've refitted the train and cleaned it and even changed cars in that time."

"Not really." Stella's eyes drooped wearily. "The guy who owns Quilter's Square, also owns the train. It's a passion project of his, and when someone died on it, he was going to put it into storage. He thought it would scare people. It wasn't until Thomas decided to film again that they started repairs. He wanted it kept as much the same as possible so they could reuse all the B-roll."

Jenny frowned. "Still, it's been a year. So much has changed. I'm not sure what we can do."

"We have Eleanor," Stella said, intensity coalescing into tears at the corners of her eyes. "Both you and my brother saw her. She appeared to you. We can't ignore that."

"I understand, but evidence doesn't stick around because we want it too. It's been a full year." Pity rose in Jenny's chest. The poor girl had lost her sister, and no one seemed to want to find out what really happened. "I don't know who was here or what happened—"

"That's just it." Stella's eyes widened, excitement bubbling into her speech. "Thomas did all this for the movie, but Bonnie's made it a memorial. Everyone who was on the train or in the cast when Eleanor died will be back on the train again. At first, I thought Bonnie had been part of getting you here too, that maybe she wanted to find Eleanor's killer, but then I saw how she treated you, and well, she really didn't want you here."

"Part of getting me here, *too*?" Jenny asked.

"Oh, I, uh, knew that Eleanor had used your videos to learn to quilt. I actually have one of her quilts with me. She made it with my mom." Stella licked her lips and leaned back a step. "So, when Thomas cast me to replace her, I looked up your tutorials so I wouldn't look crazy, trying to talk fabric and quilts, and stuff. I happened on an article about you finding that killer, um, Hugo Handsome, or Henson, or something like that. No one knew it was him, but you figured it out."

"I was just helping a friend." Jenny shook her head. The memory of facing Hugo was a sudden and clear reminder that murders weren't just puzzles to be solved. There was real danger.

"Please," Stella begged. "Be my friend. Help me. We're on a three-day train ride with everyone that was here when my sister died. We can ask them questions and see what they know. Maybe someone's hiding something. This is my chance to find out what really happened. It may have been an accident like they said, but I need to know for sure."

THE COMPARTMENT DOOR slid closed between them. Stella's stoic disappointment stayed on one side while Jenny and Ron exchanged uneasy glances on the other.

"You promised," he said without looking at her.

"That's odd, I don't remember promising anything about helping or not helping or ghosts or—wait—" Jenny tapped a finger on her arm. "No, that's not right, I did promise to help."

"Jenny," Ron grumbled.

"What? You've always said one of my best qualities is that I help others."

"Yes, but . . ." Ron closed his eyes for a moment, "you promised this trip would be just you and me." He turned and shifted the tufted chair away from the wall. Pulling the fringed curtain back, Ron pointed out the window where only a few people remained milling around the platform. "This is like no trip either of us have ever been on. Look around you. This door is hand-planed bias-stripped wood paneling inset with mirrors." He'd released the curtain and patted the side of the glossy cabinet. "This is a once-in-a-lifetime experience. Please, you promised to do this with me. I don't want to be second place to a dead woman."

"Well, technically, being haunted is a once in a lifetime deal too." Jenny took a seat in the tufted chair he'd adjusted and Ron groaned. "Don't worry," she said. "I'm here for a vacation, a getaway with my husband."

He gave her a hesitant look as he shut the door. "You mean that?"

Jenny stood, crossing the tiny room in two steps. "I know I can't get involved. I feel terrible, but all she has is questions and suspicions. There's nothing to go on, and I didn't come here to play Nancy Drew with someone else."

Ron slid his arms around Jenny's waist, pulling her close. "You mean that? You wouldn't rather be doing something more exciting?"

"You are all the excitement I need." Jenny closed her eyes as Ron brushed her hair back. "I miss you, Ron."

Ron tightened his grip, and she leaned her cheek against his chest. His heartbeat, slow and steady, begged her to temper her own and join him.

"I've missed you too," he said.

Jenny set her hand on his bearded jaw, looking up into his blue eyes. "No one would appreciate this like you. Thank you for coming with me." It wasn't that she'd thought he wouldn't, but they'd been so busy lately that somehow it felt like their relationship had staled. It was no one's fault, but it happened and Jenny couldn't ignore it. They went through the motions of hello and goodbye without actually seeing each other. She fell into bed after Ron was sleeping and when she woke, he was already gone.

When she'd gotten the invitation to join the train ride, they'd both been excited to spend three days with no work, no Cherry, and no kids, or quilting. They were going to focus on each other.

Ron's eyes sparkled as he looked at her. "I'm feeling pretty lucky to have a trip with the most impressive train—and woman—" He corrected himself when she protested. "I've ever seen.

"Good save." Jenny smirked and turned back to her vintage tufted chair. "We were pretty lucky to be invited, except for the gho—"

"Don't say it," Ron mumbled, his brows lowering. "I know better than to think you'll be able to let it go."

"Don't talk like that. I'm on vacation." Jenny tried to look him in the eye, but her grin was ridiculous, and she turned to face the wall till she could control her expression. When she was more serene, she looked back. "Do you want to go explore? I've heard it's a beautiful train."

Ron paused, his lips turning up. "I'd love to." He started as a knock sounded on the door. "And never mind."

"It's probably the porter." Jenny's eye fell on the red light near the door. "You hit the buzzer when we came in." Jenny stepped away. "And if it's not, I'll tell them to leave." She grinned at Ron, who shook his head and leaned against the armoire.

Jenny slid the door open, ready to tip the porter, only to be met by Thomas Quinn.

"Mr. Quinn? I'm sorry, we're a bit busy. Can you leave . . . please," she said with a grandiose flourish after she caught Ron's look of doubt.

Thomas nodded and looked over her shoulder, trying to see into the room. "Is Stella here?"

Jenny automatically stood a little taller, attempting to block his view. "She just left. Is everything all right?"

"Bonnie said you've been together all morning."

"I don't know where she is. I told you she just left." In her attempt to close the door, Thomas' hand shot out, stopping her. With her best glare, she wished dull rotary blades and lost seam rippers on the man.

"Great." He clenched his jaw and smacked a fist against the wall. "No one's seen her, and we're about to leave."

"She's here somewhere." Jenny didn't see what he was getting all worked up about. "She helped us find our room."

"But Warren swears she got off the train and I need—" He cut himself off, turning a glare on Jenny as if she'd forced him to talk to her. He pushed away from the wall. "It's going to delay the train if she doesn't show up. If you see her, tell her to find me in the first-class lounge car."

He turned and walked down the hall without so much as a hello or a goodbye.

"Well, that's not his usual pleasant attitude." Jenny slid the door shut with a satisfying thunk. "I hope she's okay. She didn't mention going back for anything, did she?"

"Don't worry, Jenny." Ron's soft voice calmed her racing mind. He reached over, taking her hand and stroking her fingers. "Stella's going to be fine. She's got lots of people to worry about her. You don't need to."

Jenny let out a breath, exhaustion knocking the wind out of her. "What am I allowed to worry about, then?"

Ron pulled her out of her dark cloud with a laugh. "Nothing. You need to relax."

"I don't think I know how to worry about nothing." Jenny looked around the room. She'd brought handwork, but that wasn't enough for the whole trip. She'd go crazy. "We could go explore the train."

Ron stood, moving to the door. "All right. Relaxing can wait until later."

As they moved into the hallway, the train jolted, whistle blowing. Jenny steadied herself with a hand on the wall. Through the nearest window, the arches of Quilter's Square moved slowly away from them.

"It's time." Ron's face carried enough excitement for both of them. "Just feel this machine working. We're riding the rails. Tomorrow, we get to see the mining town where they filmed. Do we stop anywhere else?"

Grateful he was distracted, Jenny shrugged.

"Maybe the conductor will know." Ron moved down the hallway at a good clip.

Jenny followed. She wanted to enjoy the trip with him. She could still do that, ghost or no ghost.

The temperature dropped as Ron stepped into the vestibule between the cars. Frozen breath hung in the air, accentuating the chill. It was nothing, she assured herself, but she didn't look back. The ghost hadn't appeared behind her, the hall was empty, she told herself.

She followed Ron into the passage and glanced over her shoulder.

The hall *was* empty.

But, frost climbed the tiny window of the vestibule's door, arching delicately into the shape of a five-petaled flower.

3

FIFTEEN MINUTES.

She'd been smiling for fifteen minutes, trying not to worry about ghosts or gunshots or anything but the conversation at hand.

Ron leaned forward, enthralled, as the conductor, a Mr. Chris Wiley, talked about pistons and boilers and the train's fireman.

Jenny checked her watch. Yup, it had been fifteen minutes since either of them had spoken directly to her. And that was only, "Nice to meet you."

It was time to go.

It was probably time fifteen minutes ago.

Jenny stood, her smile doing its job. "Gentlemen, if you'll excuse me. I'm going to get a drink."

"Of course," Ron said. "Get me a hot chocolate, if they have it, please. Chris? Did you want something?" he asked, turning to the conductor.

Jenny kept her smile in place, waiting for his response.

"No, thank you. I'll need to be on my rounds soon, but the lemonade is my favorite." Round cheeks pushed at the bottom edge of the conductor's wire-rimmed glasses. "You should try it."

A polite nod was all she could manage in return.

Nothing to worry about, Jenny thought grumpily as she walked into the next car. Why am I not allowed to have something to worry about? She needed *something*.

Stella came like a magnet to her mind. Jenny scanned the room. Stella wasn't there, but she must be somewhere if Thomas had let the train leave.

The bar stools were warm maple brown on wrought iron spindles bolted to the ground. A gentleman with thick, square glasses and dirty blonde hair occupied the center stool.

"Do you have hot chocolate? And, I guess, a lemonade," Jenny asked the approaching bartender.

"Did Wiley give you that recommendation? Don't listen to him." The gentleman tipped his head in the direction of the conductor. "I always get a gin and tonic to start a trip. Soothes the nerves."

"Thank you." Jenny slid onto the stool next to him. "I'll stick with lemonade."

The man shrugged, pulling the lime off a stocky glass, squeezing and discarding it in a quick motion. "You're Jenny Doan, right?"

"Have we met?" She held out her hand in greeting, trying to remember if she knew him or if they'd interacted on the movie set.

"Nah, you're the quilt lady." His smile curled pleasantly, as he shook her hand, revealing a sliver of pristine white teeth. "I've heard about you."

"From who?" she asked, considering him.

"Bonnie. I'm Carey Mills, Bonnie's agent."

"Oh," she said. A wash of understanding colored her view of the man and his pleasant expression. "So, you've heard all the really good stuff."

Carey chuckled, lifting his glass. "I know how to tell when she's being real and when it's all emotion. And I research . . . everyone. I know everything. If I didn't, I wouldn't be able to keep her working."

"So, is that why you're here? Research?"

"I'm here because, I'm not the only one who likes to get what they want." He took a long drink of the clear liquid in his glass and settled back against the bar, his elbow propped so he could spin the drink on the counter. "Bonnie's a determined woman. She wanted me here."

Realization dawned and Jenny stood, swapping stools. "Oh, you're waiting for her. I'll move."

Jenny didn't need to be even further on Bonnie's bad side. It didn't matter that Jenny was old enough to be Carey's mother.

"Don't worry about it. I'm not waiting. She'll find me when she's ready. Like all women in show biz, she does what and who makes her happy."

Jenny cringed. She felt bad for this man, drinking away worries on behalf of a malicious and careless woman. The bartender put Jenny's drinks down, and Carey raised a hand to someone at the far end of the car.

"Nice to meet you, Jenny." Carey picked up his drink, taking her hand in his free one and kissing her fingers in an old-fashioned gesture. "I'm sure I'll see you again." He crossed to the train car to the brunette he'd waived to and greeted her with a similar kiss.

Jenny picked up her drinks, certain that Bonnie's agent wasn't on her list of *nothings* to worry about.

She handed Ron his drink and Mr. Wiley claimed her lemonade. Jenny let him. The drinks had only been an excuse to escape. She glanced at Carey, who would surely get a kick out of the conductor and his lemonade, only to see him at a table with the woman he'd met. She turned away briefly and his smile drooped, but like flipping a light switch, it was in place again when she looked back.

Jenny returned to the bar and kept walking. Her restlessness had taken charge over her worries. She could not sit still any longer. Ron would talk to the conductor, and she could go looking for Stella.

The lounge car was next to the bar. Couches and chairs lined the walls, upholstered in maroon and gold floral tapestry. The large windows glowed under the soft light of pendant chandeliers decked in hanging crystals and curling metal. Jenny passed several intimate groups and even more boisterous parties in two lounge cars before she made it to the empty hallways of the sleeper cars. Still no sign of Stella.

After passing her fourth train car of hallways, Jenny nodded to a conductor stationed in the corner. She was headed toward the engine, she was certain of it. She could go only one of two directions, but she hadn't found Stella or the dining car yet. She thought over Ron's directions and kept walking.

To her relief, the next car was a dining car. Tables dotted the walls, the swirling woodgrain tabletops polished to a reflective gleam. It would most likely fill up at dinnertime, but for now, only a handful of people lounged at the tables, propped against warm wood and thick fabrics. No one even glanced her way.

Two doors stood in the corner beside a polished cherry wood stairwell leading up to a second level. If the view was good, it could be a good place to sneak away with Ron. *There,* she thought, *that's a good something to worry about.*

Jenny made it only a couple of steps from the landing before footsteps and the soft growl of a man's voice stopped her progress. The voice was behind another door at the top.

"You don't get a say. You need me, so I'm here, and I'm not leaving."

Jenny took another step up and then changed her mind, retreating down the steps.

"Don't screw this up for me—" The second voice was feminine, and just as insistent.

"It's not about you."

"No. It's about her," the woman responded. "It's always about her."

Jenny glanced around. Several people had left, and no one else seemed to be paying attention. She took several more steps away and stopped cold as the woman spoke again.

"I told you I'd find the killer. Isn't that enough?"

Jenny knew exactly who was behind the door. Only one person on this train was looking for a killer.

Except if Ron knew she was listening to Stella's conversation, he might consider murder to be a viable alternative. Well, not really. And that's a good thing because looking for one killer was challenging enough.

Jenny had stupidly thought that without her, Stella would let the search go. She hurried down the remaining steps, reaching the bottom as the door to the upper-level room opened.

Jenny ducked under the stairs as footsteps moved down.

"Jenny?" Stella tapped her shoulder from the opposite direction, and Jenny did a double take.

"Stella." Jenny glanced at the young woman as someone in a long coat exited the stairwell. "I thought you were upstairs." She looked behind her to the woman, crossing the room. Whoever she was, it wasn't Stella. "Excuse me for a moment."

Jenny circled back to the steps and hesitated only briefly, watching the person in the trench coat walk away. If she'd paid a little more attention she would have known. The elbows of the coat were so worn they'd faded to an off-white. A leather strap hung off the arm zigzagged together in red thread that dangled precariously from the fabric. Not your typical movie star coat.

Above her, the door to the upper-level dining room cracked open. She hurried up the steps and pushed inside. The lights were out, but the entire room was bright with daylight. Floor to ceiling windows lined the outer wall, curving overhead into a partially domed roof. It was gorgeous and completely empty.

The other person involved in the argument was gone.

"Did you see anyone come down the stairs just now?" Jenny asked as she descended the steps.

"I don't think so." Stella looked confused. "Were you hiding?"

"No." Jenny scanned the room. She'd assumed anyone looking for a killer would be Stella. Now she had unwitting knowledge that another pair of people were looking for a killer, and she had no idea who they were. Goosebumps prickled over her arms as she realized she couldn't be sure who the victim was. All she knew was someone was looking for a murderer.

"Stella?" A miserable-looking young man stumbled into them, saving Jenny from explaining what she'd overheard. "Where've you been? Everyone's looking for you."

"Warren." Stella didn't sound impressed. "Exactly the person I didn't want to see."

The heartthrob that played opposite Stella in Quilted Battle Stars didn't look like himself. Warren's usual rugged appeal, from stubbled chin to mussed hair, now leaned toward unkempt, highlighting his desperate eyes.

Stella turned away, her brisk movement giving Jenny no choice but to follow. Warren did the same.

The three of them squeezed down the aisle toward the sleeper cars while Warren pled helplessly with Stella.

"Come on. You can't believe what they're saying. We were just friends. You're the only girl for me."

Stella turned to Warren, catching her breath as he stepped closer. "Not now. Please?" She turned away and grabbed the handle of the door, leading into the next car.

"Stella." He groaned her name, and Jenny chastised herself for the empathetic distress rising under her skin. Warren pushed forward. "You can't keep walking away, Stelle. It's a rumor. That's it."

"A terrible rumor." Regret flavored the words as Stella stepped into the passage. "But most rumors are founded in truth." She let Jenny in with her and slid the door closed on his anguished pleas.

Stella led Jenny into the next car before Jenny stopped her. "Is everything all right? What happened? Can I help?"

"You can." Stella steadied herself against the wall of the narrow corridor. "Help me find Eleanor's killer."

Jenny kept her voice low and shook her head. "But Stella, there's nothing—"

"I might have something. It's just not what I thought. I found out that Warren had an affair with Elle before she died."

"Warren? I thought you two were—"

"Almost." Stella glared at the vestibule door. "Thomas just said that Warren and Eleanor were together before she died. They were still married." Stella's breathless explanation reached a peak of pitch and emotion. She gasped a breath. "Eleanor had been saying for a while that she was going to leave Thomas. What if Warren got mad that she wouldn't leave Thomas and murdered her."

"Or, an affair could've been the motive for Thomas to be the murderer." Jenny held her breath, waiting for Stella's response. She'd accused Stella's brother-in-law of murder. Even with strained family relations, that kind of accusation was dangerous.

A young man stepped into the hall near the end of the corridor, and Jenny pulled Stella from her frozen position. With her fingers wrapped tightly around Stella's arm, the two women walked toward the vestibule and hopefully Stella's room.

"It always comes back to Thomas." Stella's voice was low and bitter, the hurt tainting Jenny's sympathies. "There are so many reasons it could be him, I know you're not sure about all this, but I am going to find out who killed Eleanor.

This might be my only chance. Right now, everyone is here. After this trip, people are going to spread out. Bonnie's going to film overseas. Thomas goes back to California. And who knows where Elle's old agent will end up. Jenny, my sister was murdered. Even if nothing comes of it, I have to try."

With everything she learned Jenny felt more certain Eleanor had been murdered. "I didn't want to believe it," she said. Stella's exuberance faded as Jenny spoke, but Jenny steeled herself for what she was committing to. "But I think you're right. We have to try."

Stella's eyes snapped up, catching Jenny's determination. "You'll help me?"

Jenny nodded, glancing up and down the corridor. "I will, but first," she whispered, holding a finger to her lips. "I need to see where Eleanor died."

FIRST-CLASS MEANT SOMETHING entirely different to Thomas Quinn than it did to Jenny.

The elite section of the train had been designed for the high-class society they'd represented in the movie but was currently being enjoyed by Thomas, his co-producers, and stars.

After crossing through the regular sleeping cars and the bar, Thomas had met and joined Jenny and Stella, leading them through the second half of the train.

Parlors adjoined a luxury lounge that gave way to sleeper cars boasting large beds, damask curtains, and carved moldings around marble sinks with golden fixtures. Music played softly from hidden speakers as they entered the converted caboose.

"Eleanor died here?" Jenny asked, walking past what looked like tuffets on stools, round, blue velvet pillows with thick fringe hanging from the cushions to the floor. Silver-blue wallpaper melded the walls with the sky in three-sixty windows. "Did it look like this before?"

"Almost exactly." Stella stood in the doorway. She hadn't crossed the threshold, and it was easy to guess why.

"There?" Jenny followed her gaze to a comparatively average corner.

Stella stepped into the caboose turning in the aisle. "She wanted to talk, and I didn't want to. So, I made her come to my room. And I was so mad when she didn't show up. And then I found her—"

Silence hung between them. Jenny glanced at Thomas. He stood with his feet planted wide and his arms folded, his silence was different than Stella's. Thomas was keeping the world out, and Stella seemed suffocated by it.

"She was already gone?" Jenny asked.

"Yeah." Stella's lips barely moved. "There was so much blood."

"Ruined the costume," Thomas muttered.

Stella scoffed. "The costume?"

"You found her in the corner? Where's the bullet hole?"

Thomas passed Stella, gesturing to the lower part of the wall. "Right in here, but we patched it and replaced a huge chunk of the wallpaper during repairs."

"Just the wallpaper?" Jenny scanned from the wall to the ground. She didn't expect to find anything, but she looked anyway.

Thomas crossed his arms over his chest, walls going up thick as bolts of fabric. "There's a pretty important scene in this car when they hang quilts over all the windows and hide the soldiers. And it's not like they gave me a whole new budget."

"When did you get here?" Jenny asked.

"I don't know. Not long after Stella."

"You're kidding, right?" Stella cocked an eyebrow. "I was only a few cars over. Elle was supposed to meet me at quarter to four and just a few minutes to the hour I heard the gunshot. I came running and found her dead, splayed out over a velvet cushion. Thomas didn't get here for an hour."

"I came as soon as I heard," Thomas snapped right back at Stella.

"You weren't in your room?" Jenny asked.

"No. I wasn't in my room. I was filming a movie, and we didn't have much time left with the train." Thomas fierce glare fired heat in his eyes, tension tightening his neck in his collar.

"That wasn't an accusation." Jenny stepped back, leaving room for his emotion to flare at a safe distance.

The boiling point of his anger visibly lowered as Thomas took a breath and nodded. "Right, sorry."

Jenny's pulse slowed as she realized he'd scared her. Scared wasn't a normal state of being for her. She reshaped the emotion to focus on what had happened. "Do you either of you remember anything else?"

Stella glanced at Thomas and shook her head.

"Stella." Thomas moved to the door. "We've got an interview scheduled for you and Warren before dinner. You ready?"

Stella shot Jenny a loaded glance and turned to the door. "We'll talk later. I'll see you tonight."

"Tonight?"

Stella hesitated as Thomas pulled the door to the vestibule open. "Bonnie's hosting a dinner tonight. It's supposed to be for Eleanor. I must have forgotten to mention it. But you'll come, won't you?"

"Are you sure I'd be welcome? Bonnie and I aren't exactly close." Jenny had been to parties where she wasn't invited. They didn't turn out well.

"You should be there. I want you there. I'll make sure it's okay." Stella left with Thomas, leaving Jenny alone in the pristine room.

Jenny circled and stepped into the corner where Eleanor had died, then sat on the cushion where she'd been found. The temperature dropped, and a breeze ruffled the fabric of her slacks. Blue petals drifted over the dark wood floor, fluttering against the fringe of the benches. Jenny reached down to pick several up, stopping suddenly.

Something glinted under the edge of the baseboard. She reached for the slip of metal, trying to unwedge whatever had been lost. With the help of a pen from her pocket and careful movement, she pulled a thin gold ring from under the wooden trim. A tiny diamond pressed into the metal.

Inside was an inscription, *Always have, Always will.*

4

LUXURY VANISHED LIKE heat sensitive ink under an iron as Jenny walked from the first-class parlor car into the bar where she and Ron had met the conductor. The pendant chandeliers and polished wood tabletops had seemed so glamourous before she'd seen the rest of the train.

Stella and Thomas sat in the lounge car on an embroidered couch with Warren and a man holding a notepad and pen.

"Jenny?" Stella jumped up off the couch as Jenny passed.

"What is it?" Jenny turned back, the two men from the couch watching as Stella slid past and stopped her.

Stella pulled Jenny into the lounge seating on the opposite side of the car. "Dinner is at six-thirty in the upper dining room, but if you have time, can you meet me at six? Just by the stairs."

Jenny's mind jumped to her husband and the plan to spend the trip together. Hopefully, he'd enjoyed his visit with the conductor and it wouldn't be a problem. "Of course."

Stella smiled widely and kissed Jenny solidly on the cheek. "I'll see you tonight." With a flourish, she spun back to her interview and found her seat on the couches.

Jenny reached for the ring and paused. The reporter had already begun questioning the movie stars again. She slipped the ring loosely on her pinky finger. It spun as she contemplated interrupting to show her, but she'd see Stella soon. She could show her the ring then.

Jenny followed the string of vestibules and corridors and made it back to the car where her compartment was. Pulling her sweater tight across her chest, Jenny hoped Ron had made it back already. If he wasn't there she'd have to keep walking all the way to the other end of the train to find him. It would be just like him to want to be as close to the engine as possible.

A shiver struck Jenny as she shut the vestibule door behind her. Cold seeped into the corridor around her. White clouds of her own breath diffused before her. "Eleanor?"

Cold and regret fused Eleanor's name to Jenny's tongue. She wasn't even sure she'd said it out loud. A breeze rustled past Jenny's hair, and something clattered to the floor. Jenny pivoted to the sound.

A portrait lay on the floor.

A row of framed articles and pictures lined the wall below the windows. Nearest Jenny was an old image of the exact train they were on or one quite like it, with a ribbon spread in front of it. Next to that was a framed news article labeled *Inaugural flight of "The Flying Bear"*. Jenny stretched her sweater tighter in the cold corridor, a gasp of uncertainty on her lips.

She picked up the frame. Bright red lips and a porcelain face smiled up at her on the face of the woman from the platform. The picture slipped from her hands, cracking against the wood floor. It didn't break, thankfully, but when she picked it up, a chip had broken away from the simple wooden frame.

But that wasn't what held her attention.

"Eleanor?" She wasn't sure if she was asking the woman or the ghost. A breeze answered, and Jenny hung the picture on the empty hook.

Vibrant, overly saturated color tainted her purple suit and pill box hat. A sparkling blue pin in the shape of a five petaled bloom over a swirl of diamonds was pinned to her lapel, completing the vintage look.

A tag hung next to the portrait. *In Memory of Eleanor Grace.*

"It's really you," Jenny mumbled to herself. "We're going to need your help."

"It's gone," a woman said behind Jenny.

Jenny spiraled toward the voice and found only empty air.

No one was there. A chill ate its way over her frozen skin. Unexplained fear swirled at the base of her spine, tingling in her bones.

"Eleanor?"

Silence answered Jenny.

It's gone.

She rushed back through her bedroom door and closed it on the hallway, shutting herself in the warmth of her room. If Eleanor really did want her to help, Jenny would need more strength than this.

Her bedroom compartment was as empty as the hallway. She considered Eleanor's ghost and amended her assessment. Hopefully, her room was emptier than the hall, and without Ron in the room, she needed a distraction.

She needed to think through her current situation.

She needed her quilting.

Jenny fished her luggage from the armoire, removing the handwork from inside, along with a change of clothes fit for a dinner party. Jenny perched in the thick chair and laid out tiny, colorful, hexagons of English Paper Piecing on a small table.

The unsewn hexies were only two inches across—too small to be full blocks, but they'd have to do. Jenny placed a mini purple hexagon against the wall. It stayed.

It always helped Jenny to visualize things when she laid the patterns out in front of her. Quilting made order of chaos. Today it would be order in miniature.

Jenny tapped the little cotton shape. "You're going to be Eleanor." She put a blue block next to it with a deeper blue one creating a trio of hexagons. "And Stella. And Andrew. The Grace family."

The little purple and blue hexagons clung to the wall, twisting her heart with pain. The entire family was tangled in tragedy.

She picked up an orange hexie, "Thomas Quinn." His patch of fabric was fussy cut around a lone tree. How appropriate.

"And Warren." Sadness washed over her as she pressed a piece of green cotton to the wall. *Oh, Warren*, Jenny thought.

She dug through her quilting bag and pulled out a pink hexagon. "That's the affair." Pressing it in place, Jenny frowned at the block. "For now," she muttered.

It was strange. She'd known people suspected of crimes before. It was always sad, but this time the people on her list of suspects were first known through the glitz and glamour of Hollywood. Their fame made them larger than life, and every accusation, every suspicion, gave her the feeling of heroes falling at her feet.

37

With pursed lips and determination, Jenny sat back and looked at her mini-design wall. When all your suspects pretended for a living, how could you know who was telling the truth?

The Grace family. Thomas. Warren. The affair.

Jenny reached out to move a block and froze. She couldn't bring herself to touch them. Something wasn't right, but she couldn't move them. Not yet. She pulled back.

It's gone. The chill of the words whispered down her spine, raising the hair on the back of her neck. The temperature had dropped noticeably.

The door slid open, and Jenny jumped.

"You're here," Ron said, letting himself in. "I hope you enjoyed your tour of the train as much as I did."

Jenny exhaled and chuckled. "I saw most of first-class."

"Oh, now you've got movie star friends you're moving up without me, huh?"

"Not exactly." Jenny picked up her needle and thread and started stitching a pair of hexagons together. "What about you? Did you get to ask the conductor all your burning train questions?"

"Steaming." Ron grinned at her expectantly. "Steaming questions. Because it's a steam engine!" Ron laughed to himself as he unbuttoned his cuffs and rolled them enough to be out of his way. "That was funny," he muttered, leaning back. "Chris gave me that one."

"Chris? Oh, the conductor." She winced as she jabbed her finger with the needle.

Ron narrowed his eyes at her. "You seem distracted."

Jenny sighed and put her needle and fabric down. "I am. I got an invitation to dinner tonight."

Ron's eyes lit up. "Right! Chris invited us. The night crew takes over at the dinner shift, so he asked if I wanted to join him."

"He asked you?" Jenny didn't mean to sound so relieved, but even without Bonnie's dinner, she didn't think she could handle a full meal with the two train-obsessed men.

"Not just me," Ron grinned, "he asked us. He knows we come as a pair."

Jenny's mind spun, trying to find a way out of dinner that wouldn't hurt her husband. "That's very sweet. But I'm sure you two would have more fun if you don't have to worry about me."

"You know I wouldn't leave you to eat alone." Ron settled onto the bench that would be one of their beds that evening.

Jenny picked up her needle, taking a wide stitch that would probably need to be removed and forced herself to pick up the motion of sewing again. "Actually, I got a dinner invitation too. Stella asked if I could join her at a dinner party."

"Stella Grace?" Ron's expression darkened. "Is this because of her sister? I thought you weren't getting involved in that."

"I'm not involved so much as concerned. After all, Eleanor died a year ago. Stella is still hurting, and I'm humoring her. I'll still be here with you. She's asking questions and if I can help her answer them, why wouldn't I? She's just a friend having a conversation about her recently passed sister."

"And all her potential killers."

Jenny didn't answer directly. "Of course it sounds bad like that. It's not wrong to care about someone. Nothing may come of it anyway. It's not like we're home and I can send Cherry to research for me."

Jenny's needle stalled. She could ask Cherry to do some research, though. Do some internet searches and such.

"You're smiling." Ron slumped lower in his chair.

"Am I?" Jenny made several quick stitches while attempting to tame her expression. "Why don't you go with Chris tonight, and I'll go with Stella. Can we plan on breakfast tomorrow?"

Ron's lips tightened, disappearing behind his facial hair. "Fine. I'll go talk trains tonight. Tomorrow is all about us, though."

"That shouldn't sound like torture," Jenny teased.

"Maybe it wouldn't if we'd made us a priority today."

AS PREDICTED, THE dining room had begun to fill as waiters in white coats and bowties attended the guests. Jenny and Ron wove through the slowly filling crowd, searching for their dinner partners.

It wasn't quite six, and Jenny had spent an hour with Ron, the two of them awkwardly trying to appease the others' unknown needs. They rarely had moments like this. Jenny was usually very good at expressing what she needed. Ron seemed more hurt than she'd expected, and as she. They made their way into the dining room, Ron found Chris first. He'd traded his conductor's uniform for a dinner jacket, and Ron left her with barely a kiss on the cheek.

She bit her lip, worry piecing its way across her heart. Ron was hurt, and Jenny had to figure out how to make it right.

She stopped at the base of the stairs. Stella would be there soon, and Jenny would have to shift her focus again.

Thomas and the reporter made their way upstairs, both dressed in full suits and the reporter wearing a vintage fedora with a press pass stuck in the band. Jenny almost laughed, but it wouldn't be appropriate.

"Jenny?" Stella tapped her shoulder from behind, the same way she had that afternoon.

Jenny gasped in surprise when she turned around. Instead of Stella, Eleanor stood before her wearing her deep purple suit with the ruffled cream collar. Her pill box hat had a swath of netting over the front, and she clenched a camera in her gloved hands. It was Stella, but she was the image of Eleanor down to the pearl buttons at the edge of her short white gloves.

"I know," Stella said, tugging at her hat. "It's a bit much, but Bonnie insisted we wear our costumes to continue the dedication of the movie in Eleanor's honor. Do I look all right?"

Jenny blinked, processing Stella's duplication of her sister's character, and nodded. "You look perfect."

Stella had opted for pale pink lipstick instead of the red that Eleanor had been famous for, but otherwise she looked almost identical. While not an exact replica, dressed like this, they could have passed for twins.

"Thank you." Stella blushed. "Come this way. I need to speak with you privately."

In the shock of Stella's appearance, Jenny hadn't noticed that she held a door open behind her.

The door hid under the stairs. She'd noted it that morning but hadn't given it a second thought. Following Stella inside,

Jenny was surprised to find a bustling galley kitchen prepping for dinner.

"Should we be in here?" Jenny stepped aside for a woman carrying a large plate.

"Of course." Stella beckoned her forward. "But come quickly, or we'll be in the way." Across the kitchen, Stella opened another door. This one led to a dark stairwell.

Jenny peered up the steps to a sliver of light in the distance transformed the blackness to gray. "Where does this go?"

"The upper dining room. Hurry, we need to close the door."

The upper dining room. That's where Jenny had overheard the people looking for a killer. A back stairway was a convenient way for the second person to leave without getting caught.

The dim lighting was enough to make steps visible.

Stella didn't stop till she reached the landing at the top. In hushed tones, she explained. "I'm sorry for the cloak and dagger act, but I've overheard more than my share of conversations through the compartment walls, and I didn't want to share this with Thomas."

"Is it something about your sister?"

Stella nodded in the gray light, holding a finger to her lips. "Since you're ready to help now, I wanted to share a bit more of my suspicions. The morning before Elle died, I overheard her talking to my brother about packing a bag and quitting the movie. She wasn't even going to finish filming."

"Are you sure? That could ruin a career." Jenny hadn't heard anything like that before.

"It could but I don't think she cared. If I heard her right, she was going to leave Thomas." Stella let the accusation hang for a second. "He was already massively over budget and to lose Eleanor in the middle of filming would have put a huge black mark on his career. Professionally and personally."

"Killing her wouldn't fix anything, though." Jenny blurted the words out in a whisper.

"But it did. The backers of the film were all sympathy. They gave him more time, and another shot at filming." Stella looked toward the door where light filtered into the stairwell. "My room is right next to Thomas', just like last time. I wasn't a star in the movie then, but she's my sister. It probably also helped keep the rumors down. They fought all the time. I don't know if he was ever physical, but Eleanor was scared of him. And . . . he had a gun."

"On the train?" Jenny was surprised but not shocked. "I'm surprised he'd have it while you were filming."

"He started carrying a small pistol after getting mugged a few years back." Stella bit her lip, her whisper getting softer. "It was while he and I were together."

"I didn't know you two dated." Jenny chased her eye contact, but Stella wouldn't look at her.

"It was brief. He met Eleanor through me. She shot to fame with him, getting bigger and bigger roles, and I couldn't even get auditions. I guess he picked the right one." She shook her head and looked past Jenny into the dark hall. "I should probably be grateful. Look at her now."

"Always suspect the spouse," Jenny muttered.

A sniffle accented Stella's movement as she held her camera out. "Here, we should get inside. You're helping with pictures. It's the only way I could get you an invitation."

"Oh." Jenny took the camera. The thin gold band from the caboose was still on her baby finger. "I'm not much of a photographer, but I'll try." She spun the ring on her finger. "Did Eleanor wear any rings or jewelry?"

"Not really." Darkness shrouded Stella's face as she looked back from the door. "Just her wedding ring. And sometimes she wore a floral thing that Thomas gave her. She hated it, though. It was huge, with five big blue jewels as petals."

"Wow, sounds like he had great taste."

Stella giggled. "It was actually a pretty set, the ring was just massive and hideous. I think he only bought it because it was so expensive. He could smell money, that's part of why he picked Elle. He just knew when something was gonna be valuable."

"What about her wedding ring? Was that big and gaudy too?"

"Not as bad, but still a couple of carats at least. He wanted people to know he could afford it. Why do you ask?"

Jenny held out the band. "I found this in the caboose. It was caught in the baseboard. Could it have been hers?"

Stella narrowed her eyes looking at the thin ring. "I don't think so, I've never seen it anyway."

Disappointment settled in Jenny's chest. It had been her only hope of a clue. Still, she didn't want to give up on it yet. She dropped it in her pocket as Stella moved to the door.

Stella gripped the door handle and paused, turning back to Jenny. "Please, make sure I'm there when you tell Thomas we know Elle was leaving him. Maybe he'll get scared and confess."

Jenny flinched. "Maybe we shouldn't tell everyone what you're trying to do yet. We don't want to make the killer nervous. People do desperate things when they're scared."

"Oh." Stella looked disappointed. "Right."

Jenny could almost see Stella planning her next move. If Jenny wasn't careful, Stella would gonna grab the first person she suspected with a dramatic, *Gotcha!* And have them arrested and sentenced before the night was through.

5

"**T**HIS IS GORGEOUS, Bonnie, as usual." Thomas brought Bonnie's fingers to his lips in his go-to female greeting, and Jenny snapped a picture.

Bonnie barely noticed Thomas. She had turned a glare on Jenny.

"Don't post that," Bonnie snapped, "I wasn't ready."

Face-to-face with her least favorite starlet, Jenny smiled brightly and held up the camera. "I'm just doing what I'm told." She pointed the camera at Bonnie and clicked the shutter. "Smile."

"Again," Bonnie snarled, a clipped warning in her tone. "I wasn't ready."

"Oops," Jenny said innocently and turned to Stella. "Smile."

Stella posed, and Jenny took the picture. "That's all I needed," Jenny said, giving Bonnie a pleased look.

Bonnie's glittered lashes flashed, narrowing at Jenny.

"It is a gorgeous event." Jenny picked up a tiny puff of bread sprinkled with golden brown shreds of crisped cheese. "Of course, a lot of that has to do with the train." From crystal goblets and flowers to windows that curled from the floor all the way overhead. The skyward view of the coastline sunset radiated more lavish expense.

Jenny took a bite of the tiny pastry, and her mouth filled with savory cream and seasonings. "Oh gosh," she muttered, her mouth still partially full. "And the food." She turned looking for Stella. "This is delicious."

"Maybe you can bring Ron up here for a date night later." Stella winked at her. "When the stars come out, it's even better."

"Oh, sweetie." Bonnie swept over and looked dramatically out the window. "Some of us are already here."

Bonnie held her pose as if someone might jump out from behind the curtain to take her picture while Jenny and Stella exchanged a look over the self-indulgent comment.

"That's right." Carey applauded beside a platter of glazed fruit, slow and deliberate. "Brighter than the North Star."

More credit than Bonnie deserved. Except that Jenny thought she detected a momentary eye roll. What was Carey's relationship with Bonnie, anyway?

When she finally broke character, she glared at Jenny. "What? You didn't want that picture?"

"Oh, sorry." Jenny jumped, pulling up the camera and clicking a picture of Bonnie.

She growled and spun on her heel. "Carey? Where's the food? I'm tired of this."

"Well done." Warren stepped over beside them, his eyes on Stella. "I don't know when Bonnie's been the first one to want to leave a party."

"It's a gift." Jenny brushed her shoulder. "A terrible, repulsive gift."

"Stella? Could I talk with you, alone?" Warren slipped a hand behind Stella's elbow.

"I'll be right over there," Jenny said, setting the camera at the table. She walked toward Thomas where she could keep an eye on the pair. "Thanks for showing me the caboose earlier. I appreciate being able to see where Eleanor was found. Stella's been really concerned about finding out who killed her sister."

"She needs to let it go," Thomas said, not looking at Jenny. "Eleanor's not coming back."

"I guess you don't miss her as much as Stella does. I've heard you and Eleanor fought a lot."

"Who told you that?" Thomas looked at her sharply. "It's not my fault I couldn't make her happy. It doesn't mean I didn't love her." He held Jenny's gaze for a moment. "It doesn't mean she didn't love me. And now Stella's headed for another spiral. She was never good at looking to the future. She fixates on things. Eleanor didn't see things like that, but she indulged Stella. Took care of her like a mother hen and wanted me to help. Stella was one of the many things we fought about."

"That didn't bother you?"

"Sure it did. But Eleanor was worth it. She was good for me. Beautiful and talented, she understood me. She didn't put up with it when I was stupid. And she let me know it. I'd be a fool not to miss her."

"Someone shot her on your production, on your train. You don't want to find out who?"

"Of course I do, but if the police couldn't do it, why do you think Stella can?" Thomas made a face and pulled Jenny to the side. "Stella's the one you should be talking to anyway. She was jealous of everything Eleanor had. All Eleanor did was take care of her, and it was never enough for Stella. They fought like crazy when Stella didn't get her way. Ask her. And while you're at it, ask for Elle's necklace back."

"Her necklace?"

"I bought it for Eleanor on our anniversary, blue diamond forget-me-nots. Her favorite flower. I haven't seen it since she died."

Jenny hesitated, jeweled forget-me-nots sounded a lot like the ring with the five blue jewels as petals that Stella had described earlier. "Was the necklace part of a set?"

"Yes. A necklace, pin, and a ring. She wore it every day. It was an expensive vintage set. It's rare to find a full set of jewelry like that. She loved it and the team made it part of her costume. You've probably seen the pin in her pictures." He waited for a sign of recognition, frowning when Jenny shook her head. "Well, it disappeared when Eleanor died and I'd caught Stella trying the necklace on the night before."

"You think Stella took them?"

"Well, the necklace is all I saw her with, but yeah, probably. Eleanor was in full costume minus the pin when she died, and Stella was the first one there. She always wanted what Eleanor had. If she killed her, it would have been easy to finally take what Eleanor would never give up."

"The necklace?" Jenny asked skeptically.

"And her career." Thomas snipped. "She was very jealous. She got it too."

"You gave it to her."

"I didn't have a choice. If she'd waited till the film was finished, she'd have never been able to take over."

Jenny glanced at Stella, caught up smiling at Warren, she didn't look worried about the affair rumors any more. "But she's the one trying to find Eleanor's killer. Why would she be trying so hard if she was the one who did it? It's been a year. The attention on the murder case was going away."

Thomas laughed. "Who knows what she's thinking. Maybe something made her nervous and she's trying to pin it on someone else. Maybe she feels guilty and wants to get caught. Whatever it is, she's the one who wanted Eleanor dead. Not me."

"Did she know where you kept your gun?"

"My gun?" That seemed to shock him more than any of her other questions.

Jenny watched him closely. "Yeah. Stella told me you had a gun with you. Did she know where you kept it."

"We had tons of fake weaponry. My gun never came out of its case. It's just for protection."

"But did she know where it was?"

Thomas snarled. "I don't think so." He looked across the room as Stella turned and his snarl pulled at his upper lip. "I have to go."

Thomas moved away, leaving Jenny alone with her questions. She moved to the trays of appetizers, snagging a fruit skewer as the waiters picked them up and carried them away. Warren was at the table moving name cards around and Stella had been caught in conversations with a smiling woman in a dusty purple dress that looked like a modernized copy of Stella's costume.

"If everyone can take their seats." Carey stood near the end of the table. "We're ready to get started."

"Is this yours?" Warren picked up the camera from the seat where she'd left it. He held it out hovering as if nervous someone would take his seat.

Bonnie scoffed. "That's so unprofessional. Your seat is over here, Jenny." Bonnie wiggled her fingers at a chair on the opposite side of the table from Warren. "That's my best angle."

"Excuse me." Annoyance and embarrassment plucked a fake smile from Jenny's lips. She took the camera and sat as quickly as possible.

Jenny had been placed between Carey and a dark-haired young woman she didn't know. Beside the dark-haired stranger sat the reporter in his comically vintage hat. Thomas was at the end of the table. Another unknown guest, sat beside him on the other side of the table, the unknown gentleman whispering a steady stream of conversation while Thomas tried to talk to the reporter on his left.

"He was one of the soldiers," the young woman beside Jenny whispered. "Garrett Brandt, I think."

"Who?" Jenny asked as the woman looked pointedly at the stranger across the table. "Oh, I didn't need to—"

"I just noticed you looking curious." She held out her hand. "I'm Vivian, or Viv. I helped with costumes for both rounds of Mr. Quinn's film. I've passed you a few times on the set."

"Well, thank you, Viv. It's nice to meet you. I'm Jenny." She took Viv's hand briefly as Bonnie finished settling everyone at the table.

"I know." Viv giggled. "I'm a huge fan. I've been quilting for about three years now. It's different than costume sewing, but I love it."

Warren sat beside Garrett, then Stella and one more stranger. A woman with short blonde hair, but before she could ask about her, Bonnie clapped her hands, calling everyone to attention.

"It's so nice to have you all here." Bonnie announced.

Viv's lips clamped shut, her eyes turned to Bonnie in quick reaction.

Jenny turned to face Bonnie more slowly. Hopefully looking more in control of herself and less like a puppet being pulled by Bonnie's strings.

"We'd like to start things off with a toast. No one is perfect, including Eleanor, but with the film we've just finished, I'm hoping to put her memory to rest. We've created a beautiful legacy, and I think we all deserve credit for that. With most of us in costume—" Bonnie stopped her gaze on Jenny, sparing a glance over her beaded sweater and slacks.

It was the nicest thing Jenny'd brought, but it certainly wasn't vintage 1940s. Vague embarrassment tinged Jenny's thoughts, making her wish she had gone to dinner with Ron instead.

Bonnie looked back to the table and continued. "Let's honor Eleanor and the legacy we've built for her. If you'll all raise a glass . . ." She waited while everyone grabbed their glass. "This is a night of healing and letting go. To Eleanor." She tipped her glass toward everyone at the table and drank with the rest of the group.

Thomas stood at the other end of that table. "Elle loved acting, and she loved her friends." He fell silent, turning the glass in hand. Then he lifted it. "To Eleanor."

Bonnie grimaced, repeating her name. "Sure, she loved her friends. Especially Warren," she scoffed. "That's how I knew she had so much acting potential. Lying and acting go hand in hand. To our favorite little actress. To Eleanor."

"She wasn't a liar." Stella spoke softly, but it stopped Bonnie. "She was the most caring person I know."

"That's a pretty nice pedestal you've got her on. It keeps everyone below her. Maybe some of you belong there." A half smile tugged at the side of Bonnie's lips, her snarky tone sounding almost like laughter. "To Eleanor." She raised her glass to Stella specifically, taking a solid gulp from her glass.

"You're kidding me." Warren dropped his napkin, pushing away from the table. "Eleanor wasn't perfect, but she was a good person. Let it go, Bonnie."

"I've been passed over for more roles than I can count because of Eleanor. Because of her secrets. I'd think you know that better than most, Warren."

"Some secrets deserve to be buried. There's no reason to hurt anyone else."

"He *would* say that." Carey commented to Bonnie, but the whole table heard.

"What is your problem?" Warren leaned forward. "Just because you were too much of a coward to tell her you were in love with her doesn't mean—"

"Why would I tell a married woman I loved her?" Carey snapped. "I make it a point not to ruin relationships. Unlike some people at this table."

"You don't know what you're talking about." Warren slowed his speech, enunciating carefully. "She wasn't always married. Coward. I know you knew her then."

Carey glared for a second and spat. "She wasn't always pregnant, either."

Thomas gripped the edge of the table. Garrett, the man who'd been so excited to talk to Thomas before, tugged at his collar looking anxious. It didn't stop him from whispering though. The stranger leaned over to say something, and Thomas released his hold.

Thomas' hand clapped down on the table. "That's my wife you're all talking about. She didn't cheat on me and she wasn't pregnant. You're all liars, and there's no point to it. She's dead!"

"Oh, she was pregnant all right. I guess she just didn't want you to know." Bonnie ate up the tension, and Carey seethed beside her.

"You're wrong." Thomas' neck had warmed to a violent shade of red.

"Very well done, everyone. I hope that was as cathartic for you as it was for me." With a smirk, Bonnie laid a hand possessively over Carey's. "Now, I have one more event planned for our evening. Waiters?" She gestured to the staff standing in the background.

Each white jacketed waiter wore a black bowtie, carrying a silver tray with a dome over it. The trays swung in front of each guest, and the waiters lifted the covers to reveal a tiny white card.

Bonnie clapped. "Perfect. Now I want us to read these together and release Eleanor's spirit."

"What is this? A séance?" Warren grumbled, picking up a white card from his tray. His eyes went wide, and he looked at Bonnie. "This is a sick joke." He tossed his card on the table.

The rest of the guests read their cards and looked like they agreed, but, regardless, Jenny suspected they would put on the necessary show for Bonnie's satisfaction.

Only they didn't.

Stella placed her opened card face-down on the table. Blanched skin betrayed her nerves, leaving her pale and short of breath. "If you expect me believe this has anything to do with honoring Eleanor or releasing her spirit, you're crazier than I thought."

Anyone who hadn't opened their cards did so quickly. Garrett cleared his throat, coughing and Thomas patted his shoulder.

Jenny looked at the little white card in her hand. Letters wove across the paper in beautiful, gold-embossed script, the message searing her fingers like she'd been burned.

I killed Eleanor Grace.

The room grew still. Bonnie's pride faltered for a moment. "What's the matter? I thought you would enjoy — it's a great idea, right?"

Carey cleared his throat and held out his card. "You should look at this."

She only had to scan the card before red splotches blossomed across her chest.

"Who did this?" Anger radiated from her voice, slicing through them like the deep cuts of a rotary blade. "It wasn't me."

Carey stepped away from the table, leaning toward Bonnie as he passed. "It's time to go. This was a mistake."

"I didn't do this." Bonnie jerked away from him.

"Then who did?" Thomas marched up to her, hands on his hips, pushing the edges of his tuxedo jacket back with the confidence of a man used to getting what he wants. "It looks to me like you're confessing to her murder."

"This isn't a confession. Someone else made those cards. Mine said *'In Honor of Eleanor Grace'* I was being selfless. All of you had the same card anyway. Who says I'm the one who killed her? Whoever did it, did us all a favor, and I won't apologize for saying so."

"Um, excuse me." Garrett leaned forward, propping himself against the table while loosening his tie.

"Not now, Garrett." Thomas didn't look back, but Warren stood and spoke quietly to the man while Thomas glared at Bonnie. "If this isn't a confession then what is it? Were you trying to get some kind of communal bashing? Then what? Send away anyone who dared to love her? That's me, Bonnie. I loved her. Did you want to send me away?"

"No. It wasn't about that." Bonnie protested.

Behind Thomas, Warren circled the table headed for the door until Garrett coughed and slammed his fist into the table as he stumbled back.

A communal shriek sounded around the group and Warren propelled himself over the table, knocking over dinnerware and décor to get to Garrett's side. Several white pills rolled across the table as Garrett's body lurched and collapsed, Warren guiding him to a chair.

"He needs help." Warren yelled. "Garrett needs help."

Garrett's face turned crimson before someone shoved a drink into Warren's grip. Warren held the glass in front of the struggling man as he gasped. He swung out his hand, knocking the drink from Warren's fist and across the table.

It splashed over Jenny and Viv who simultaneously threw their hands up in a useless defense.

"What's going on? Does he have some kind of condition?" Thomas sounded appalled that he had the audacity to collapse in his presence.

"No!" Warren shouted without looking away from the convulsing man. "He's healthy. We play racquetball every week. He's fine."

"He's not breathing," Warren shouted.

Thomas finally reacted with urgency turning to the group. "Somebody get help!"

"I'll go." Viv jumped out of her seat, her belt snapped catching on a decorative edge of the table as she stood, the thin silver band fell to the floor. She gasped and dropped to retrieve it.

"Someone else?" Thomas growled. "Who's not incompetent!"

"I'm going," she scrambled to her feet and ran for the door. "I'll be right back."

Jenny picked up the belt for her as she disappeared through the doorway. Her sweater dripped with the remains of Garrett's water.

"Does anyone know CPR?" Thomas asked as people crowded around the man on the floor.

"I do." The reporter shoved past them knocking Jenny back her arm rising again in defense. Bitterness triggered Jenny's gag reflex as the wet fabric of her sleeve brushed her lips.

"What was that?" Jenny blurted out, staring at her soaked arm. Garrett had swallowed half a glass of whatever that was, and all Jenny knew was it wasn't water.

The reporter started chest compressions as Bonnie backed away and Jenny scanned the table for the glass that had flown out of Warren's hand.

It lay on its side only a couple places from Jenny's seat. She picked it up, a thin white residue pooled in the side of the glass. She flinched, remembering the pills she'd seen but they were gone. Her hand shot out moving dishes to look for them but the only thing she found was a pale line of white dust. The pills were gone.

Her gaze shot around the room. Every person in there had known Eleanor. They'd all been on the train when she died and now they were here again as this man struggled for breath.

"What is it?" Carey asked and she turned to look at him with as much fear as she'd had for each of them.

"Nothing." Jenny set the glass down not sure who she could trust. "Just thirsty."

Carey picked the glass up, obviously not believing her. "What's in there?"

Jenny just looked at the glass her head moving slowly. How could she say he'd been poisoned? Carey's jaw dropped, looking back at the glass.

"No, it's not—" Carey stuttered over the words as the glass fell from his hand.

"No!" Jenny yelled reaching for the glass as it crashed to the floor.

"I gave it to Warren." Carey muttered. "I wanted to help. Did I—I couldn't. But how—"

A man in a full black uniform appeared through the staff entrance where Jenny and Stella had come in.

"What's going on?" he demanded.

The question was answered as Garrett screamed out in pain as Viv walked through the door with a man in a conductor's uniform like the one Ron's friend Chris had worn.

"Who's that?" Jenny asked Viv as he pushed his way forward.

"The train conductor." Viv answered.

Jenny frowned. "I thought Chris was the conductor."

The man must have heard her because he turned, narrowing his eyes at her. "We take shifts. It's a big train and multiple days out here. Is that all right with you or did you want me to get Chris? Because I'm sure this gentleman won't mind waiting."

"No. I didn't mean anything." Jenny's jaw dropped as the conductor turned back to Garrett. The uniform was the same but the man lacked all of Chris' friendly demeanor. She leaned over to Vivian. "Is he always this sweet?"

Viv giggled and the conductor shot them another look. He only took a moment longer before turning to the room and sending everyone away. "All right," the conductor said. "Everybody out. This man needs medical attention and we need space and quiet to do that."

Thomas stood immediately, holding his arms out and corralled the group to the door. "You heard what he said, everybody out."

No one objected. The group of costumed adults shuffled and stumbled out to the stairs. Stella exited the room just before Jenny.

"Stella, did you know Garrett? Was there any reason someone would want to hurt him?"

"I only know him from the movie, but I don't think so. He must have been friends with Eleanor or Bonnie wouldn't have invited him but otherwise I'm not sure."

Jenny put a hand on the rail and looked at her sleeve. "Are you sure? I think he might have been poisoned."

Stella stopped on the steps turning back to Jenny. "Who would do that?"

"I don't know." Jenny urged her to keep going as Thomas shoved Warren out behind them.

Behind them, the group gathered, shifting toward the end of the car by the galley entrance where less diners were seated.

"What just happened?" The woman with the short blonde hair, who'd been between Bonnie and Stella, looked shell-shocked.

"I'll tell you what happened." Stella pointed a finger at Bonnie. "She tried to kill that man."

Jenny nearly choked on her own voice. "Stella—"

"That's ridiculous," Bonnie whined, waving one of the envelopes from upstairs at them. "Those cards were supposed to say, 'In honor of Eleanor Grace.' I didn't kill anyone."

"Yeah?" Stella stepped closer. "Jenny said he was poisoned. You made the cards. You invited us all there. If not you, then who poisoned Garrett?"

Jenny gasped along with the rest of the group.

"I didn't say that." Jenny defended her assumptions.

"I didn't poison him." Bonnie defended herself at the same time.

"Well, Garrett is up there gasping for life. So, obviously someone did. Whoever it is better come clean, or I swear you'll regret it." Stella's eyes flashed with anger as she took another step toward Bonnie.

Bonnie took a step back. "I didn't do anything to Garrett. I invited him because knew Thomas had paid people to get Eleanor so many roles. He literally bought her fame. Why would I want him dead?"

"Of course, he was there because of Eleanor. It's always about her. Why can't you let it go. Why can't you stop killing people?"

The dining room went silent, and Jenny's mind flashed to the argument she'd overheard in the dining room that day.

It's not about you.

I know it's about her, it's always about her.

She looked at Stella. She couldn't be the woman in the trench coat. But she could have gone down the kitchen stairs and come up behind Jenny. Maybe the person in the trench coat had simply been a tall thin man.

People were talking again but their eyes stayed on the group. When Carey opened the door to the vestibule, the whole group followed him into the next car. It was a second dining car. Jenny bit her tongue and followed Carey across the floor to the next door.

They entered a nearly vacant car. Storage boxes were piled in the corners, and he had to search the wall for a minute to find the light switch. "Finally, some privacy," he said when he found it. "We need to figure this out."

"I didn't poison Garrett, and I didn't kill Eleanor. There, are we good?" Bonnie crossed her arms over her chest.

"No," Warren and Thomas said together.

"I didn't do anything wrong." Bonnie stomped her foot, her lower lip protruding in a pretty pout.

"Well, someone did." Thomas stepped forward, taking a wide stance with his arms crossed. "You planned this whole night. The toast, the cards, I think you even planned the arguing."

"That's ridiculous," Bonnie said.

"You did. And then you picked where we sat and—"

"I did it." Carey announced. And all eyes turned to Carey. "I gave Warren the drink. There was poinson in it and I gave it to him."

Jenny frowned. "What poison was it?"

"I don't know. But the glass I gave them had poison and now Garrett could die."

"Shut up Carey. He didn't even drink it then." Thomas brushed off the aggressively apologetic agent. "Did you put the poison in the drinks to begin with?"

"Well, no—"

"That's what I thought," Thomas said. "Bonnie made sure everyone had a specific seat, even moving Jenny when her camera was in the way."

"No." Warren's confused gaze met Bonnie's terrified one. "I traded places with Garrett. He wanted to talk to Thomas, and I wanted to sit by Stella. Bonnie didn't poison Garrett, she poisoned me."

"I didn't do it," she shouted, eyes wide. "Whoever switched the notes, they must have done it. Someone's trying to frame me. They want me to look like a killer. They said so in my letter." She waived the card in her hand around again and then quickly dropped it when everyone focused on it.

"What's in your letter?" Thomas asked. Bonnie shook her head and Thomas held out his hand for Bonnie's envelope, after a slight hesitation she gave it to him.

He opened it and read the paper silently. Anger sweltered under snarling lips. He wadded the paper up and threw it at the wall.

"You hated her!" Thomas shouted. "And now that she's gone, you want to smear her name too."

"I didn't kill her." Bonnie bared her teeth, speaking slow and sharp. "I could've, but I didn't."

Jenny picked up the discarded paper.

> *Read your cards for me. You killed me. Now it's my turn. –Elle*

With a thump, Stella crumbled to the floor.

6

THOMAS CARRIED STELLA out of the luggage car with Warren on his heels.

"Is she gonna be okay?" Viv asked.

Carey rolled his eyes. "She passed out. She's fine."

"And Garrett?" The other woman, the blonde who'd been sitting by Stella looked anxiously between them. Jenny had never gotten her name. "He was such a sweet guy. Do you think—Is he going to be all right?"

"It's okay Mia, right?" Viv sent a glance around to the others who returned her question with sighs and nervously shaking heads. "I'm sure they'll do their best to help him."

"Help him?" Bonnie pushed through the group of them to the vestibule and turned around pointing a finger at them all. "My dinner party was ruined. I'm going to find out who did this," she said and disappeared through the door.

"Classy." It sounded like it came from Carey.

Footsteps pulled Jenny's attention back to the door.

"Why don't we go see if the conductor has any news." Viv gave Mia a nudge and walked her out of the room.

Carey stopped and looked out the window. He didn't move. Jenny almost left. She should follow the others out, or go check on Stella. But she had a question that needed an answer.

Finally, she took a step closer.

"Was Eleanor really pregnant?"

"Why do you care?" Carey turned to the side so he could keep looking out the window. His pleasant smile from their first meeting was gone. "Looking for little secrets to sell?"

Jenny flinched. "I wouldn't do that. Stella's worried about it. She asked me to help her figure out what happened. If we can figure out why someone wanted to hurt her, we might be able to find her killer." She smoothed the card in her hand that read as if it were from Eleanor.

Carey snorted. "You better hurry, cause you're not the only one looking anymore. And whoever left those notes doesn't just want to find a killer. They want revenge."

Jenny thought about the note, written like it was from Eleanor beyond the grave. She hadn't specified anyone. "You're right. The note said, *You killed me. Now it's my turn.* You think someone's taking revenge for Eleanor?"

Carey shrugged. "If it's true every one of us got the note saying we killed her." He shook his head. "Does that mean we'll all die?"

"I don't plan on dying." Jenny said. "But if we're going to find out who's killing people, I need to figure out what happened."

Carey leaned his head against the window. "They never could just leave her alone. All she wanted was a little peace." The sun was setting, and Carey shoved his hands in his pockets. "She was a private woman. I don't think she wanted to be famous. She did it for him."

He was rambling and everything he said left more questions. She didn't want to stop him from talking, though, so she only asked one. "What did she do?"

"Everything. She did everything for Thomas from the day he picked her." He paused and took a slow breath. "Until the baby."

Jenny couldn't help the breath she sucked in, but Carey didn't seem to notice. It was really true. She wasn't just quitting the film, she was pregnant too. Maybe that's why she decided to stop acting. "It sounds like you two were close. How long did you know Eleanor?"

"We grew up together. I went to school with her. We were theater nerds together. Making it through high school as theater kids creates a bond." Carey smiled, soft and sad. "When she decided to start auditioning, I realized I was not meant to be an actor and offered to be her agent." He shrugged. "We did well for a couple of high school sweethearts."

"You were sweethearts? And you stayed friends. I love that."

"Well, sort of. The story would be better if I'd told her how I really felt about her. Warren was right about that. I never did, and that's why our story changed."

"Do you remember where you were when Eleanor died?"

His smile drooped, but he nodded. "I was with Bonnie."

"I thought they were prepping to film a scene. She wasn't getting ready?"

Carey shook his head. "No. She wasn't in the shoot that day. It annoyed her I think. So she found me a little before three, and we were . . . otherwise occupied when Eleanor passed."

"Oh, I see." Heat rose up Jenny's cheeks.

"By the time we found out there had been a shooting, the whole cast knew." Carey took a deep breath, letting it out slowly. He glanced around the car. "I'm going to check on Bon. Things didn't go the way she planned tonight."

Jenny followed him out, only then realizing she should have looked for Ron when they'd come downstairs. She glanced up to the upper dining room. The door was closed. The conductor could have come out, or he might still be up there with Garrett. He could be dying from the effects of the poison right now.

You killed me. Now it's my turn.

The person behind the notes had taken revenge without caring about the identity of the real killer. Or maybe they left the notes to distract the group and keep them from finding out who really had killed Eleanor.

As she thought about the night's events, Jenny walked through each of the dining cars.

Ron was gone. He'd left his hat at the corner table where he'd met Chris before dinner. Jenny picked it up and carried it with her as she made her way to the vestibule door.

Warren sat at a table by himself. She paused when he met her eye and gave a wan smile.

"Warren? I thought you were with Stella."

"I was." He wiggled his eyebrows and swirled the ice cubes in his glass, his voice hollow. "But it got . . . crowded in the room. Thomas asked me to leave." He rubbed a hand over his jaw and turned, showing her the opposite side of his face. A fist-sized bruise decorated one eye.

Surprise silenced her for a minute, and she slid into the seat across from him. "Do you need anything? Some ice, or a first-aid kit? Maybe a bodyguard?"

"I'm touched. You think I need a seventy year old woman to protect me."

"I'm not seventy." Jenny frowned. "Regardless, I'm not the one with a black eye."

"Thanks. But I think I'm good. I've got this taking care of me for now." He lifted his drink to his damaged skin with a good-natured grin. "It takes care of the insides and outsides." He winked and took a drink before returning the glass to his damaged eye.

Jenny should laugh, she knew it. But after everything at the dinner party, and not knowing if Garrett was alive or dead, there was a ragged edge to her nerves.

"Where were you? When Eleanor died." Asking questions was almost a compulsive thing for her now. It gave her some control when things fell apart . . . like they did tonight.

Warren cocked his head. "Why do you ask?"

They sat next to the window, a stained-glass lamp spreading dim light across the table. Spots of light flashed in the distance of the darkening horizon as stars began to glow. Jenny forced a smile to assuage the worry reflected on her face over the window.

"I just want to understand what happened. Do you remember where you were?"

"I remember." He tapped a finger on his glass, watching her. "I was with Thomas and the screen director. I didn't find out she was gone for at least an hour."

"Right." Jenny had heard Stella say Thomas didn't get there for a long time. "Why didn't someone call him? Or text? Stella got there right away." Jenny didn't use her phone excessively, but she always had it in case of emergency.

"Stella was probably a little preoccupied. No one had seen Eleanor all day, and Thomas wanted to catch the light before it started to set. When it started to get late, Thomas sent someone to find Eleanor."

"You didn't hear a gunshot?" The train was big, but was it that big?

Warren squinted and looked away. His slow head shake didn't seem very confident. "There may have been something, a sound in the distance . . . but honestly . . . with filming, and it being a war movie, I was used to the odd noises and cracks of sound." He set his glass down on the table and swallowed hard. "If I heard it, I didn't pay attention."

This movie had been a noisy production. Jenny had spent most of her time with the cast in a lovely little tent room outside Quilter's Square. They'd heard the sounds, but the explosions and weaponry had been offsite. With the sounds of the train and the faux war and rehearsals, it was a miracle they could still hear at all. "Can I ask a personal question?"

Warren raised his eyebrows and took a drink from his iced glass. "Shoot."

"The affair rumor . . . any truth to that?" Jenny kept her eye on him as his eyelids lowered.

"You're worse than the reporters." His grin lied to her below doleful eyes. "Nah, despite what Bonnie might say, Eleanor wasn't that kind of girl, and I'm not that kind of guy."

"So why would they say it? If that's not you, what gives people room to say it's true?"

Warren shrugged. "Because Eleanor was having an off year."

"I don't follow," Jenny said, scrutinizing the comment.

He sighed and slid his glass slowly from hand to hand. "We'd been working on *Quilted Battle Stars* for months, and the re-shoots were taking over. Something wasn't right with her, and everybody knew it. The producers wanted me to pick up the slack, do more on set, but me doing more didn't pull more out of her. That's not how acting works." He lifted his glass and took a drink. It was getting low, and he glanced back toward the bar. "I was trying to help her relax by inviting her to lunch, making her laugh . . . so she'd get comfortable with me. And maybe our scenes would feel more real."

"You flirted with her?" Jenny gave him a half smile, and he returned it. "What did Thomas think of that?"

Warren laughed. "He called me into a private meeting. I thought I was getting fired. Apparently, we had our first good reel since the start of filming. He told me to keep it up. 'Get friendly, make her feel good.' So, I did."

"He asked you to flirt with his wife? That's an odd request for a husband to make."

"But not a producer. Acting is an emotional thing. If she isn't feeling it, I'm basically kissing cardboard."

"Or shooting it."

"Shooting it, hiding in train cars, throwing it into the river. Makes for an exciting film. Me and the cardboard actress." He held his hand out as if wrapping it around an invisible person. "She doesn't even need a name at that point."

Jenny chuckled. "She couldn't have been that bad. She's Eleanor Grace."

"She wasn't that good." He turned the glass absently on the table. "Shocking, I know, but as we talked, it was pretty clear why. She was having trouble at home. Hard to pretend you're in love on screen when offscreen your romance is on the rocks. Which made Thomas' request less strange, and his behavior now . . . more so. The crazy thing is, if we had recast, she might still be alive."

That was the hardest part of surviving the death of someone you loved. Guessing and retracing and deciding what could have made it different. "They wanted to recast?"

"Everyone but Thomas. He and Eleanor had a big fight about it one night. She wanted him to let her quit, but he wouldn't. He thought it would look bad for him." A sneer tugged slightly at his lip, and he took another drink.

"She told you about it?"

Warren swallowed and looked away. "Um, yeah. We became pretty good friends. She liked to talk to me. So, she came to my room after their fight."

"I'm beginning to understand the rumor." Jenny leaned back against the bench.

Warren snorted and took a drink before lifting the cold glass to his eye. It was mostly ice now. "She was leaving Thomas, you know."

"I heard that. Were you hoping she would?"

"I told you it wasn't like that. It couldn't be."

"Because you didn't want it to? Or because she didn't?"

"Because she was married to a man who could ruin our careers. I didn't touch her. Not once." Warren couldn't meet her eye, but it didn't sound like a lie. "She wasn't happy though. Thomas wasn't who she thought he was. She shoulda left him. Maybe if things were different. I would have—" Warren looked up, meeting Jenny's attentive gaze. "She shoulda left him."

"She was special." Jenny could feel him spiraling and she slid toward the edge of the chair. It was almost time to go.

He nodded. "She was."

"But you and Stella . . ." She pushed just a little with the memory of Eleanor so fresh. "Is that you trying to capture something you couldn't have with Eleanor?"

"No. I like Stella, but she's nothing like Eleanor." Warren tipped his glass back to finish it off.

"Sounds like it." Jenny laughed lightly. "She won't even talk to you."

Warren hesitated, shook his glass of ice, and gestured to the bar. "Do you mind? I really do want that refill, and I don't want to keep you."

Jenny stood. "Sure. I should go check on Stella. Do you know where Thomas took her? I'm sorry for all of this. I'm sorry you're having to relive it."

Warren stood and pointed to the doors. "They're in his room. Last sleeper car, closest to the viewing car."

"Where Eleanor was shot."

Warren stared for a second, his bruised eye purple in the light, and gave a quick nod before turning away.

The trip through first-class was less awe-inspiring than her first time through, but still impressive. Jenny made it through the first-class parlor and lounge cars to the hallway of sleeper cars. She walked carefully over the dense carpets. The patterns ran differently than her quilting, but she loved the art of the framed oriental styling. Every car had identical carpeting until the last. The fanciest of them all, intricate gold basket weave, framed the corners of detailed florals with silver daisies and green roses. It was like walking through a dream garden.

She stopped at Thomas' door and knocked. No one answered.

"Thomas?" Jenny called. "Stella?" Still no answer. They might not have heard her, but Jenny couldn't exactly be called a quiet girl. Anyone on the other side of this door should be able to hear her.

She knocked again and moved to the neighboring door. Stella had mentioned having the room next to Thomas' Maybe she'd have better luck here.

She knocked again, and someone screamed as a gunshot rang through the train.

TWO BODIES LAY on the ground at Jenny's feet. Two.

How many people would die tonight?

Thomas groaned, splayed at Jenny's feet. She dropped to check his pulse, wishing she wasn't the only one there.

She'd opened Thomas' door after the bullet left a hole in the thin wood panel and found him lying, one arm extended, as if he'd been coming to open the door. Behind him, Stella lay slumped against the wall, partially covered in a blanket.

A gun lay on the floor beside her.

She looked back at the man in front of her. A red wound pierced the shoulder of his three-piece suit. Blood seeped slowly into the brown woven material.

Footsteps and voices grew in the hallway. People were coming. Any second, they would be there, filling the hallway and asking questions. And Jenny had no answers.

She jumped up, grabbed a towel from the counter by the marble sink, and hurried back, pressing it against Thomas' wound.

He groaned in pain but didn't open his eyes.

"Thomas?" Jenny said gently. "Thomas. Are you awake? What happened?"

He groaned again. "Shot me," he mumbled shifting slightly.

Jenny rolled her eyes and pressed harder, trying not to breathe the scent of blood. "I see that. Hold still, okay? Someone's coming."

Jenny glanced over her shoulder at Stella. She still hadn't moved. "What did you do?" Jenny whispered.

A handful of people spilled into the doorway. Ron was at the head of the group, along with Mr. Wiley.

"I knew it." He didn't look happy to see her. He dropped beside her and took over pressing the towel against Thomas' shoulder, but the blood pooling below his shoulder continued to spread.

"Mr. Wiley." Jenny looked away from Ron's disapproval and focused on the conductor. "Do you have anyone with medical training on board? Mr. Quinn and Stella are hurt."

"Oh, yes. This is bad." His chubby cheeks puckered around pursed lips. "I heard a gunshot. Oh, and um, there's a gun." He whipped a handkerchief from his pocket and picked up the weapon, his nose wrinkling as he held it carefully. "We'll have to—um, we'll have to take them to the police in Denning. We'll be there in the morning."

"Or a doctor?"

"Right, right. Oh, right, the doctors. He's bleeding. Can we stop that? He's ruining the carpets. We don't really have a facility for this." He turned to Stella, keeping the gun out of the way, and nudged her toe. His voice rose as he enunciated with extreme precision. "Are you okay?"

Stella flinched, and the conductor's face lit up. He nodded as if he had some part in her health. "Okay. He's all right, and she's not dead."

Jenny's mouth opened slightly, not sure how to respond. "That's good." She looked at the young woman. Stella was conscious. That was good. "What about a doctor? Thomas needs bandages."

"Oh, right, bandages. We have bandages. I'm sure we do. I'll have to ask my co-conductor if he knows where they are. But we should check on him first." The conductor pushed his glasses up his nose and leaned over Thomas and tapped his cheek, then shouted, "Are you okay?"

"Why are you yelling at them?" Jenny rubbed her temple.

"Well, it worked with her." The anxious man said. "I, um, I'm really sorry. I think he's . . . well, I think he's gone."

"He's not dead." Jenny put her hands under his shoulder, and Ron adjusted his pressure, sliding a hand over to help her.

"Oh right, right. Just a moment." He knelt beside Thomas, lifting him and just as quickly dropped him when Thomas groaned. "Oh, blood." Mr. Wiley spasmed, almost dropping the gun. "That's blood. Did you see it? Oh, my. This whole room is going to have to be redone. People don't usually get shot on my train."

Thomas groaned and rolled to the side.

"Oh my. Look at that. More blood. Keep him still please."

"Chris, we could use more towels," Ron said.

The little man jumped up. "Right, right. I'm gonna go. I'll go get some towels. Oh, no."

"And bandages." Jenny said while the conductor danced away from the blood and bodies, turning circles as if he had forgotten how to get out of the room.

Jenny reached over, pressing on the towel with Ron. "Ron, will you go with him? We need them ... quickly."

"Right." Ron got up and looked back at Jenny. "Towels and bandages. Come on, Chris. You'll need to put that gun away too, won't you?"

"Oh, right, right," the conductor said. People made way and crowded back together to watch the scene as they left.

"Here." Someone handed Jenny a wadded length of gold fabric.

"Thank you." She took it and pressed it to Thomas' shoulder. "What is it?" It was softer than normal cotton, and her fingers brushed along a thick, corded hem.

"A pillow case. He can get it replaced later." The stranger had dark hair and a deep blue buttoned shirt under a dark jacket. He glanced over Thomas and turned to Stella. "Put it under his shoulder. Block the blood on both sides. Save the little man's carpets."

"Good point," Jenny said, shoving the pillowcase under his shoulder. "I'm Jenny. Are you a doctor?"

The stranger gave a quiet laugh and shook his head. "A pillowcase to stop the bleeding isn't doctor level medical skills. But it's nice to meet you, Jenny."

"I appreciate the help. I need it. I've never had to stop someone's bleeding before."

"Your patient's going to be fine. He looks to be in good hands." He turned back to Stella, looking her over before he glanced back. "Relax. Keep pressure on the wound. I can bandage him up when the conductor gets back."

Jenny let out a breath and adjusted the pillowcase to get a better grip. "Not a doctor, huh?"

"Not a doctor. I'm an EMT. I've done a lot of trauma. Besides," The stranger glanced over his shoulder and raised an eyebrow. "He's always fine. The devil himself couldn't kill that man."

"I'm awake and I can hear you," Thomas grumbled.

Jenny looked at the stranger sharply. "You did see he was shot."

"And he's not dead. See my point?" He put his arms under Stella, adjusting her so she was fully lying on the ground instead of slumped against the wall. She squirmed in the process, and Jenny's heart gave a heavy beat of relief.

"It sounds like you know Thomas?" Jenny wracked her brain to see if she remembered him from her time on set, or even here on the train.

"Too well," he muttered, removing the blanket from Stella's side. "Stelle? Can you hear me?"

He was far gentler than the conductor had been. After he got her to respond with some sounds, he put his fingers to the side of her neck, checking her pulse.

Whispers and movement at the doorway reminded Jenny they had an audience. In the corner of the crowd, a woman with the same dark hair and eyes of Viv peeked around the doorframe. In her dusky purple dress, she was the only one Jenny recognized. But as soon as they locked eyes, Viv disappeared, pushed out by unfamiliar faces.

"Has anyone seen the conductor?"—*Or my husband?* — "He's looking for bandages."

No one answered her question, and Jenny blew out a breath of frustration, spawning a look from the stranger and a louder flow of whispers. Footsteps hurried down the hall, though Jenny couldn't see who had gone.

From Stella's side of the room, the man stood and moved to the door. "Everyone needs to go back to their rooms. It's going to be fine." When he turned away from the door he muttered, "we really don't need a crowd of strangers watching us either."

"I'm not a stranger," Bonnie's voice called out from the doorway. "Can I see him? What happened to Thomas?" She stepped into the room, wrinkling her nose lightly. "I was so worried when I saw the crowd. Carey ran off looking for the conductor and now I'm alone."

Jenny let out a sigh of relief. Carey had gone for help. At least someone knew what they were doing.

"I feel so bad." Bonnie wasn't done with her speech yet. "I can't believe that anyone would shoot them."

"Him," the man cut her monologue off. "They tried to hurt him. Stella's fine. She just passed out or hit her head. And somehow, she got tangled up in a blanket."

"She really passed out?" Surprise tainted Bonnie's voice. "I thought she was just trying to get Thomas alone." She wiggled her eyebrows. "Maybe we're both right. She did end up tangled in the sheets."

"No," the stranger snapped at her. "Stella's not like that."

"How would you know?" Bonnie's teasing turned to venom. "Did she dump you? At least she has some taste."

"I'm her brother."

"Andrew?" Grit ground in through Stella's voice. "What are you doing here?"

7

"**D**O YOU REALLY have to ask?" Andrew wiped his hands off, looking only at Stella.

"I do." Bonnie pushed her way into the room, taking a moment once she was there to lean gracefully away from her extended foot and lift her chin to look down on Stella's brother. "I approved every name on our guest list. And you're not supposed to be here."

"Give it a rest Bonnie." Andrew glared at her. "You knew I was here."

That revelation caught Jenny's attention. Not even his sister had known he was here.

Bonnie gaped at him, looking around the group while she decided how to handle Andrew's honesty. "Well, you weren't supposed to be." She wouldn't meet his eye anymore. "Now someone's threatening to kill people and you're the one who's been lying to everyone. That doesn't exactly alleviate guilt."

"But you're so familiar with threats and lies, Bon." The tension between Andrew and Bonnie increased with every volley of words.

"Don't call me that." Bonnie said, not letting him have the last word. "And, it's not just threats. Garrett is dead.

Stella's gasp stuttered painfully. "He's dead?" Her breathing grew quick and shallow. "I thought they were . . ." she cleared her throat. "—they were getting him help."

Jenny didn't say anything but based on Chris' reaction a few moments ago, he wouldn't have been much help.

"Yes, he's dead and now Thomas has been shot. How can we assume it was anyone but you?"

"I wouldn't waste my time on him. I'm here for my sister."

"For your sister! So, you admit you're here taking revenge for Eleanor's death? I thought you wanted to find her treasure or something. You lied to me!" Bonnie spat the words angrily as Andrew clenched his teeth and stepped nose to nose with Bonnie.

"I said I'm here for my sister. Stella shouldn't be alone with him." Andrew gestured sharply in Thomas' direction without looking away. "She needs me, as you can see."

"Are you saying you shot Thomas then?"

"No!" Andrew shouted. "You're twisting my words."

"Well, I hope that's true for your sake. When Thomas is conscious again, I'm sure he'll tell us who shot him." She glanced at Thomas' prone form and pulled her toe in slightly when she saw how close he was.

"I am conscious." Thomas kept his eyes closed as if he was still deciding if he believed what he'd said. "And he didn't shoot me. It was Stella. She's a psycho." His voice was slow and soft in its reprimand. "It must run in the family."

"Stella's not a psycho." Andrew stepped in front of his sister.

"Was there another brunette with a gun?" Thomas grumbled.

"I didn't shoot you," Stella moaned softly, her voice grating in her throat. "If I had, I'd be dancing over your dead body, not lying on the floor with a headache."

Thomas lifted his eyelids and propped himself up looking at Stella. "No, you wouldn't. You're a terrible shot. But my shoulder can attest to that."

"I didn't do it." Stella's compliant held more frustration than venom as she struggled to pull away from Andrew while he helped her sit. "You turned to answer the door, and someone hit me. I never touched a gun."

"I guess we know how you feel," Thomas said, and Stella scoffed. Taking the bloody fabric from Jenny's hands, Thomas pushed himself up, sitting against the end of the bed. "Why has no one told me how much it hurts to get shot?"

Jenny looked between them, shaking her arms slightly to get feeling back in her fingertips. Relief flowed through her tired limbs after putting pressure on Thomas' shoulder for so long, but all she could think in this moment was, *how?* "How did neither of you see who did this?"

Thomas looked at Stella. "I saw her. We were arguing when someone knocked on the door, and I turned around to a gunshot. All I saw was the flash and a woman's dark hair. I don't remember anything else but pain." He looked up at the people standing over him and flinched. "I think I hit my head, too."

"Stella?" Jenny bent toward the injured girl. "Did you see someone?"

Stella shook her head.

"Of course she didn't see them," Andrew blustered. "She was passed out."

"Does anyone have water?" Stella's plea cut through her brother's frustration, pulling sympathy from the crowd.

Jenny jumped up and found a glass by a decanter set and filled it from the sink. "Here."

Stella accepted and drained the glass easily, pulling the blanket around her shoulders. She glanced between Andrew and Thomas before turning to Jenny. "I didn't see anyone. But Thomas and I weren't arguing." She directed her attention at him. "I asked you about Eleanor, and you didn't like it."

"You just can't let it go, can you?" Thomas growled.

"I don't like being lied to."

"I didn't do anything to your sister!" Thomas leaned forward and cringed. "Someone arrest her!" he shouted from his position reclining against the bed, the pillowcase still pressed firmly into his shoulder.

"You can't arrest her," Andrew said. "She didn't do anything."

"If you didn't hurt her—" Stella's shout pittered away into a moan. She put a hand to her neck and let out a breath. A red streak peeked out from under her fingers. "If you didn't do anything to Eleanor, then why was she so scared of you?" She watched Thomas as though she could read the answer in his face.

"Stella." Jenny leaned over the young woman again. "Can I see your neck?"

"I'm fine. Like Andrew said, they shot him, not me." Stella sent Thomas a look of frustration. As she twisted, the blanket fell to the floor and the streaks of red became visible as full lines around her thin neck.

"What happened?" Andrew put his hand by her neck, hovering but not touching the marks. "How could you not see this?"

"See what?" Stella swatted him away, and Jenny stepped to the side so she could see herself in the mirror.

Andrew stayed close, not letting his sister's objections keep him back. "Someone tried to strangle you. You don't remember? You didn't see anyone?"

Bonnie couldn't take her eyes away from Stella's neck. For the first time since Jenny had met her, Bonnie looked terrified. "I'm going back to my room." Her voice had gone breathy and weak as Ron appeared in the doorway, alone.

"Where's the conductor?" Jenny asked as Ron handed over a latched white box.

"Carey is with him. He was making a phone call. I offered to bring the first aid kit back."

Bonnie grabbed Ron's arm. "I need you to take me to Carey."

"I should probably help here first." Ron's gase darted to Jenny and back, looking Bonnie over like she was possessed. "Is everything all right?"

"No, it's not all right." Bonnie insisted dragging Ron toward the door. "Someone's trying, uh— I need . . . to talk to Carey . . . and the conductor . . . to go over some security concerns."

"Jenny?" He turned to her as Bonnie insisted.

"It's okay, I'll be done in a minute." Jenny handed the first aid kit to Andrew as Ron stumbled after Bonnie. "I'll meet you in the room." Jenny called.

"Let's get you back to your room," Andrew said, holding Stella's arm. "We'll take care of you there."

"What about me?" Thomas stood awkwardly, pressing the cloth to his injured shoulder.

Stella's perfect lip hitched up in distaste.

Andrew stepped forward. "Like I said, I'm not wasting my—"

"Maybe you should wrap Thomas' shoulder first." Jenny stepped between them. "You're our only medical professional and I'd hate for Stella to be accused of worse than being present while he was shot."

"Are you threatening her?" Andrew asked, turning to look at her.

"No." Jenny stepped over setting a hand at Stella's shoulder. "But I wouldn't put it past him."

Andrew flinched and looked at Thomas. "Fine. But he's not getting anywhere near my sister. Ever again."

"She shot me," Thomas complained.

"Quiet." Andrew turned back. "I'll help you in a minute, Stelle."

"No one needs to help me." Stella stood, and Andrew was immediately beside her.

"I'll help her to her room," Jenny offered. "You can take care of her when you're done."

Andrew's gaze moved back and forth from Thomas to Stella amid furrowed brows and short huffs of frustration. He finally tore himself away from Stella with a pained expression.

"Thanks, Andrew. You were always my favorite brother-in-law." Thomas smirked.

Andrew's nostrils flared before he grabbed the bandages from the box and gripped Thomas' shoulder. "Well, you're gonna hate me after this."

"HE'S NOT HERE FOR ME." Stella led Jenny into her room and dropped onto the bed without looking at Jenny. "You heard Bonnie. Andrew's here for Elle's treasure."

Jenny had almost forgotten that little comment. "What treasure?"

"There isn't a treasure." Stella shook her head and whimpered resting a hand over her throat again. "It's ridiculous. Eleanor appeared to him at Quilter's Square a couple months ago . . . three months at most. He came to set on one of the train shoots. He said he'd seen Eleanor and she left a treasure for us to find. The crew went crazy. They'd already been talking about things being haunted. Andrew just fueled the stories. It's ridiculous. If anything, it's probably a scavenger like she used to do with our after-school snacks. She loved games, but a treasure? It doesn't make sense. And Andrew won't leave me alone about it. I'm not letting him take her quilt if there's not a real reason. It's all I have of hers."

"What quilt?"

"Elle's quilt." Stella went to the armoire and pulled a brightly colored quilt from the top shelf. With a flip of her wrists, she spread it over the bed and let the fabric drift open. "After Eleanor came to him, Andrew was convinced she meant this quilt was the key. It was her favorite. She took it with her every time she traveled." Stella dropped onto the stars formed of squares and rails across the quilt top. "If she did leave something, it's surely gone by now, discovered in cleaning or repairs or by other passengers."

"It is interesting that she'd come to him after all this time to tell him about her treasure." Jenny looked at the quilt. "And if it's really a treasure hunt, she'd have had to set it up. But I thought she was murdered. Do you think she might have known that someone wanted to kill her. Did she ever mention someone threatening her? Thomas or anyone?"

Stella glanced at her dresser. A smattering of makeup products, a pair of glasses, and a card labeled *I killed Eleanor Grace* sat on top, brought back from Bonnie's dinner. "Well, yes, but nothing came of it. One of the wardrobe girls said she overheard an argument in the dressing rooms. Someone saying she'd make Eleanor pay for ruining an opportunity. But it said that they never found out who it was."

Someone in wardrobe. Viv flashed in Jenny's mind. Maybe she knew something. "What said they never found out?"

Stella's eyes went wide. "Oh, just from a police officer— when he was checking in . . . once . . . recently." Her brow furrowed as she spoke.

"Really, do you usually reference officers as 'it'?" Jenny watched her carefully. "What is 'it' referring to?"

Stella's shoulders drooped, and she walked over to the dresser, opening the top drawer. She pulled out a brown folder and held it out. "It's the police report on her death. I made a copy months ago. I was going to show you. I just wanted to be sure you were on my side first."

Jenny took the folder and flipped to a page with a picture of Eleanor's body. Draped over the chair almost as she'd imagined it. The only difference was her hand extended to the baseboard where she'd found the ring. She could have shoved it under there. Or maybe she was trying to get it back. "I can't believe you have this. We'll have to be careful. If the Eleanor's avenger gets ahold of this it would be a gold mine of victims to add to their list."

"You killed me. Now it's my turn." Stella repeated the words softly. "But what I don't understand is why now? No one cared before. I've been trying to figure it out for months."

"Maybe they have, too." Jenny closed the folder. "We need to find out who wanted Eleanor dead. And who would kill to bring her justice."

Stella bit her lip and looked away. "I would."

"I know. And you knew about Bonnie's party."

Stella nodded. "But I don't want to kill everyone. Someone else traded the cards. Someone else killed Garrett. I wouldn't do that." Stella pushed away from the dresser and turned a full circle around the room, ending with a kick at a door beside the dresser. It popped open, revealing a second door that likely gave access to the adjoining room. "Thomas," Stella growled at the door. "This is supposed to be locked." She snapped the lock on the door shut and spun around. "I'm tired of all these games. I just want justice for my sister. I want to find her killer."

"And we will," Jenny said, no longer focused on Stella, but the locked door behind her. "Where does that lead?"

Stella looked bitterly at the eight-foot slab of wood and kicked it again for good measure. "It connects to Thomas' room."

"And it was unlocked." That was how the shooter could have left without anyone seeing. Jenny turned back to Stella, filing her little revelation away. "Stella, I have to ask. Thomas mentioned the blue diamond jewelry set he gave Eleanor."

"Not surprising. He probably gave you an inflated value on it too. I've heard everything from a few thousand to tens of thousands."

Values that high could be added motive and wouldn't help Stella's case. "He said you were in their room, trying it on before Eleanor died."

Stella didn't respond right away. "I mean, I may have put it on once. I was curious about the metal. I'm allergic to most metals they irritated my skin and if that one is really worth as much as he says I wanted to know if it would hurt me. That's all. I don't even like it. But when do you get to wear ten grand on your neck?" The stench of guilt clung to her laughter. Her hand went to her throat. Jenny couldn't tell if she was remembering the moment or holding her neck against the raw pain she must still feel.

"So you didn't take her pin when she died? Not even for nostalgia? She was your sister after all. It would have made sense to stop by their room on your way to hide it and grab the other pieces?"

"No!" Stella shouted and glanced at the wall separating them from Thomas and her brother.

"Are you sure?" Jenny kept her voice down, keeping tabs on Stella's fear. "You were alone with Eleanor for a while before anyone else found you. Isn't that what you said?"

"Yes, but I didn't steal anything from my sister." Stella looked away and immediately back, pointing a finger at Jenny. "No one came for like an hour. I was alone with her dead body that whole time because I wouldn't leave her. Viv found us."

"Okay, I believe you. I just had to ask," Jenny said. Stella's eyes clouded and flashed. Her frustration was packed in dangerous reserves, like lint in a tinder box. "It's going to be okay. We'll find Eleanor's killer. We'll start with what we know. Thomas and Eleanor had a rocky relationship—"

"She was terrified of him," Stella blurted out.

"I remember. We'll work through it." Jenny put an arm around Stella's shoulder and walked her back to the bed. "Do you mind if I borrow the police file? I'd like to look it over. And can I take a picture of the quilt? I'm not sure if it's related, but if Andrew thinks she's come back from the grave to tell him about a quilt and a treasure, we shouldn't ignore it."

Stella straightened the quilt while Jenny took out her phone to take a picture. "This reminds me. I left your camera in the dining room in the commotion. We need to remember to get it."

Jenny snapped a picture of the quilt and tried see a key somewhere in the pattern. It was all stars and simple shapes. "It's a beautiful quilt. I have a pattern like this. It's called, Sweet Stars."

"I like that." Stella smiled and cleared her throat gently. "She made it with my mother before she passed away."

"And then you lost Eleanor. That's a lot for your family."

Stella gripped the edge of the quilt. "Andrew and I are the only ones left. He thinks he has to be my protector. I just want justice for Eleanor."

"And that means finding her killer?" Jenny asked the obvious question.

"Finding them and making them pay for what they did to her."

8

JENNY SAT ON her bed reading through the police file detailing Eleanor's case.

Thomas, apparently, had been at the top of the police's list of suspects. They had pages of notes and copies from an appointment book that showed his daily activities for the entire filming period. Most notable of which were repeated calls with a competing studio. The last few were labeled with notes like "Get E on board" or "she's gonna kill me"

Then there were the notes on Warren. Relief and suspicion tangled over the pictures of him and Eleanor at lunch or leaving each other's homes late at night. Their list of texts between the two stars filled several pages saying things like,

—I may not be your hero, but I'll try.

And

—I need someone to count on if I go

—I'm here. I love you. Remember that.

Nothing directly incriminating, but a relationship that went further than Warren had let on. There was practically a whole private investigator file on him, until it cut off abruptly, with one word: *cleared*. No record of confirmed alibi or a reason they took him off the list of suspects, just *cleared*.

The hexagons she'd been arranging earlier still clung to the wall. Her miniature quilt on a vintage train design wall. She might have enjoyed it more if it wasn't helping her organize suspects, clues, and motives. The trio of purple and blue hexagons representing Eleanor and her siblings hung in the center of several other blocks. Thomas, Warren, and the affair all pressed up against the three stoic hexagons.

Jenny picked up another brightly colored block and pulled her heat sensitive pen out of her supply bag. She wrote "Pregnant" over the yellow background fabric setting it on the wall against the blocks representing the affair and Warren. Taking a moment to label the original hexagons she realized she'd stitched the affair and Warren's blocks together, only according to him it was all a rumor. Still, rumors don't have to be true to cause real damage.

Jenny looked down at the file in her lap and plucked out another hexagon. She labeled this one as "Competing Studio". She wasn't sure who the studio was but if Thomas had been anxious enough about it that he'd made notes in his appt. book to warn himself then she needed to consider that.

A green piece of fabric stared up at her. She took a deep breath and wrote the word that was still rolling around in her mind, "Cleared". It should have made her feel better, after all the notes and investigation they'd made into him, the police had cleared Warren. But with no explanation it only made him look more suspicious.

It didn't fit in the quilt any better than it did in her mind. She didn't want it on top, next to Stella's block, or angled between the affair and Eleanor. Finally, she set it beside Warren's block, sticking straight out of the side. It was an extension to the pattern that didn't fit anywhere else.

After stewing over her oddly shaped quilt, Jenny turned back to Eleanor's case file.

The next page held a statement from a woman named Karah Stewart. When Jenny realized she worked in the wardrobe department Jenny's interest piqued. She'd apparently overheard an argument between Eleanor and another woman while doing a fitting for one of the soldiers. It could be the threat Stella had mentioned.

"I was fitting one of the soldiers with a new coat and I had to go in the back for some new buttons when I heard Eleanor's voice through the wall of the tent. She was arguing with another woman. They were talking about an audition. It sounded like Eleanor was given this person's spot. She accused Eleanor of ruining her career. But Eleanor wouldn't do that. Then the woman said something like, 'you shouldn't have done that' and 'I'll make you pay'. Then something hit the tent wall, and Eleanor screamed. I screamed too and ran away before they found out I had overheard."

Ms. Stewart claims she spoke to her coworker about it shortly after. Ms. Vivian Teagan.

The door to Jenny's compartment slid open, and Jenny slapped the folder closed, dropping it onto the table.

Ron stood in the doorway, breathing heavily. He slid the door closed behind him, locked it, and tugged at the handle to be sure it held, before stumbling into the room.

She stood to meet him as he wrapped her in his arms. "Are you all right? It took longer than I thought for you to get here. I thought you'd beat me back." Concern pinched the start of a headache in Jenny's jaw when he didn't respond. "What happened?"

"Please, just tell me you're being safe." Ron held her tighter, the smell of must and varnish suspended the moment as he stroked her hair. "Bonnie told me what happened at the dinner. Jenny, what is going on?" He paused and picked up the file from the little table. The hexagons clung to the wall and when Ron shook his head, Jenny was certain he'd noticed. Only a few pages into the file Ron shut it and looked at Jenny. "I need you to stay out of this. Someone died tonight."

"I know," Jenny said, "but some things can't be helped. This is a small train. We're both in it. Whether we like it or not."

"This isn't about an old murder anymore. Garrett was poisoned. I was there when Darren told Chris. There's a killer on this train, and I'm not going to lose you. We need to stay together."

"You're not going to lose me. This is exactly why I can't stop looking. I don't know if this is purely revenge or if Eleanor's killer is back but we need to figure out who is responsible."

Ron took Jenny's hand and held her gaze with his clear blue eyes. "Promise then. Promise me you'll be safe.

Jenny frowned. "I promise."

"And that we'll stay together." Ron added and Jenny flinched. "Please?"

His eyes turned pleading, and Jenny softened. "I'll try, but sometimes we have to split up. Like tonight. I was helping with the injury, and you had to help Chris and Bonnie came in all upset, and—" she paused, as Ron started to shake his head. He wasn't usually this close to murder. "Okay," she said gently, putting her hand over his. "We'll stay together."

"RON," JENNY SAID patiently as they walked away from Viv's table, "you can't just tell her we think she tried to kill someone."

"Why not?" He sat down at the first empty table he found.

Jenny glanced from the seat in front of her to the woman they'd just insulted. She circled the table and sat on the other side where Ron's body would mostly block her from Vivian's view. If she leaned over her food like she was starving, anyway.

"Because we don't know that." Jenny hunched forward and kept her voice low. "And I needed her to talk to me. Now she thinks we already believe she's done something terrible. Next time, let me do the talking."

Ron huffed a little and stabbed a clump of eggs with his fork. "I just wanted to know where she got the gun."

Jenny rolled her eyes and took a deep breath. "I understand. But it's possible she didn't do it at all."

"But you said—"

"Forget what I said," Jenny hissed frantically. The gun is the last thing we should have asked about. All I *know* is that she was in wardrobe when Eleanor died, and she had the same job for this round of filming. She was nearby when Thomas was shot, she was at the dinner, it's suspicious, but that's all. I have no idea what her motive would be or if she even had the opportunity." She peeked over Ron's shoulder to see Vivian shooting daggers at them. Jenny scooted closer to the table, hiding from the dark-haired woman. "Everyone is on edge today. Eat your eggs, and next time we're on one of *my* visits, just . . . just listen."

He glared at her as he stuffed the food in his mouth and chewed.

Jenny ignored him.

The sweetness of Ron's concern had disappeared with the reality that he really wanted to spend every moment together.

His concern was valid. Discussions about Thomas and the shooter were everywhere. There wasn't a single person on the train not worrying that Eleanor's killer was back or wondering who among them had a gun. She'd even heard people contemplating if it would be safer to get off at the next stop.

"Maybe it's a good idea." Ron was halfway done with his breakfast, while Jenny had only eaten a few bites.

"Maybe what's a good idea?" Jenny toyed with her fruit, not sure she'd heard him right.

"Getting off. Denning is coming up soon. We can find a way home from there and let the police handle the murderers." Ron set his fork down and pushed his plate aside.

"Can we talk about it later?" Jenny glanced over Ron's shoulder. Viv was gone. She relaxed for the first time since they'd gotten to the dining car. "I understand your concern but—" Jenny jumped as Viv slapped her hands on the table and leaned over them.

"I didn't shoot him. And I don't have a gun," Viv insisted, bracing herself against the argument she must be expecting.

"Okay." Jenny glanced at Ron. His lips disappeared behind his facial hair as he pinched them together in silence.

"I know you saw me in the hall, but that doesn't mean anything." She moved around anxiously, bending her knee and leaning to the side as she propped her body against one arm, then the next. "Stella was the one in there, I thought it was obvious that she shot him."

"Except, that someone attacked her too. And neither of them saw who it was. Except that they were dark-haired." Jenny paused as Viv's eyes widened.

Vivian pulled her hair back as if she could disguise it. She opened her mouth several times as she continued to shift anxiously. It felt like there was something she wanted to say but couldn't decide what or how. "I see," was all that finally came out before she turned away.

Disappointment knocked the hope out of Jenny's chest, like a bobbin suddenly and unexpectedly out of thread.

Then Viv turned back, putting a hand on her hip, her chin jutting out in defiance. "I didn't do anything. I wanted to see if Thomas was hurt, I mean, if he was okay. I don't know how to shoot anyway." She waited a second, her gaze darting everywhere but directly at Jenny. "Who do you think it was? You know, who do you think shot Thomas?"

"I don't know." Jenny waited to see if Viv would look at her for longer than a few seconds. She didn't. "You didn't see anyone suspicious in the hall, did you? Maybe going the opposite direction, or—"

"No." She pulled back, offended again at just being questioned. Jenny's annoyance at Ron dissipated as Viv continued to be uncooperative. He'd simply asked a question. One that someone who wasn't guilty shouldn't be bothered by. "I should go." Viv turned to leave, knocking her hand against the tabletop. "Ouch." She grabbed her injured hand, shaking it against the pain as a beautiful ring with five blue jeweled petals fell from her finger.

"Where did you get that?" Jenny reached for the expensive bauble. It had landed on the table in front of them and looked exactly like the descriptions of the ring from Eleanor's jewelry set.

Vivian snatched it up before Jenny could take a closer look. "It was a gift," she said quickly. "Anyway, talk to Stella. She would do anything to help her career. I know, because she tanked mine."

"And how does shooting her producer help her career?" Jenny glanced at Ron.

"It doesn't," Viv said, and she swallowed hard. "But shooting the actress blocking your success changes everything."

"You think she shot Eleanor?" Jenny asked slowly.

"That's what I heard." She shrugged, there was only a moment of hesitation before Viv spun on her heel and left.

"Wait," Jenny stood to follow, but she was running down the aisle.

Ron pushed away from the table looking from Vivian to Jenny. "Are we going after her?"

Jenny coughed in surprise. "No. I don't chase people. Besides, she can't go far, and we still don't know what happened. That ring though . . . it's just like Eleanor's. If it was really a gift, I wonder who gave it to her."

"I don't know." Ron held out a hand to Jenny and she took it. "So, we don't chase people." Ron coughed lightly and grinned. "And we don't know where Viv went. Where's our next stop? Stella?" Ron asked. "Or Thomas?"

Jenny leaned into Ron's shoulder. "Thank you. Stella. I was hoping I'd get a chance to visit her before we stop at Denning. I have a few more questions for her."

They moved down the hall in the same direction as Vivian, though she was long gone before they made it into the next car. They passed the bar and lounge cars as they headed to the first-class section of the train.

Suitcases were stashed every few compartments along the sleeper cars. As if they were waiting to be taken off the train. More people than Jenny realized must be planning to make Denning the end of the road. They crossed through the bar into the first-class cars. It wasn't a true first impression, since Ron had been there the night before, but it had been dark, and he'd been chasing a gunshot. Based on his reaction, it was fair to say he hadn't noticed much of the finery the night before.

Outside Stella's door, Jenny knocked and pointed to an article hanging on the wall across the hall. "When you get a chance, read this one about the palace car. The most luxurious train car ever made. At least it's assumed to be. Even the plumbing was gold plated."

A loud crackle burst over the background music. "Arrival at Denning in fifteen minutes. Duration of stay four hours. Departure at three pm."

The background music resumed, and Ron glanced at the door. "We should probably be quick so we can see some of the town before the tour."

Jenny knocked again, and Thomas opened the neighboring door. He leaned into the hallway and looked both ways before exiting and putting on a layer of confidence like a comfortable sweater.

"Good morning," Jenny greeted him. "Your shoulder looks good."

He stretched it a bit and cringed, pulling it right back in. "Thank you. Andrew said the bullet went clean through. I want to make sure it heals right, so I called my doctor and I'm going to see him when we get off."

"Oh, are you leaving, too?" Jenny hadn't expected him to disappear with the rest of them.

"No. My arm is fine. They said a clean shot can wait a couple days. There's no reason to go. Who said I was leaving?" Thomas held his arm close, watching them.

"No one. It's just . . . people—" Ron looked behind him. The hall was empty. "I mean some people—"

"People are talking about getting off the train at Denning and renting cars or calling for rides to go home," Jenny said.

"No." Thomas' eyes flashed panic and he stumbled back, his injured shoulder hitting the doorframe. "Aagh!" He hit the wall with a slight crunch of plaster. "They can't do that!"

Jenny gripped Ron's arm. "Actually, they can."

"Wait, . . . let me think." Thomas' good hand went through his hair, gripping the back of his neck. "The gun is locked up, right? We don't know who shot me, but that's okay because we're being more careful now. Added security and more group activities. I refuse to be the cursed movie producer. No one will hire me. No! No one will work for me. They don't have to leave. They can't leave. I need to fix this. I have to go. You're staying, right? I'll see you tonight."

Jenny nodded in quick response. And Thomas stormed down the hall.

"We're staying?" Ron asked, a healthy waver of unsurety in his voice.

"I wasn't telling him we're leaving while he's in that state," Jenny muttered.

"Let's go back to our room." Ron turned them around. "We should pack up, just in case."

The door to Stella's room was ajar, and Jenny swore it hadn't been a minute ago. "Did Thomas open Stella's door?"

Ron shrugged. "Maybe he hit it on his way past. He was in a hurry to get out of here."

The lights were off inside, and Jenny broke free of Ron's arm. "Just a second. I want to check on her."

The door opened easily. The cool familiar scent of flowers spilled into the hallway. Thick and heady, like Stella had sprayed the room down with perfume. It hadn't been like that the night before. Jenny knocked on the wall. "Stella?" Her fingers found a light switch, and she flipped it on as she stepped inside.

The room was trashed.

"Wow." Ron followed Jenny, stepping over a pile of clothes. "I hope she can afford a cleaner."

Jenny went to the sitting room near the bathroom. "Stella?" She scanned the empty room and turned back. On the far side of the room, the adjoining door that led to Thomas' room was open. She crossed to the door, swung it shut, and ticked the latch closed. "She locked that last night. I watched her do it."

"I hope she's okay." Ron said. He reached the dresser and inspected the contents scattered along the smooth surface. "Who would have done this?"

"I wish I knew." Jenny had been in Stella's room one other time. She looked around trying to understand. Nothing seemed damaged everything had been tossed around. Like a teenage girl had come inside, searched for her keys, then tried every article of clothing on, and left it all on the floor. "Where are you, Stella?"

"She's not here. Should we go back to our room?" Ron asked.

"I guess so, but on the way, we need to stop by the conductor's office and let him know about this." Jenny only made it halfway across the room, in the time Ron took to get to the door. Below her feet pale blue flower petals danced over the chaos. "Hang on."

Ron looked down the hallway impatiently. I'm going to go get the conductor. I'll meet you back at our room. Do not go looking for new suspects, okay?"

"I'll be right there." Jenny half watched Ron and half watched the petals battering her feet as they danced around her.

Ron didn't seem to have noticed. "Okay," he said. "If I don't see you when I get there, I'm coming back."

"I love you too." Jenny smiled.

He hesitated a moment before blowing her a kiss and leaving.

Jenny bent, picking up several petals. They were just like the ones she'd found in the viewing room of the old caboose. They felt so real. "Eleanor?" she asked softly. The petals swirled like a mini tornado over the chaos of clothing and belongings on the floor. The temperature dropped, and the floral scent grew stronger. "Okay, Eleanor. What are you trying to tell me?"

The breeze turned into a full-blown wind, sending petals crashing into the closet door like a wave.

A lamp tipped, knocking over a stack of electronics on the desk. Jenny stumbled as the wind pressed her forward "All right," she said. "I'm going. Calm down."

The wind obeyed, the petals falling into a pile in front of Stella's closet. Jenny stepped forward, suddenly nervous. Eleanor's intensity had been unexpected, and the fear of what she would find behind Stella's closet door made her hesitate.

Her hand hung in place over the handle as her mind painted terrible pictures of Stella crumpled in the corner. Below her, the petals shot up like fireworks in the wind. Smattering against the door.

Jenny grabbed the handle and pulled.

The closet was empty.

"Seriously?" Jenny muttered as the petals disappeared. She took a moment to calm her breathing. "Of course, it's empty. Everything is on the floor."

Jenny looked it over one more time and turned away, working her way back to the door with no objection from Eleanor except for the cold. Jenny turned around one more time, wrapping her arms tightly across her chest and scanning the room.

A huge mess of clothes on the floor, the newly tipped lamp, blankets pulled off the bed.

The bed.

Jenny's gaze shot around the room and ended resting on the closet. The door had closed, but she knew it was entirely empty.

With everything in chaos around her, it had been hard to tell if anything was missing—but it was.

Stella was gone.

And so was Eleanor's quilt.

9

"**H**OW OFTEN DO your quilts stay home?" Ron asked, zipping his suitcase.

"Almost always."

"Unless you're showing them off, loaning them out, picnicking, or sharing them, or taking pictures, or one of the kids wants to borrow them—"

"All right. But Stella also said her brother thinks the quilt is the key to something Eleanor left for them. If it's some kind of treasure map it could have been stolen."

Ron raised an eyebrow and went into the little bathroom to gather his personal items. "Not typical quilt use, but okay. It's a possibility."

A crackle in the hall caught Jenny's attention, and she opened the door.

"Welcome to Denning. We wanted to inform all our passenger the results of the incident last night. Everything has been handled, and the responsible party has been apprehended and is currently in custody. And to avoid any similar incidents, security across the train has been increased. Your safety is of the utmost importance. Enjoy your time in Denning, and we will see you back on the train at 3:00 sharp."

As the background music sputtered back over the speakers, Ron's hand slid over her shoulder. "We need to go."

Jenny shut the door. "I know. We can talk to the police and tell them what we know about Eleanor. I'll find Stella and make sure she knows what happened to her room."

Ron lifted both their suitcases to the floor and turned to look at Jenny. "You don't think Stella was taken into custody, do you?"

"I hope not." Jenny looked at her own suitcase. "Maybe Chris worked on finding the suspect during the night. It would be nice to know what he knows."

Ron's fingers worked over the handle of his bag.

The train pulled to a stop, and Jenny looked out the window. "Well, if nothing else, we may be able to create our own fairytale here."

Ron pulled the curtain back and laughed. "Perfect, if we get lost, we can find little children to bake into gingerbread."

"Oh, Ron, you didn't." Jenny let the curtain go. "You just turned us into the villains."

"How's your cackle?" Ron asked handing Jenny her bag as he wagged both eyebrows and stepped from the room.

DENNING WAS TOO PERFECT.

Window boxes filled with flowers and dark wood beams decorated every building. Colorful signs hung over business doors throughout the town with scrolling trim across the eave. The sweet scent of pastries and savory breakfast foods filled the air. If "It's a Small World" had started playing, Jenny would have believed they were in a theme park.

"You can't be out of rentals." Ron leaned over the counter of the only rental car agency in town.

"I'm so sorry," the man said. "We're a small town. And we got a lot of requests with your train's arrival. Can I offer you a discount on your next service?"

Ron groaned, and Jenny just held out the handle of her bag.

"Do you have a bus station?" she asked.

"No. I'm sorry," the man said. "They canceled bus service here two years ago. Not enough demand."

"Well, there's demand now," Jenny said with a smile.

The clerk gave her a thumbs up and grinned.

"Well." Ron looked around. "Do you want to find some souvenirs?"

"Whatever you think." Jenny was only half paying attention. A small ambulance had pulled up beside the train. She couldn't see who was in it though.

"Okay. I don't know if you want any souvenirs from the town we got stranded in after getting shot at."

"We're not going to get stranded," Jenny muttered. She chose to ignore the *getting shot at* bit. It was an exaggeration, and Thomas happened to be coming off the train with Bonnie on his heels.

Jenny squinted through the bright sun as he stopped to talk to the conductor and the paramedics. After the ambulance left, Thomas and the conductor started pointing and arguing.

Without taking her eyes off the heated moment, Jenny waved at Ron. "Is that Chris?"

"Excuse me?" Ron sounded offended.

Jenny glanced at him. His pinched brow matched pursed lips turned down into a frown. He was indeed offended by something. "I asked you if that was Chris Wiley. The conductor." She pointed at the men arguing while Bonnie pouted beside the train. "Over there. Is that him or the other one?"

"You didn't hear anything I said, did you?" Ron's expression hadn't changed, but he'd crossed his arms over his chest and leaned back in his chair.

She thought back to the last things they'd said. "We were joking about getting stranded."

"No, you missed everything about the hotel and Cherry and what I thought we could . . . you don't want to go, do you?"

"What are you talking about? We're here." Jenny had missed something important, but her gaze kept drifting back to the train. "None of the cast seem inclined to leave." Jenny's observation didn't appear to make Ron feel better. "They trust Thomas."

Warren had headed into town, and she even spotted Viv. The collection of unfamiliar suitcase holders gathered around the benches where Jenny and Ron were currently sitting.

Ron grunted. "So we're staying on the train." He leaned forward. "Because you decided we should."

"I don't know what you want me to say." Jenny's mind tangled in a baffling web of threads and circles as she tried to figure out where she'd gone wrong. "Is there a better option?"

"I suggested getting a hotel." Ron's voice had turned icy. "That was a good idea. We could stay here and enjoy this rustic little town and wait till a rental car comes back or call someone to come get us."

She took a breath. They needed to de-escalate whatever was happening. "Okay, how long would that take?"

"Depends," Ron said, like it was a guessing game. "Maybe a week . . . at most."

"A week?" Jenny stared at him, shocked into giving him her full attention. All she could see were the passing days of the calendar and everything she had scheduled. "You know I can't randomly be gone a week. People are counting on me. On us. We need to be home. I have filming and guests coming in three days. And I still have to make all the quilts for next month. I have already been gone so much with the movie—"

"Oh, I know. Believe me, I know." Ron glared, and Jenny's eyes narrowed.

Being cruel wasn't in Ron's nature, but when arguments built up, frustrations boiled over and even simple words started to hurt.

"I know you know." The pointed words cut him off, and Jenny leaned forward to finish. "So, you shouldn't be surprised when I say, I can't stay here for a week."

"Then I guess we won't stay here. I'll go put my bag back on the death train and wait to be murdered." Ron stood, gripping the handle of his suitcase.

"Ron." Jenny put her hand out to stop him. "You're being dramatic."

"That doesn't make it untrue."

"Except it is untrue," she said. "We are not going to be murdered on the train."

"Eleanor was," he snapped.

"A year ago."

"Stella is missing."

"I know." Jenny's gaze shot back to the train. "But we'll find her."

"We probably just missed her." Ron sighed. "She might be in town sightseeing already." He sounded drained, and Jenny understood. She dropped her defenses.

"That's possible," Jenny said more to herself than anything. Her worries about Stella bubbled up and took over all her thoughts. "So why am I still anxious about it? My gut is telling me something is off, and my gut feelings tend to be right. Something is wrong here."

"And yet we're getting back on the train. I'm so glad you're so in tune with whoever wants to hurt Thomas and Stella." Ron spat the words like ammunition, and Jenny pulled back. Ron's whole body tensed. "Where's your intuition about us? I'd love for you to pay that much attention to our relationship. Maybe then you could see that something is wrong here too."

"Ron," Jenny said. "Don't be like that."

"Like what, Jenny? You've been so stuck on solving an old murder that I've barely seen you since we started this trip. This was supposed to be a couple's vacation for us to reconnect." Pent up tension finally exploded, a cupboard full of sewing supplies so carefully packed she hadn't even noticed it was overflowing. "Maybe, now that I've told you what's going on, your intuition can kick in and explain what's happening with us."

"This is not the place, Ron." Heads were turning. Jenny didn't know if it was disapproval or concern, but this attention was not the kind she appreciated.

"Where, Jenny? Where is the place? Because it's not at home. It's not in our room. It's not on the train. For months, I've tried so hard to get even a little bit of your focus, and it feels like there's just nothing for you to give."

"We just need some time together. I've had some big projects. You know it's not always like this." Jenny lowered her voice. People were full-on staring. "I only have one more thing coming up. It will calm down."

"Will it?" He leaned forward, not angry or yelling, but so frustrated he was shaking. "There's always a next thing. And another, and another after that. I want to be the next thing."

"Ron," Jenny hissed, gesturing around them with her eyes. "Not here."

"Right. Then I guess I'll go somewhere else." He grabbed her bag with his and stalked off, dragging them both back to the train.

"Ron!" Jenny barely knew what had just happened. She stood in shock, waiting for him to turn around and not leave. To come back. To say he was sorry. To ask her to come with him. Anything.

He didn't look back.

By the time she processed what had happened, Bonnie stood in front of her. "Give him a minute."

She wore a look of sympathy Jenny hadn't known Bonnie was capable of.

"I can't. We need to talk. You heard that. We just can't talk here." Jenny sidestepped Bonnie. "I need to figure this out."

"No," Bonnie said, stopping her. "You really don't. Give him a minute. Why don't we go for a walk?" Bonnie linked her arm through Jenny's and walked her toward the shops, actively moving her away from the train, and Ron. "You two have been having some struggles, haven't you?"

"Some, but I didn't think they were that bad. I've been busy. It happens, though. He knows that." Jenny tried to look over her shoulder several times in those few sentences. Bonnie kept her moving forward.

They turned a corner, and Jenny sighed.

"Relax. Neither of you are going to disappear. Let him calm down. You'll be back together before the train leaves, and so will you."

"I know. We just argue so rarely that it's a shock when it happens. You don't think he's going to be more hurt if I don't find him? I can fix this—"

"But should you?"

Jenny stopped talking as she questioned her instincts. "I don't know. There's so much. I just want him to feel better."

Bonnie patted Jenny's arm. "It can be hard, but I've been through this so many times. I'm guessing you two have been together a long time?"

"Almost forty years." Those words alone softened Jenny's frustration.

"Not bad." Bonnie sounded pleased. "So let him have his tantrum. He'll get it out and eventually remember that he's crazy about you no matter how busy you are."

"That seems a little one-sided." They turned to a window filled with dried florals and soap. It was beautiful.

Bonnie apparently agreed, walking them inside. "Not at all. These are his feelings, right? He needs to resolve them. Didn't you say you thought things were fine?"

"Yes?" Jenny picked up a bar of white soap with pink and peach swirls, not sure if that was the right answer at all. Her desire to fix the problem battled with Bonnie's words. "I guess I can see what you mean. He's allowed to feel hurt."

"That's right. Ron's a big boy. He knows he hurt you with what he said back there—"

"That's not what I meant," Jenny interrupted but Bonnie didn't pay her any mind.

"Just let him deal with that, and when he comes back, he'll be in a much better place."

Jenny paused, lighting on those last words. *He'll be in a much better place.* "You think so?"

"I know so." Bonnie exited the building and walked them right into the next one as if she already knew where she was headed. Old and new items crowded the shelves of the small shop with little-to-no organization. Bonnie picked up several items, her eyes constantly on the back of the store. "In fact," she went on. "He'll probably be so penitent he'll beg for your forgiveness. That's when you know it'll last."

Jenny followed Bonnie's meandering path through the store. Nothing much caught Jenny's interest, and when she did reach for something, Bonnie was already moving on. "Is that how you and Carey have managed things?"

"Carey?" Bonnie scoffed. Her eyes turned immediately back to the store's rear wall. "I'm not with Carey. I'm not in a relationship at all, at the moment. I'm just waiting for the right guy to recognize that he needs me."

Jenny caught the profile of a salt and pepper-haired man in the back, right in Bonnie's vision. Jenny was willing to bet that if they got closer, he'd have a bandage on his shoulder.

Thomas had apparently finished arguing with the conductor and was now doing the same with the store clerk.

"I didn't realize." Jenny could see quite clearly who Bonnie thought the right man was. "You're always with Carey. I just assumed you were together because, well, you always are." Jenny glanced around, for the first time wondering why Carey wasn't padding after Bonnie like a puppy.

Bonnie groaned. "I know. I like him to be there when I call, but some days . . . oh well." She walked them over to a clearer view of Thomas and became engrossed with a miniature tea set featuring pink cats. "Besides, haven't you been listening? When a man loves you, you have to let him know that you're the one in control. If you lose that, you'll be apologizing for his hurt feelings. Make him remember that it's his privilege to be with you."

Bonnie waved the cat-shaped handle of her teacup at Jenny. "You are worth a little begging. Love is not free, and it is not common. You deserve to be fought for. So, make him fight."

The force of her statement took Jenny by surprise. She nodded, if only to appease Bonnie, and Bonnie's intensity cooled.

"Good." Bonnie seemed to finally register the cat teacup in her hand. She set it down and threw her shoulders back. "Now, I'm going to follow my own advice and show a certain gentleman what he's missing." With powerful strides, Bonnie walked to the back counter of the shop where Thomas stood arguing with a clerk.

Jenny watched her go. Conflict and contradiction churned inside her, discrediting Bonnie's passionate speech.

His weakness didn't make her feel strong. There was truth in there too, Jenny was worth being chosen and fought for, but she didn't want to make Ron beg for her love.

Bonnie flounced up to the counter beside Thomas, as Jenny took a cleansing breath. Just because Bonnie said and believed she was right didn't mean she was and Bonnie's knock-them-down-and-show-them-who's-boss plan made Jenny sick to her stomach.

"I didn't know you were interested in bedpans." Ron's voice spoke softly beside her.

"What?" Jenny startled, turning and finding him only inches away. "I'm not," she said, but, to her surprise, Jenny's fingers were wrapped around the seat of a vintage chamber pot. She let go, dropping it as soon as she realized what she had been holding.

As her chosen bedpan fell to the table, it knocked the whole pile off balance. In a grand cacophony of sound, dozens of bedpans fell to the floor.

"Oh, no."

Voices all around them expressed concern, and shop personnel ran her way. It only took a glimpse of Bonnie's smirk in her periphery to know how Bonnie felt about leaving Jenny on her own.

"I'm so sorry." Jenny stacked bedpans haphazardly with Ron's help as the clerk frowned. "It was an accident. Is anything damaged?"

The clerk scanned the stack and gave her a disapproving glare. "It looks like everything's fine."

"Those are very nice portable toilets. Thank you for your time." Ron grabbed Jenny's hand, and they hurried out of the store like teenagers who'd been caught pulling a prank.

"I leave you alone for five minutes and look what happens," Ron teased.

"That was more than five minutes, and after our last conversation, I was trying to give us some time. How did you find me, anyway? You couldn't have seen me from the street."

"I didn't." He paused on the sidewalk. "I don't know how he knew, but Warren told me where you were."

"Warren?" She hadn't noticed him on the street. "What was he doing?"

Ron sobered. "Keeping tabs on your suspects, I see."

"Ron." Jenny kept step as Ron slowed. "It's not—I'm not ignoring you."

"I know. You're just focused on a problem. You'll figure it out. I know you will. Warren talked to Andrew and the woman from breakfast, Viv—Vivian. Something about quilts, actually."

"Jenny, Ron." Thomas walked up beside them, stopping beside a tall van parked at the curb with the logo of a tour company painted on the side. "We're going to tour the mineshaft that inspired the one in the film. Would you like to join us?"

"We'll be right there." Jenny glanced at Ron. Ron smiled, but he kept his hands in his pockets and only looked at her briefly before heading toward the tour bus.

Things were not back to normal yet.

10

DARKNESS HAD BEEN EXPECTED. It was the water that surprised Jenny. Cold damp air clung to her skin and clothes as rivulets of groundwater seeped down the walls.

Worn wooden beams lined the dirt and metal walls of the old mine tunnel. Jenny's knuckles turned white gripping the edge of her shirt hem as she peered through the darkness. Keeping watch behind them for the guide, Thomas worked quickly, shoving Warren's body into the hidden gap. The fissure was worked into the space behind a wall of corrugated metal that still held shovel marks from years past. Warren's broad shoulders barely fit, but with a little effort, his body disappeared behind the wall.

Shadows flickered with the lights. For a handful of seconds Thomas' heavy breathing was the only sound in the tunnel. Then Warren coughed and reached an arm out of the cubby. It was barely large enough to hold a stash of a few tools, let alone a man.

"All right, I believe you." Warren grabbed for Thomas as he squirmed out of the tunnel, his arm wet from the groundwater seeping down the walls. "It's the same size as the studio replica. I didn't fit in that one very well either. And it's freezing. It's a good thing we didn't have to film here."

Water dripped from the ceiling, coated the walls, and pooled on the floors of the mine, chilling the tunnels and leaving the entire shaft cold and damp.

"What did I tell you?" Thomas puffed out his chest having proven his point. "I do things right. No one can say I don't take care of my people. I always do."

The cast members and crew moved around Thomas with a certain amount of distance there. Even Warren's challenge had been more of a joke that Thomas had allowed likely because he knew he'd win.

"Great. Help me out of here, will ya?" Warren reached again for Thomas' hand. "Or are you gonna take care of me when the tour guide comes back, too? How will you take care of things when she asks what I'm doing climbing through the walls of her mine?"

Thomas grabbed his hand, and with a swift tug, Warren came scrambling out from behind the wall. With both hands he brushed off the damp remains of his hiding place and straightened to his full height once again.

Only a few feet from where he'd been hiding, the corrugated metal holding back the mountain had been punctured. The metal support was overcome by mother nature in several places. Rocks and coal tore into the metal barrier, like a child poking holes in a sheet of tissue paper.

The mine shaft continued on, like railroad tracks, caged in unending boxes of repeating wooden frames and corrugated metal.

"That was a stupid thing to do," someone muttered from the edge of the group.

Jenny had half expected to find Stella at the other end of the blunt reprimand, but Carey's dimly lit skepticism claimed it. Stella had never appeared to join them. Carey waved at the hollowed out hiding place. "Quite the combination of old metal and rusted nails in there. It's like you're begging for tetanus. And with the water dripping over tubes of *updated wiring* . . . that's nice way to die."

"Is now the best time to joke about dying?" Warren asked. "You might be giving someone ideas."

The group quieted as Warren's teasing resonated with truth.

"I'm sure it's safe. Or they wouldn't bring people down here." Viv scooted closer to Warren not bothered in the least by Stella's absence.

"Except no one said it was safe to climb inside the crack of an underground wall." Bonnie's bored look had been perfected during their tour.

"There's nothing to worry about," Ron said. All eyes turned to him, and for a second he was speechless. "At least, from the wiring point. That's outdoor grade electrical conduit. It's protected from the water. And you're right, they wouldn't bring people down here if it wasn't safe. I'm guessing they expect us to use common sense to stay out of dangerous situations. Of course, common sense isn't always very common."

The group laughed, including Warren.

"I found it!" The young tour guide reappeared holding a small, circular badge like a trophy. "Thank you all for waiting. I'm sure no one moved while I was gone, like we discussed." She chuckled and pinned the badge to her lapel. "Now, like I was saying, I need this to monitor the air quality, which was one of the most important jobs in a mine, and it was given to the smallest members of the crew. Back then, canaries helped to detect dangerous gases . . ."

The group followed the guide, but Jenny still had her eye on the cutout where Warren had tested his hiding place. It was a gap in the dirt behind a sheet of metal, hidden by angles and dim lighting.

In the movie, Warren had played an antihero that won over a local seamstress. Through multiple deceptions and crossed loyalties, they hid him in the mine shaft when his enemies were about to discover him. In the movie, it had been clear who the hero was. As Jenny looked around, she knew too well that in real life heroes weren't always so obvious.

"WAIT FOR IT," Andrew whispered.

The small group curled around Thomas and the staff of the coal mine. Jenny had joined Andrew in the back and only had to shift a little to see what he was talking about.

As Thomas finished his speech about the challenges of creating his historic film, he paused and looked around at the crowd.

"Wait for it," Andrew repeated, leaning forward ever so slightly.

Thomas took a quick breath, closed his eyes, and turned to the owner of the preserved coal mine. "Thank you so much for everything you contributed to help make this film into a reality." He reached out, shaking the man's hand as a single tear dripped down his cheek.

"Boom!" Andrew made a mini blast-motion with his hands, grinning under the sound of his whispered explosion.

"Look at those tears. The boy pulls it out every time. He was a great actor once." Andrew's enjoyment of the moment faded quickly, his nostrils flaring while he watched Thomas clap Warren on the shoulder. His emotion only brought up more questions for Jenny.

"I'm thinking he still is," Jenny whispered back.

"If only he wasn't such a terrible person." Andrew's voice teetered between sarcasm and bitterness as he slow-clapped behind the enthusiasm of the crowd.

Thomas talked about what a great cast and crew they had. With as much ceremony as he could muster, Thomas then presented the owner with a framed picture of the cast in full costume. Jenny had seen it earlier, and the image captured a dirty group huddled together, arms around shoulders, smiling in their torn uniforms and bloody aprons in front of the mine shaft entrance.

Around them, the extras and stage crew began talking more freely as the presenting cast shook hands and signed autographs.

Jenny looked side-long at Andrew. "I wish Stella had made it. She seemed surprised to see you last night. Are you two close?"

Andrew glanced at Jenny and shoved his hands in his pockets. "She didn't know I was on the train."

"Were you going to tell her?" Jenny shrugged, playing off the question as more casual than it was.

Andrew's eyes darkened. "Not until I had to," he said, keeping it just as casual. "But it would have come out eventually. It's a small train."

"Exactly my point." Jenny didn't step closer, but when he leaned in, she didn't move away. "So why hide?"

His gaze faltered and he looked away, turning to the front, regardless of the fact that the presentation was over. "No." he finally answered her question. "I wasn't planning to tell her, unless she needed me, which she did. Last time we talked, she asked me not to come."

"But you came anyway." Jenny raised an eyebrow. Stella hadn't told her that. "Do you know what happened to her this morning? She was planning on joining us today, but when I stopped by her room this morning it was a mess, and she was gone. She didn't make it to the tour at all."

"She texted me this morning and said she wouldn't make it." He sneered when Thomas laughed. "She was probably just sick of him."

"I don't know. I didn't see her at all when I went by—" If Stella stayed on board, she'd be practically alone ... with access to everyone's rooms. "She's been on the train this whole time?"

"That's what she told me."

Oh, she's good. Jenny grinned.

Andrew crossed his arms. "She did get strangled last night. Are you gonna hold it against her if she decided to rest for a day."

"Not at all," Jenny agreed as the crowd began to dissipate. People left to explore the upper area of the mine, some headed into the tiny museum, while others gathered in groups to visit. She turned to Andrew, hoping for a few more answers. "So, tell me about this search for Eleanor's treasure."

He sputtered a laugh. "I don't know what you're talking about."

"Yeah, you do." Jenny's no-nonsense tone quieted his laugh. "Don't worry. I don't want it for myself. I was just surprised to hear Eleanor had left you something. She was murdered unexpectedly. How would she have time to hide something for you to find? Why would she even hide it in the first place?"

"She had to be planning it before she died. To be nostalgic or something." Andrew hesitated, looking her over. "I might as well tell you the whole story. Stella seems to trust you anyway. I don't know what you've heard, but this isn't just about a treasure. Eleanor took care of us for years after our mom died. She passed just after Elle went to college. I was barely a senior in high school, and Stella hadn't even started freshman year. At the time, I thought the treasure hunting was dumb, but Elle loved it. She would hide our books and games before we hung out together, snacks, new clothes, whatever. That way it didn't matter how much there was or if the clothes weren't really new. She tried to make everything fun. Elle watched out for us. Kept us together."

It matched what Stella had mentioned but Andrew seemed more invested in the story than Stella had. Things that she'd passed off as nothing Andrew squeezed with details.

"It sounds like you were really close." Jenny said.

"We were. Before." Andrew turned toward Thomas. "Our problems started when that man walked into our lives."

"Stella told me she was dating Thomas when Eleanor met him. After what you said, I'm surprised Eleanor would marry him, or even date him, knowing it would hurt Stella."

"It didn't just hurt Stella, it destroyed her. I guess it destroyed them both." He raised an eyebrow and followed the crowd toward the exit. "You've met Thomas, right? He's very convincing. Thomas Quinn always gets what he wants. For Elle, after challenges in her life, I think she just couldn't give up the security. She always said she would make it up to Stella. It just didn't work out like she'd planned."

"Jenny?" Ron paused on his way to the parking lot. "There's a car going back now. I told Chris I'd help out before the train leaves. Do you want to go back now, or shall we meet up later?"

Jenny glanced at Andrew. "I'm not quite ready yet. I'll meet you there." Jenny kept her voice low as Ron moved to the exit. "Is it possible she knew about someone who'd wanted to hurt her? The treasure hunt makes it look like she was planning for the possibility. Maybe this treasure hunt will give us a clue about her killer."

Andrew scoffed. Jenny knew exactly who his first thought would be.

"You think it will help us take down Thomas?" Andrew's eyes darted to the group fawning over his brother-in-law.

"That's not what I said." She didn't need everyone jumping to conclusions. "But I do think it might help us find out who killed her. Last night at dinner, threats were made, and someone was poisoned. I'd rather collect facts and prove who killed her than keep guessing."

Andrew sobered. "I heard things got pretty bad at dinner. I talked to Stella for a while after bandaging Thomas. I needed to keep her awake and make sure she wasn't in shock."

Jenny examined the change in his face. He had been bitter and cold and accusing, but when he talked about his sister, he looked sincere. "We can't assume it was Thomas. Not yet. I don't know who killed Eleanor, but if we assume it was him, we could lose the real killer."

"I'M NOT SAYING you killed her." Jenny and Warren stood almost nose to nose in the hallway outside his room. "I'm just asking why the police would clear you, point blank, when the rumors about you and Eleanor are the biggest motive for murder outside of her rocky marriage. Together, it stitches up a pretty solid case against someone."

"Not me," Warren insisted.

"Unless you and she had plans to leave together." Jenny couldn't see why the police would take Warren off the suspect list without giving a reason. "How many people knew she was leaving Thomas? Not even her sister. But you did. Stella found out by accident. Why would she tell you if you weren't part of it? Did she change her mind and you got angry?" She pulled back, as his eyes narrowed and his jaw clenched. "Or maybe it was an accident. Maybe you just wanted to protect her."

"You're not listening to me. I wasn't in love with Eleanor. And I didn't kill her, not even by accident. We were friends."

"Do *friends* kiss each other goodbye after staying the night at each other's homes, or text I love you?"

"So, we were affectionate."

"Warren." Jenny looked at him with all the pleading she could muster. "I need answers. You can't expect me to believe that you and Eleanor were nothing more than friends. You said yourself—if things had been different . . ."

"Yeah, Jenny, if things had been different. I cared about her, but I'm not talking about timing." He looked down the hall and pulled her into his room. "There are things about my private life that I don't want everyone to know."

"Things you told Eleanor?"

He nodded his head. "My career is based on who the public thinks I am. My jobs are based on what movie producers thinks I can do, for them and their movie. Who I'm perceived as is my brand, and I'm not allowed to change that."

"I understand. Your image is who people want you to be." She knew what it was like to live in the public eye. Not as extremely as an actor or actress, maybe, but people commented on her clothes, or the movies she'd gone to see. There was a lot of second guessing in the decisions she'd made in her life. It didn't change who she was, but she understood. "But you built your image. I don't understand how telling the police 'I didn't do it. It's not part of my brand' would clear you."

Warren let out a sharp breath and crossed his arms. "The police were looking at me. Pretty hard, in fact. Thomas was pointing them my way, even though he'd been part of instituting our relationship." He paced across the room and back, stopping in front of Jenny. "I need to know I can trust you to keep this in confidence."

"Is there a reason I would feel obligated not to?" Her hesitation grew as he deliberated. Jenny and Ron were supposed to check in with each other before dinner. Warren's stubborn secrets were going to make it difficult to keep her appointment with her husband.

"No, I haven't done anything wrong. It just changes who I am, to all of them." He waved past her, and Jenny pushed through her hesitation, nodding her agreement.

"You know that I was with Thomas that evening. We had a meeting that was scheduled at four. Just a few minutes before, he rescheduled it, pushing it back to five. We were prepping for a night shoot, but all of us basically knew what to do. Thomas said he had some issues with an upcoming contract to deal with. After Elle died, he asked me to corroborate his story. And I agreed . . . because it helped me too."

"So, you're protecting Thomas? The man who was making your friend's life miserable?" Jenny stared at Warren as he set his jaw, nostrils flaring.

"Not exactly," he said. "I agreed because it was helpful to me too. When Thomas pushed the time back, I met someone in wardrobe."

"I don't see how—"

"A man, Jenny. I met a man who I'd been dating in wardrobe. And neither of us was there for a fitting."

Jenny furrowed her brow. "So, your secret is your sexual preference?"

His expression didn't shift or even twitch. He just looked at her. "I'm not ashamed of being gay. I just don't want to change the way I'm seen and cast and paid. I like my life. One day I'll tell the world, but not until I find someone I'm ready to change the world for."

"Okay." Jenny was a little excited she would finally be able to knock someone off her suspect list. "And who did you meet? I'm assuming he can confirm your alibi?"

"Not anymore." Warren stepped back. "I was meeting Garrett."

"Oh, I'm so sorry." Thinking back, Jenny could see the connection she'd missed in his reaction the previous day.

"Thank you. We haven't been together for a while now, but it's hard to see someone you cared about die." That had apparently happened to him twice now. "When I finally told the police, I asked them not to include it in the report. I'm asking you the same thing. Please keep this to yourself."

"Of course." It was an easy answer. "Would you let me know if you think of anything that could help with Eleanor . . . or Garrett? I just want to find out who's behind all of this."

"I think I've shared everything I know, and if you have the police report, that has the rest of it."

The police report . . . it wasn't enough to convict someone then, and with stories like this, it wouldn't be enough now.

Warren started to close the door, and Jenny turned back.

"Warren? You said you met Garrett in wardrobe, right? Don't they keep that locked when no one's there? Who let you in?"

"Wardrobe took over the first baggage car. Like the empty one where we went after Garrett's—Anyway, yes, they kept it locked, but Viv showed me where they stashed the extra key."

"Viv?" Jenny kept her face neutral. Viv's name had been coming up more and more. She'd need to add Viv to her list of people to talk to . . . sooner rather than later "You make a lot of friends, Warren."

"I'm a friendly guy." He grinned, one side of his lips curling up. "I've helped her out with some things in the past, and she lets me schedule the room for private fittings, occasionally."

"Helped her out?"

"Connections. She's trying to get started as an actress and just hasn't found her break yet."

"So you scheduled this *fitting*? Can she confirm you were there?"

"She knows I asked if the room was available, but scheduled is probably a strong term. I don't think she'd confirm. She could lose her job for handing out keys."

Jenny raised her eyebrows and nodded. "Let me know if you think of anything else. I'm going to be looking for Stella."

"Why?" Warren grabbed his phone and scrolled through several messages. "Isn't she in her room?"

Jenny looked at him hoping he'd read the question in her eyes.

He did. He pulled his phone out and scrolled. "Look, she's taking a diva day." At her cough Warren grinned. "Sorry. You could also call it a mental health day. Point is, we were supposed to do dinner but she canceled because she's got a headache."

"Oh." Jenny turned slowly and gave him a last look as several questions ran through her mind. "I know you're a friendly guy and all, but I like Stella. She's got a good heart. Don't break it."

11

JENNY WOULD NOT get frustrated with this man. He was only defending his staff. But he'd been doing it for twenty minutes. She was supposed to be getting answers.

The kitchen manager stood, sliding his chair in. "Mrs. Doan, as I said, no one on my staff would touch a client's property."

With over an hour left until the dinner rush, the dining room was fairly empty. She kept her voice low anyway. "I understand you believe that, but the cards were tampered with. Mr. White," Jenny said pulling herself up to her full height. "Someone was poisoned."

His lips pressed into a thin line before he spoke. "And yet no one but Mrs. Beale and Mr. Mills gave any indication of knowing the cards were even there."

"No one amended her request? Or maybe they just called your people away." Jenny followed him to the kitchen door.

"Mrs. Doan." He turned to face her. "Is there anything else? I should be helping prep for dinner."

"It was a busy night. But a man died. He was poisoned. Don't you want to clear the reputation of your company and staff? Don't you want to find out what happened? Garrett and his family deserve to know."

The manager pushed the kitchen door open, then pulled back, letting it close behind him. Scents of sizzling butter and garlic washed back through the opening. He stood staring at the floor as if he were finally considering her question. "I'll check with my staff. As you said, it was a very busy night."

"Thank you."

As he pushed through the door, Jenny remembered the other reason she'd come to see him. "There's one more thing," she called, catching the door before it could close. "The door to the upstairs dining room is locked. I left a camera up there after the party. Did you find one when everything got cleaned up for the night. It was Mrs. Grace's, and I wanted to get it back for her."

Mr. White looked into the kitchen, the bustle of white coats danced with the sound of vegetables disintegrating under sharp knives in the background. He pressed a smile on his face. "You're just doing favors for everyone, aren't you."

"I can go look. I just assumed you would have already found it."

"No," he said quickly, pulling a handkerchief out to wipe his face. "Don't do that. The conductor has closed off the room. It's a crime scene." His stern tone carried a chastising authority, and Jenny pulled back slightly.

"So, you haven't even cleaned? Could I . . ."

"You really can't. It's locked up," he said. She glanced to the stairwell in the corner of the kitchen, and he bristled, adding, "—on both sides. And I didn't see a camera anyway. There's nothing for you to find in there."

Jenny doubted that very much. With the room being left as it was, there would be plenty to learn. Her whole body itched to get past those doors. "Are you sure? I'd really appreciate it if you'd let me check. I'd just be a moment, and you could come with me."

"No," he said with finality. "Good evening, Mrs. Doan."

The stubborn kitchen manager had taken longer than she'd planned, and she still needed to meet Ron before dinner. She'd just wanted to know if someone suspicious had been around before the party. It became an inquisition of "he said, she said," as if she were accusing him personally.

Jenny checked her watch and started down the long corridor. The pictures on the walls were becoming familiar as she passed from car to car and found herself ticking off the ones she knew. Coral Grant, one of the quilting girls. The soldier who always got lunch for himself and a friend. Bonnie's portrait with her pristine smile, and one she'd seen earlier today. She paused in front a picture that looked identical to the one Thomas had presented to the owners of the old coal mine.

It was disturbing to see so many familiar faces covered in blood and grime, the buttons and sleeves ripped away on vests and uniforms, and none of it bothering anyone.

The entire group smiled, except Stella.

Only . . . it wasn't Stella.

It was Eleanor. Jenny could tell from her bright red lips. The dead woman stood in miner's pants with a buttoned shirt, and a hard hat, her bright red lips turned down. It was so different from the purple suit Jenny had come to think of as her uniform. On the opposite side of the group photo,

Stella wore a floral house dress and coal-brushed apron. The young woman looked so happy in her supporting role.

Flanked by both Thomas and Carey, Eleanor looked miserable. Thomas' arm gripped her shoulder, and Eleanor stood stoically beside him . . . holding Carey's hand.

Frost curled up the windows along the outside of the car.

"It's gone." There was a gasp of breath behind her, and Jenny spun around to see a little card on the floor, with gold letters scrolled across the front. *I killed Eleanor Grace.*

Unsure where the card had come from, Jenny reached to pick it up. Blue petals danced around her fingers, getting in the way as she snatched it off the ground. She had several petals pinched against the card as the rest of them blew wildly about. She followed the path of the petals as they slipped under a door. The door directly in front of her carried a brass twenty-three.

She knocked.

Voices whispered behind the door, intense and fast. Jenny knocked again, and the voices got quiet.

Silence settled around her, and Jenny looked down either side of the car. The frost and petals had vanished, and no one else was in the corridor. She looked back at the door and let out a breath. Blue flowers danced over the floor again.

"What do you want?" Jenny asked, kicking at the loose petals. She looked at the card in her hand and stuffed it in her pocket. "Someone killed you. I understand. Who was it?" she hissed at her invisible friend. If she could have yelled at her without sounding crazy, she would have.

The door of the neighboring cabin opened, and the petals vanished. Jenny froze as Carey exited the room with a distracted look about his eyes. Her smile popped into place.

"Carey." She paused, as if his name was all that was needed. She tried again. "It's good to see you."

"It's good to see you too. He glanced from her to door number twenty-three. "Are you visiting Andrew?"

"No."

Her quick, defensive response got a reaction from him. He stopped on his way down the hall, furrowing his brow.

"I was just returning . . . something." Jenny's mind had gone blank at a terribly inopportune time.

He looked at her empty hands. "Tell me the truth. You're here to kill him, right?"

"What?"

"No, no. Don't let me interrupt you." He winked and held his fingers to his lips, twisting a pretend key and tossing it away. "I won't tell anyone."

Jenny gave a stiff laugh, glancing at the door beside her. "No, really." Desperately she reached in her pockets, retrieving the disturbing note she'd found on the floor. She held it up, attempting to hide the message on it. "I was just returning this. He dropped it."

Smooth embossing slid over the textured linen cardstock beneath her thumb.

The blood drained from Carey's face. "Where did you find that?" He knew exactly what she was holding. "I thought we threw them all away."

"What?" Jenny looked at the paper innocently. "This? Oh, it's noth—" A blue smear, the color of forget-me-not petals, stained the back corner. Was it on her fingers? She almost dropped it trying to check. "—nothing. I was just leaving my phone number. Stella wanted to talk to him about Eleanor and—sorry, we don't need to go into all of it."

She bit her tongue. That was unnecessary.

"No, it's fine. Where is Stella? I haven't seen her. She missed the mine tour, didn't she? That's too bad." The skin around his eyes tightened, and Jenny nodded.

"Yeah, I guess she's not feeling well." Something crashed behind Andrew's closed door and Jenny turned to it curiously. "Is he in there? I knocked, but he didn't answer."

"It may not be a good time." Carey glanced at the door. "He's been spending some time with an old friend." He flicked his eyebrows up and adjusted a small bag on his hip. "Vivian," he whispered loudly.

"Vivian. Like, costume, Viv?"

"Yeah, exactly. You should probably warn him off if you get the chance. She's looking for any way she can to get into the acting side of things, and she'll do whatever it takes to make it happen. Except get better at acting."

"What makes you say that?"

Carey shrugged, his thumb starting to tap against his bag. "She's Bonnie's best friend about every other day. She hangs off Warren and sends me a birthday card every year. The strangest was when she sent me a get-well card last month after my dental surgery . . . I don't even know how she knew about it."

"And Andrew's family is well known in the acting community."

"Yeah. Thomas is the only one who's managed to keep Vivian at arm's length. Not sure how, but she doesn't bother him. Ever." Carey stepped past her, headed the way she'd come. "I should get going. Nice to see you, Mrs. Doan."

He left, and Jenny squinted at the door suspiciously. Vivian and Andrew. That was not who she would have expected.

She knocked again, waiting only a few seconds before giving up. Ron was waiting on her. She hurried to the end of the corridor, looking back as she opened the door.

Pale blue flower petals blew in a mini cyclone of color over the deep red carpeting, frost again on the windows.

THE HEXAGONS ON Jenny's wall had expanded. There were enough little patches of color now that she couldn't remember what they represented without their labels. It was a real murder quilt.

A cream colored hexie with a bright flower center labeled "Treasure" sat between Thomas and Eleanor. Floating a bit to the side, Jenny had placed a new block with "What is 'IT'?" written across it.

The words *"It's gone."* Floated through her mind. Jenny had been hearing Eleanor's voice since she got on the train, but that was all she ever said. "What's gone?" Jenny hovered her fingers over another block without looking away. "The treasure? Love? Your family?"

She shook her head and picked up another piece of fabric, a purple hexagon in graduating colors from lilac to a ring of deep purple on the outside. *Karah*, she wrote, glancing at the police report. The girl who'd overheard the confrontation in wardrobe. She pressed it to the wall beside block she'd labeled "Viv."

Someone had confronted Eleanor about ruining her career and threatened her. Jenny looked at Viv's block. She really needed to talk to her.

Jenny twisted her watch on her wrist. Five minutes after five. She looked at the door. Nothing.

Ron hadn't even shown up. She let her eyes wander around the room. The suitcase against the armoire. Ron's bathroom supplies on the counter in the tiny cubby of a bathroom. Her own bags on the overhead shelf.

She settled back in with her fabric and took two of the hexagons and started stitching them together. This investigation was literally coming together whether she had answers or not.

She had Eleanor and Thomas stitched together. She could probably stitch Warren to Eleanor's block as well. She wrote, *Friendship* below the label "Affair" on the pink hexie. But where did she put the treasure, or Bonnie, Andrew, Carey, or Garrett? Had his drink really been meant for Warren? And why? Why threaten so many? She picked up Bonnie's hexagon.

"It was your party. Your cards. Your placement! How can it not be you?"

She glared at the tiny block and tossed it against the wall. It hit it and fell to the ground.

A thin paper slid under the door. Jenny dropped the disconnected hexagons and stood, releasing a frustrated breath.

She opened the unsealed flap on the envelope. A piece of cardstock with gold lettering across the front fell out. *I killed Eleanor Grace.* Jenny glared at it and picked it up. "Someone mistyped their print order."

She opened the door and stepped out into the hallway, looking both ways.

Empty. No prank message deliverer. No porter or conductor. No Ron.

Still.

"I didn't even know Eleanor!" Jenny yelled at the empty hallway. Obviously, her frustration hadn't eased.

With a crack, the door slammed behind her. And the hallway dimmed as if clouds had overtaken the sky and night had fallen. A gust of wind blew from one end of the hall to the other, flower petals flying against her in a barrage of color that wasn't pretty or sweet. They hit her face in waves of floral potpourri. The wind whipping her hair and clothes as the temperature accommodated Eleanor's spirit.

Jenny waved away the mess, blocking her face from the delicate bullets of ghostly flowers. "Fine. I'm sorry. I'm still here!"

The wind relaxed and the petals fell to the ground, dancing in swirling patterns across the floor. *"Help me. It's gone."*

Jenny's breath came heavy and fast, the chill of her skin only partly from Eleanor's confrontation. Her heart beat was so fast the nerve endings in her skin fired at every breath, sparking fear through the pores of her goosebump-covered skin.

Jenny looked behind her. Nothing.

A door opened, and a young man leaned out, looking at her curiously. "Did you knock? I'm sorry I didn't know what that was."

It took a moment to find her voice again. "No. I'm still here, but I'm going now. Thanks."

Jenny turned and went back inside her room. She grabbed a pen and the envelope with the gold-embossed card.

Ron,

I'll be in the dining car at six-thirty.

—Jenny

That was it.

If he wasn't coming back when he said, she wasn't waiting around. She needed to breathe.

In the hall, the sun had come out, and the brass fixtures sparkled. There was no sign of Eleanor.

That meant nothing.

Jenny had convinced a ghost she would help her.

She started walking until she made it to the bar at the end of the lounge car. "Lemonade—" Blue petals danced at her feet, and she smiled up at the bartender. "Never mind."

She started walking again, hurrying away from the ghostly petals. It wasn't that she didn't want to help. She was constantly wondering what had happened. She just didn't want to fail. Not that she hadn't failed before, she had. It was hard and disappointing. But failing in the normal world was entirely different than failing a ghost.

She couldn't be indebted to a woman who walked through walls and appeared out of nowhere, freezing the blood in her veins, and destroying an entire train car because she was stuck wanting only one thing, and thought everyone else should want it too.

Before she knew it, Jenny found herself standing in first-class outside Stella's door. The "do not disturb" sign was up. "That's new," she muttered. Maybe Stella was really there.

The Haunting of Quilter's Square

Jenny knocked and waited. There was no sound inside, no footsteps, or anything. She glanced at the hangtag and sighed and stepped away from the door.

Dinner was an hour and a half from now. She could check on her then. She glanced down the corridor. She could go back to her room, but she wasn't ready yet.

She looked the other way. The caboose—Eleanor's murder site—was just through those doors.

"All right, Eleanor. You win."

12

TREES AND WATER rolled by one side of the converted caboose with the mountain rising above them on the other, casting shadows as the sky grew dusky. Windows surrounded three sides of the train car. Jenny could see why Eleanor had liked coming here. It was a beautiful place to ride and watch the view, if it wasn't also a murder scene.

Jenny sat on the tufted cushion opposite Eleanor's resting place. Her toes brushed the long fringe of the bench beside her. She replayed in her mind several of the scenarios from that afternoon a year ago.

Eleanor came to the room before meeting with her sister. She was in costume, ready for the filming that night, except she was missing her pin. Had she forgotten it? Or had it been taken?

Jenny could see Eleanor perched on the cushion watching the world, anxious about her plans to leave her husband, and preparing to make sure her family got whatever it was she wanted to leave them.

If he found out she was pregnant, or that she was leaving him, would he have done it? She now knew he had the time. In the hour difference of when Thomas had scheduled his meeting and when he moved it to, he could have seen Eleanor pass their room on her way to the caboose, gotten his gun, and shot her out of spite or anger.

With his temper, it seemed entirely possible. Jenny could imagine him standing there over his wife's dead body before the scene reset in her mind.

This time it was Bonnie, the spiteful friend who hated her, that followed Eleanor into the room. The image of Bonnie in one of her glitzy dresses and heels prancing in after Eleanor was almost comical. She'd probably ask someone to come with her to shoot the gun because that could cause strain to her delicate fingers. Of course, the image of Carey padding after his beloved starlet fit beautifully.

In her mind, the gun went off and Bonnie screamed, latching on to Carey, begging him to help her with the stress.

And then it reset again. A dark-haired woman entered her imagination. Vivian, asking about Thomas and auditions as she begged for help to start her acting career. It was a good theory, but her motive was frail, and the scene was fuzzy at best.

The reset on Vivian was easy as Stella ran through next. Poor Eleanor stood in her corner in shock as Stella screamed at her for taking the life she'd wanted, finally breaking when Eleanor decided to leave Thomas. As Stella raised the imaginary gun, Jenny shut the scene down. She couldn't even pretend to watch Eleanor die at the hand of a sister she loved.

Then Andrew walked in. Jenny sighed, resigned to the next scene. Not sure why he'd want to kill Eleanor, she let her mind play out the scenario, considering his motives. Jealousy? Doubtful. Anger at betraying their family, maybe. He seemed to hate Thomas. Maybe something else had happened she didn't know about. Eleanor sat on her perch and Andrew walked across the floor, stopping only a few paces in, when Jenny remembered he hadn't even been on the train last time.

"Jenny." He nodded, and she jumped. "I didn't expect to see you here."

"Andrew?" She forced her expression to relax as he sat on the bench opposite her. He was real. "I'm sorry, I didn't realize it was you."

He lifted one eyebrow at her. "Who did you think it was?"

"Sorry, not like that. I knew it was you, I just—" Jenny shot a glance to Eleanor's corner, a short laugh betraying her nerves. "You know what, never mind. I sound crazier the more I talk. What are you doing here?"

"Looking for Eleanor." Andrew's expression shifted from confusion to silent laughter. "And no, I'm not crazy either. Did Stella tell you how I heard about Eleanor's treasure?" His eyes drifted around the room, ending on the same corner where Jenny had been fixated.

"She said you saw her in Quilter's Square and told you the key was on the train."

He looked at her, wide-eyed, and dropped his head into his hands, massaging his temples. "The whole thing, huh?"

"I suppose." Jenny hadn't told many people about seeing Eleanor at Quilter's Square. They were the only two who'd experienced it. She looked at Andrew, trying to decide if it would help him to know. "It's not so strange. I've seen her as well."

He lifted his head, eyeing her warily. "You've seen her? Why would she come to you?"

"I don't know. I saw her run through the crowd and jump onto the train as it was leaving. She didn't speak to me, at least not then. She screamed. I can still feel it. Like all her fear siphoned into me."

Andrew frowned, watching her like she'd become his competition instead of an ally.

Trying to make him feel a little better, Jenny told him the rest. "There have been a few times on the train that I've felt her, but all she's said to me is, *it's gone*, or *help me*." Jenny half-smiled at him, shaking her head. "I'm assuming it was Eleanor, anyway, because if it wasn't, I've become a ghost conduit and I'll never have any peace again."

A smirk toyed with Andrew's lips, and he steepled his fingers, leaning forward to rest his elbows on his knees. "Quilter's Square was the only time for me. I wasn't in the movie, or even helping with it, but I came every day after that, hoping to see her again." He looked over Jenny's shoulder, out the window. The air grew heavy in his silence. "It's strange, but I can feel her here on the train, as well as I could on the platform."

Jenny could feel her as well. Andrew's emotions seemed to call to his sister's spirit.

Jenny rubbed her arms to warm them. All the scenarios of Eleanor's death that had played out in Jenny's mind before Andrew arrived seemed to come together, unfolding simultaneously. Friends and acquaintances, walking through like ghosts until Eleanor died, over and over again.

Jenny's heart slowed with every shot, her body going cold. But it was only her imagination. She could feel Eleanor, but Jenny and Andrew were alone.

"Maybe it's the train and not the platform that she's tied to," Jenny said.

Andrew took a laden breath, running his hand across the back of his neck and over his jaw. "She died here. I wanted to see where she was and if I could figure out what to do next."

"And have you?" Jenny asked.

He shook his head, looking her in the eye. "No. She came to me on the platform, asking me to find her treasure. But I couldn't do it. Now Stella is trying to keep me out. Elle has stopped talking to me. If I can just find the key, everything will work out."

"And that's why you want to find the treasure." Jenny hesitated. "You don't care what it is, do you?"

"Not really. Anything valuable Thomas would claim it belonged to him, anyway." His eyes glistened with a thick layer of unshed tears. "I just want my family back."

"How does that happen, though? What could she have left?"

"I don't know." Andrew's lip trembled, and he took a fortifying breath. "I've been looking everywhere. I had a friend sneak me the invite list for the whole voyage and looked into everyone. I've snuck into people's rooms, including Thomas' and a few others."

"You're not serious, are you? Breaking into peoples rooms?"

"Yeah, I am. It's not what I expected, either. I'm looking for something that already belongs to me, well, my sister. I was so certain the quilt was the key, and then Stella wouldn't even talk to me. She chased me off the train right before it left."

"Wait, she knew you were here?" That wasn't what Jenny'd been led to believe.

Andrew shrugged. "She saw me and tried to make me leave. I thought I was going to miss it. She barely made it back on and I had to sneak onto the caboose. Bonnie helped me hide, but I had to promise to share the treasure with her. Then, when I finally got to look at the quilt, there was nothing there. No key at all."

"What made you so sure it was the quilt? How would it be a key to anything?"

Andrew's eyes went distant, and he smiled. "Eleanor said, *the key to my treasure is with my favorite star.* That's Stella. Elle started calling Stella her favorite star as soon as she got accepted to acting school. It's got to be something Stella has. I worried maybe she gave something away, but nothing else fits. And the quilt is just a quilt."

"Is there anything else that Stella got from Eleanor? A jewelry box, journal? Is there a locker code somewhere?" Jenny couldn't imagine there was nothing.

He shook his head. "The quilt is the only thing we have of hers. At least, I don't know of anything else. Thomas kept it all. So, now I'm guessing just as much as you."

"What about the forget-me-not necklace and pin? Thomas doesn't have them. He thinks Stella took it. Is it possible she could be hiding it? Did anyone ever look for that? It seemed pretty valuable."

Andrew frowned. "I didn't know that. I had sort of hoped that might be the treasure. Stelle was definitely jealous of it, but I don't think she'd take it. She doesn't do jewelry. She's allergic to the metal. Her skin gets all red and irritated."

Jenny couldn't wear most earrings because of a similar problem. "Are there earrings in the set? I thought it was a necklace and a pin—" *And a ring* . . . that Vivian had. Vivian, who Andrew was spending a lot of time with.

Andrew shook his head. "There're no earrings. But even necklaces leave red marks. All of it bothers her. She went to the hospital a lot before mom figured it out."

"Red marks . . . where the metal touches her, or everywhere?"

"Just where it touches her. It looked like rashes or bug bites, depending on what it was."

"A necklace could leave lines that look a lot like she was strangled, then, couldn't they?" Jenny could see the lines around Stella's neck from the night before. Maybe she hadn't misjudged how bad Stella's injury was, but misjudged what it was. An allergic reaction after trying to steal from her ex-brother-in-law. "Maybe, she stole the necklace after all. And he wanted it back. What if he found her, and she shot him for it. What if he wasn't lying."

"No way." Andrew shook his head. "He wouldn't let that go. There's no way he'd let her try and steal from him and just say sorry for the misunderstanding . . . unless—"

"Unless he didn't let it go." Jenny could feel the possibility settle into her bones. "He would have wanted payback. And no one has seen anything but texts from Stella all day."

Andrew swallowed and turned to the door. "We need to go check on Stella."

ANDREW'S FIST BANGED on Stella's door.

"She's not going to answer." The irritation in her voice made her sound more aggressive than she intended. Jenny stood to the side. It had been too long, and she'd made too many excuses. "If she's there at all, we would have seen her by now."

Andrew's breath flared through his nostrils as he landed his fist one last time on the door and let his body slump against the wood panel. "How could I be so stupid? I'm supposed to be protecting her. She texted me this morning. I didn't even question it. I was grateful. I thought it meant she was talking to me again. But she never texts me. She lumps me in with Eleanor as having abandoned her."

Andrew fished two thin pieces of metal from his pocket and knelt beside Stella's door.

Jenny leaned against the wall, watching his hands slide the thin metal into the simple lock. Stella's brother had an interesting skillset. "Just carry that around with you for emergencies?"

His fingers paused long enough for Andrew to glare up at her and turn back to his work. "Such as this one," he muttered.

The thin shafts of metal moved obediently, an extension of his hands. When they caught inside the lock, her breath did the same. The room and everything in it seemed to turn with him, spooling the fibers of proximity closer, Jenny included. She leaned in slowly until a metallic click released her.

She straightened along with Andrew. Putting his tools away, he turned to her. "You're welcome."

"I'd report you," she teased quietly. "But there's not many people to tell, and it's your sister's room."

"Report all you want," he said, sliding the door open. "Would you rather I break the door down?"

"No, it still looks like we're thieves."

"I'm not a thief. Just a talented property recovery specialist."

"What does that mean?" Jenny asked, following him inside.

"Thief," Andrew said, grinning. He moved into the room, scanning surfaces and headed for the bed.

"It's clean," she said in surprise.

"That's Stella for you. She's the youngest, but she was the pickiest about a nice place. She always wanted to impress people."

"But it was trashed this morning." That morning it had been covered in clothes and chaos worse than when her kids were teenagers. Jenny crossed the room slowly, pausing at the dresser.

The dresser was cleared, with only a few bottles on the surface. Stella had eye shadow, makeup remover, face wash, body sprays, and more hair products than she could remember. "This isn't right." She pulled a drawer open and stopped. "Where did it all go? The dresser's empty."

Behind her, Andrew swore. "She's gone, and I had no idea. She's probably hurt."

He moved quickly, checking the rest of the room. Jenny did the same, finding several drawers stuffed full, while others were empty like the first one she'd found.

"This morning it looked like someone was looking for something. All the drawers and closets were empty. Maybe they were looking for the necklace."

"Well, I haven't found it, or the quilt," Andrew muttered, dumping the trash across the floor. He sent the contents skittering apart with his shoe, looking through them as if he didn't expect to find anything.

"Hang on," Jenny said. She reached in front of him, pulling a floral pajama top from the trash. "That's what she was wearing when I left her."

"You're right." He lifted it up, and his face went pale. He held the shirt out to Jenny. "Did you notice the blood when you left? Because I didn't."

13

"THERE HAS TO be something," Andrew said. "Some clue about where they went or who took her."

He yanked the closet open. A vertical wall of packed clothing stood proudly like a garden wall without supports. It held its shape for several seconds before collapsing to the floor at his feet. "We're never gonna find anything in this, are we?"

Jenny started picking through the new pile on the floor. "Not without knowing what to look for."

"So, what are we looking for?"

"Something that doesn't belong to her. A note . . . a bottle of chemicals labeled with the owner's name. That would be helpful."

"Great. You look for the flashing sign." Andrew stood, tense as a knotted bobbin spool, thread ready to snap. "I'm going to start knocking on doors."

"Everything was so different this morning." Jenny looked around the room, trying to remember what she'd seen that morning versus now and even the night before when she'd visited with Stella. "There was a lamp there. And books, and electronics over there."

"None of that has to do with a necklace or the burns on her neck."

"Okay." Jenny took a breath, watching Thomas pace. "But are we trying to figure out what happened to her neck or her life?"

"Will one help the other? He'd only be looking for the necklace if she hid it." Andrew moved to the marbled surfaces of the bathroom and leaned his forehead against the glass shower wall. "But why would she have been wearing it in the first place? I have a hard time believing she just came in and tried on something like that."

Jenny cleared her throat. "Actually, she admitted it to me. She said she just wanted to see what it was like to wear something that fancy."

"You mean valuable." Andrew leaned to the side. "I know she liked expensive things. I just didn't think she had a death wish."

"You think Thomas killed her for trying on a necklace?" Jenny looked around. "She was hurt, bloodied, and taken from her room. Jenny straightened a few things off the floor and folded a small stack of clothes. "We're assuming this is about the necklace, but Stella didn't seem to know anything about the burns, and Thomas never mentioned the necklace."

"Or they lied." Andrew stopped pacing to stare at Jenny, lips in a tight line. "But if she stole the necklace, he would have flipped. He would have shot her himself."

"Are you sure?" Jenny's mouth went dry. "I saw Vivian in the hall along with my husband and Bonnie and lots of other sightseers. With the door unlocked to access the room, it really could have been anyone."

"You think your husband did this?"

Jenny shook her head. "Of course not."

"You said Thomas and Elle found her trying the necklace on before Elle died. If she did it again, he might have wanted to teach her a lesson. Andrew paced, moving across the room back and forth from closet to shower to the door and back. "Elle's not with him anymore, and he's most cruel without witnesses."

Those words ate at her belief of decency in the world, sitting atop the knowledge that real cruelty was alive in the places she least expected it. "But that contradicts the situation, doesn't it?" Jenny asked almost hopefully. "If Thomas saw Stella wearing Elle's trust-fund necklace, Thomas should have been doing the shooting. But yesterday it was Thomas who got shot."

"You know, this door was open last night." Jenny walked over to the adjoining doors, moving the debris that had built up in the random search of the room. "Maybe Stella did it, shot Thomas after fighting him off and hid the necklace."

"Only to come back and play the wounded bird?" Andrew shook his head. "This is feeling more and more unrealistic."

Jenny took a breath and gestured around the room. "Something happened after we left last night. How strong a possibility is it that Stella stole Eleanor's necklace?"

"It's possible," he said quietly. "But not probable. She's not a thief."

"Okay." Jenny examined the pile of clothes from the closet. "The quilt is missing too. Maybe someone came for that. To try and find the treasure. And they took her too."

"Except no one else knows about the treasure."

Jenny tripped on her thoughts. "Andrew ... Between you, Stella and Thomas ... I think everyone knows about the treasure."

Andrew quieted and set to work then. Things went more smoothly, since Andrew wasn't panicking. "It's hard to believe she thought she would need all this for three days," he said.

"Or that she could fit it all in a suitcase," Jenny said.

"She's got several suitcases." He stood, gesturing to the closet. "They were under the wall of clothing."

Jenny chuckled and stepped over to the door leading to Thomas' room. "I think we're done," she said, leaning her ear against the door. "What time is it?"

"After six. Why?" His skepticism bled heavily from across the room.

"Because I think Thomas might be at dinner. And I was hoping you could put your property restoration skills to use again."

"We're breaking into Thomas' room?"

"I would never. I just think I lost a very important piece of quilting fabric under the door. Would you be able to help me do a quick search for it? Or anything else I may have mistakenly lost."

"Mrs. Doan." Andrew knelt by the door. "I think I like you."

"Not the kind of approval I usually go for." Jenny stood by the dresser watching him curiously. The thin metal was doing its work again. "You said you stayed up with Stella last night, right?"

"Yeah, for several hours. Probably near midnight."

Jenny nodded as the metal bars caught and pulled the lock gently. "So, she didn't go missing until somewhere between midnight and morning. I think Ron and I were here around seven-thirty or eight."

The lock gave a final twist, with a satisfying click completing the movement. Andrew stood and opened the secondary door in slow transitions, checking to see if Thomas was indeed gone.

When it swung open fully, Jenny followed Andrew inside.

"So, is this a smash and grab?" He wiggled his eyebrows.

Jenny shook her head. "Don't you dare. I'm not looking to break laws or steal things. I'm just looking for information."

"That's good because, in spite of from my hooligan vibes, I don't enjoy ransacking people's things."

"I agree," Jenny said, looking carefully over surfaces and drawers. "I just like kidnappings less."

"It's like you're reading my mind." Andrew picked up a decanter set and opened it to smell the liquid inside. "So, what are we looking for?"

"Clues," she said simply. "We couldn't find anything in Stella's room, so consider this an extension of the scene. Something that indicates if Thomas was in her room this morning or of what might have happened."

"Maybe he took pictures." Andrew moved over to the large dresser and picked up a camera, turning it over.

"Oh my gosh." She joined him, and he gave Jenny the camera. "I thought this was locked in the dining room." She pushed the power button and flipped over to the stored images. Color lit the screen. The party appeared in stage after stage of Bonnie. She'd somehow managed to be in nearly every picture, and Jenny didn't even care. "I think it's all still here."

She clicked through several more and backtracked. She could have sworn there was an image of the table before everyone had gotten there. Thomas and the reporter had been talking and— "Oh my gosh." She clicked through several more. "He's worse than Bonnie. He deleted every picture of himself."

"You're kidding." Andrew lifted the lid on a black box with metal grommeted corners, like a mini trunk.

She slung the camera strap over her neck and tried to think what she should be looking for. One of Stella's belongings wouldn't do it unless they were bloody, like the floral pajama shirt. But everything was organized and carefully placed.

She opened a drawer of perfectly folded clothes beside a desk organizer containing a stack of three by five cards, three triangularly folded handkerchiefs, and four bowties clipped to the tallest divider.

"I don't know what's more surprising." Jenny laughed. "That he's more organized than my assistant or that he wears clip on bowties."

When Andrew didn't respond, Jenny closed the drawer and crossed the room to join him. "Is everything all right?"

He stood in front of the mini black trunk, now with a book in his hands. "It's her journal." He held it out for Jenny to see. Roses were sketched in cream over a sage green background, a thick locked band wrapping the book. "I bought this for her, years ago."

There was the emotion again.

"Wow. It's too bad you can't keep it."

"Why can't I?" He waved it like he was hoping Jenny would give him permission. "You're taking the camera."

"I'm returning the camera to Stella. It's not his. That's his wife's journal."

Andrew flinched. "Well, it's my sisters. And I doubt he'd even notice. It was buried in a box of power cords."

"I don't know, Andrew. It's not like he's living here. He chose to bring this stuff—oof!" Jenny stumbled as she moved away, knocking over an old army munitions box. "Why would he still have props in his room, especially if they can hurt you?" She rubbed her leg and froze.

There in the middle of scattered papers and office supplies lay a small handgun. As far as Jenny could tell, it was the same one she'd seen on the floor last night.

The one the conductor had put in the safe.

"WHY DO I have to keep it?" Jenny peeked into the deep purple bag she'd taken from Stella's room. A large camera sat atop a pair of dark blue corduroy pants, also borrowed from Stella's room, and folded vaguely in the shape of a triangle. *Still there, still safe.*

"Because I'm not supposed to be here and I don't want the conductor to throw me off." Andrew's whispered confession brought a questioning harrumph from Jenny.

"What do you mean? I thought your room was only a couple cars down from mine." Jenny took a double step to keep up with Andrew. Her height and long legs normally gave her an enviable stride, but Andrew was almost running. "Number twenty-three, right?"

Andrew ignored her. "And doesn't your husband have a rapport with the conductor?"

"Slow down." She forced a laugh as they passed by the casual visitors in the lounge. Her voice lowered to a hiss. "I'm not running through the train with a gun."

"Shh." The alarm in his eyes was louder than his hushed warning, but he slowed his step and let her catch up. "Sorry."

When they'd made it back into the corridors of the sleeper cars, Jenny asked again. "I thought your compartment was only a few away from mine?"

Andrew nodded. "Sort of. I don't have my own room. Viv is letting me share a bunk."

"She wasn't visiting you?" She thought back to her conversation with Carey outside Andrew's door and frowned. He'd been being discreet.

"What are you talking about?"

"Never mind." She didn't know yet if the things she was hearing were true, or if Vivian could potentially be mixed up in all of this. "I guess you're right, then, you can't take the gun."

"Because of Viv? What does that mean?"

"I've heard some mixed commentary on her character. And she lied to me." She could have just been nervous or misremembering, but so far, the reviews were not favorable.

"She's always been honest with me," Andrew whispered. "Have you even met her?"

"I have, but not much else." Who he spent time with was not something Jenny wanted to argue about. She'd just keep her secrets close. "I'm glad you can trust her."

They made it to Jenny's cabin first, and Andrew waited while she opened the door. Ron didn't come rushing to meet her and, considering she was holding a concealed weapon, that was good, but it was also bad.

Squinting to see inside the dark compartment, Jenny searched to see if Ron was waiting for her. But no one was there, and her spirits drooped.

Andrew patted the doorframe. "Okay. Figure out what to do about that." He gestured to the bag. "And I'll meet you after dinner, if I don't find Stella first."

"You're going to look now?" Crazy eyes felt perfectly appropriate as she stared him down. "You can't go by yourself. What if her kidnapper or attacker follows you, or if Thomas figures out one of us was in his room? You shouldn't go alone."

"I'm not waiting while who knows what happens to my baby sister. Can you guarantee that she's still alive?" Andrew took a step back, shaking his head as he moved down the hall. "No. I have to go. I've got people on my side. You're the one who needs to be careful. I don't want to come back and find you've gotten yourself caught—or worse."

He was already halfway down the corridor when she called to him.

"I'll be careful if you will." She took a few steps toward him and he turned back. "Andrew? Ask Viv if she knows Karah Stewart, in the wardrobe department. I have a question for her about Eleanor."

Andrew touched his fingers to his forehead in a light salute as he'd done in the movie. "Yes, ma'am."

Then he turned away, leaving Jenny alone in the hall with a camera and a gun. She shivered and turned back to her room.

A single blue petal danced in with her.

"I'm glad you approve." Jenny shook her head and smiled into the hallway.

She shut herself inside, giving the room a quick scan. She needed to get rid of the heavy bag. The luggage rack over the bed was too risky. She didn't want a gun falling on her in the night if she couldn't get it back to Chris soon enough.

The armoire was too obvious. Beside it, sat the suitcases that they'd packed to leave and unpacked again to stay. She carefully unzipped the smaller of the two suitcases and set the purple shoulder bag inside, zipping it again.

"Is everything all right?"

Ron's voice made her jump. Her fully alert nerves were sending all sorts of mixed signals.

"You're here!" Jenny said. "I didn't realize."

He stood in the doorway of the bathroom and smiled. "People have started talking about Stella's quilt."

"It's Eleanor's," Jenny corrected, not sure how other people knew about it. "What are they saying?"

"That there's a treasure attached to it. That it's a map." He stepped into the room. "I think people are expecting pirates."

"They may not be far off." Jenny let her head tip to the side, thinking about Thomas and Eleanor's avenger. It was a silly title, but what else did you call a killer with a personal vendetta on someone's behalf?

"Hmm." Ron scooted closer. "You're staying safe, aren't you?"

Jenny lifted her eyebrows in pretend shock. "Of course." She'd checked that Thomas was out of the room before they'd gone in. Then Ron picked up the suitcase and put it back in place and Jenny's heart stopped. Safe wasn't much of a possibility at the moment.

Ron released a heavy breath and pressed his cheek to her head. "I'm not sure I believe you."

He shouldn't, but it was for a good cause. "Stella's missing." She shook her head as Ron opened his mouth to object. "No. I appreciate having a voice of reason, but she's really missing. I think she's been gone since this morning or even late last night."

"How do you know? Couldn't she just be somewhere else on the train?"

"I hope she is. I just don't know where." She looked up into his blue eyes.

They shifted from doubt to concern. "Maybe there is some reason to worry." His breath filled the empty space, and Jenny could have listened to his steady comforting breaths all night. "I was just talking with Chris. He said there was an argument with Thomas earlier."

"You mean when we were in Denning?" A thread hung off the hem of her sleeve. She wrapped it quickly around her fingertip, as Ron nodded. The vague image of the two men standing beside the train waving their arms at each other was all she could recall. "I may have seen that. What happened?"

"Thomas wanted his gun back."

"Oh." Jenny's eyes fell on the suitcase she'd just zipped, holding Thomas' gun inside.

"Chris refused, of course. It wasn't supposed to be here in the first place."

"But he took it anyway." The picture of how the gun had gotten back to Thomas' room began to fill in for Jenny, colored in deep swatches of lies and deceit.

Ron ran a hand along her shoulder. "He's denying it, but now both the keys to the safe, and the gun are missing."

With the ache of truth in her breath, Jenny looked up at him. "That's not completely true." Her eyes fell to the suitcase. "The gun's not missing."

14

"I thought you said he'd be in the sleeper cars."

They'd walked the length of the entire train looking for Chris. The only staff they'd seen were waiters in the bar and the porters, delivering room service.

"That's what he told me," Ron grumbled, opening the vestibule door to the dining car. "Maybe he's in his quarters."

"Where's that?" Jenny stopped walking and glanced behind them. "I thought we'd been everywhere." They'd gone all the way to first class and back.

"This way." Ron led them through the dining cars and into the baggage car and kept going.

"There's more?" Jenny had assumed they'd run into the coal car or engine if they went any farther.

She wasn't far off. The conductor's quarters were only one car farther, right next to the coal car, or tender, as Ron called it. There were only a few employees relaxing in the bunk car, and they eyed Jenny and Ron warily.

"I haven't seen him." A lanky man dropped to the edge of one of the thin beds. "Passengers don't usually come back here. Not without Chris or Darren."

Jenny turned to Ron and murmured, "Who's Darren?"

"The second conductor," he whispered out of the corner of his mouth. "He and Chris work together."

With an exaggerated chuckle, Ron leaned against one of the bunks like it was his own. Jenny bit down on a laugh. He was trying so hard to be one of them. All he needed were some striped overalls and an engineer's hat to complete the picture.

"I was just talking with Chris," Ron said. "I thought he'd be walking the train this morning and then back here."

"No idea," one of the workers said. "We don't keep track of his schedule."

Ron grinned. "He keeps you pretty busy, doesn't he?"

"Only when we're on a shift." The man sitting in the corner chair of a round table gave them a dirty look. It was a not-so-veiled hint that they weren't working at the moment.

"Okay," Jenny said. "When did you see him last?"

"Last time we were off." The lanky man on the bunk was taking his boots off.

"Thank you." She wasn't getting any details. "That's very helpful." Her monotone sarcasm was only caught by one of the men.

"Sorry about them." The man from the corner adjusted his cap. "We're pretty exhausted. None of us have seen Chris, though. You'd have had better luck twenty minutes ago, before the shift change."

Ron seemed disappointed that there wasn't more to keep them there.

As she turned to leave, Jenny noticed a low box with a thick door hanging slightly ajar. "Is that the safe?"

"Yeah," the lanky man snickered. "But Chris lost his keys again. You stick something in there, and it's never coming back."

Ron had said Chris lost the keys, but they'd said *again* . . . If she thought she could trust them, she'd have handed off the gun now and let them figure out Chris on their own. "He's lost them before?"

The car quieted until the man in the corner stood and walked to a bunk. "Aw, whatever, it's not like it matters." He slung himself onto the mat and rolled over, looking at Ron and Jenny. "He lost 'em last time these guys were filming.

"Movie stars make him lose his mind." Another man answered. "That's why some of the guys call him 'Witless Wiley.'" The belly laugh of rumbled across the cabin until a shoe flew from a neighboring bunk. "Hey, I don't."

"We'll get out of your way," Ron said. "Let him know Ron and Jenny came by, if you see him."

They left the men joking. Before the door closed behind them, someone had begun snoring.

"So, does Stella really have a treasure? Is that why you wanted to know about the safe?" Ron asked on their way back to the main section of the train.

"I have no idea what the treasure is. Only that Andrew thinks Eleanor's quilt will lead them to it, and whoever took her likely took the quilt too." Jenny hooked Stella's bag under her arm. "It's possible they think she can help them figure it out."

Ron stopped at the dining car. "Can we wait a sec and grab food while we're here?" He pulled a chair out and gestured to Jenny.

"You want to eat with a stolen gun in the seat next to you?" Her eyes darted around the room to see if anyone had heard her.

There was a gun in her bag. How could they not know?

No one looked. No one even noticed. Aside from Ron, no one knew what she was talking about.

"Yeah, it sounds pretty bad like that," Ron said. "We'll keep looking for him. I promise. I need to eat though. We were supposed to meet for dinner and hour ago."

"Okay, but I can't." The fibers of Stella's bag resisted the clench of Jenny's fingers. She had to get rid of it. "We've looked over half the train. I'll head the other way and find him. If I don't, I'll put it back in the room for now."

Ron's stomach growled. "Ignore that." He laughed and glanced down at the buttons of his blue striped shirt. "I'll go with you."

Jenny let her tension go with Ron's laughter. "No, you order." Jenny kissed his cheek. "I'll be right back."

It took a moment, but he finally claimed a table, and Jenny hurried from the room. She'd barely made it to the first sleeper car when the air chilled, pale blue flower petals dancing over the floor.

"Eleanor." A breeze sent the petals flittering across the carpet in response. "You've got to be kidding me. You want to help now? Where were you when I was with Andrew, looking for your sister?"

She picked up her pace, crossing the hall. There were too many things to worry about, and Eleanor's visits had done little to help her.

The door caught as Jenny pushed through the enclosed vestibule to the next car, frigid air stalling her progress. The windows were already coated in a sheen of ice, patterns of tiny flowers across the glass. Her breath froze in her lungs. It crystallized as ice wove trails through her veins. The thump of her heartbeat fought the cold, reverberating in a hypothermic race.

She crossed her arms over her chest, gripping her biceps as she turned a painstaking circle. Beyond the faded sheen of frost in the air, everything looked normal. Jenny forced another step and stopped breathing as a pale woman appeared in front of her, petals circling her feet.

"*It's gone.*" Her porcelain skin shimmered with the perfect translucence of a woman no longer of this world.

Eleanor turned away, stopping mid hallway to look at the doors beside her. She turned back to Jenny, her eyes were dark wells of blue and black. Tears spilled down her cheeks, icicles of pain streaking her face. "*Help me. It's gone.*"

Sharp needle points of foreboding pierced Jenny's chest. She only managed a few steps before a crack of sound knocked her to her knees. Eleanor screamed, and the needle points in Jenny's lungs exploded in cold pain. Her chest was on fire as Eleanor ran down the hall, disappearing in her purple suit with the echo of a gunshot.

"No!" Jenny knelt in the hallway, panting from the intensity of her silent scream.

The blast rang in her ears as the cold retreated, her heart thundering against the pins and needles inside her, every beat an excruciating echo of Eleanor's final pain.

But it was Eleanor's pain.

Warmth tingled through her body, thawing the ice that had incapacitated her during Eleanor's visit.

She was fine.

No blood or gaping wounds.

The corridor was inexplicably empty, as if no one else had heard her terror or the gunshot.

The gunshot.

Dread and panic blasted through her, sending feeling through her bones all the way to her trembling fingers.

"Please, no." She whispered a barely audible prayer and pulled Stella's bag from her shoulder. The smell of acrid smoke played in the hall, a taunting indicator of her fear. With a glance down the hall, Jenny opened the bag.

No holes disrupted the heavy fabric, and the wrapping of blue corduroy around the gun hadn't even shifted.

Her breathing slowed, and Jenny got to her feet. Eleanor was gone, but the experience was seared in her mind. Goosebumps propagated her skin, a relic of the ghostly cold, ignorant of the sunlight now spilling from the windows.

She rubbed her arms, turning in the hallway like a rotisserie chicken, waiting for heat to penetrate her skin. Sunlight reflected off the dark wood trim boards and polished fixtures, warming the hallway. The brass number twenty-three flashed against the door in front of her.

Andrew's door.

Andrew and Vivian's door.

Eleanor had stopped to look at these doors. She'd stood very close to, if not exactly, where Jenny stood now. Cold seeped around the edges of Jenny's body as she stared at the bright metal, a new fear settling into her thoughts.

But Andrew wasn't there when Eleanor was murdered.

He wasn't supposed to be here now, either.

"Andrew, what did you do?"

He seemed so sincere about missing his sister and wanting his family back together. Of course, if he'd killed her, it wouldn't stop him from missing her or wanting to keep Stella safe.

Voices drifted behind the door in muffled conversation. Jenny knocked, and they fell away. She didn't stop knocking. "Andrew? It's Jenny."

The door opened a moment later. Vivian stood on the other side. "Jenny? Can I help you?"

"I'm looking for Andrew. Can I talk to him?" Jenny clutched her bag. She tried not to think about what was inside. If she didn't act guilty, no one would know she was.

"He's not here."

"Really? He said he was staying here." Jenny glanced over Viv's shoulder. "And I thought I heard voices."

"Neighbors." She gestured to Carey's door. "Agents and actresses are a noisy crew. Should I let Andrew know you came by?"

"I'd appreciate that," Jenny said. "Are you and Andrew close?" If they were, Andrew might have been upset if Eleanor had caused problems for Vivian's career.

Viv raised her eyebrows. "Sort of. We're friends, mostly."

"Just friends, rooming together?"

"Okay, fine. We're close, but I'm focusing on my career." Viv shrugged. "So, sort of."

"Right, you're in Wardrobe."

"That's not my career." Viv folded her arms and shifted her weight to the side, staring at Jenny. "I can sew, but I wasn't meant to be a costume mistress. That was a foot in the door to acting. A way into this world."

"Sewing may have been your foot in the door. But don't discount creativity." Jenny couldn't help feeling a little sad for this lost girl. "Sewing will do a lot for you. Even when your acting more."

Viv huffed a laugh. "Well, thanks I guess. But I act plenty. And I've got friends helping me more than sewing ever will. It was a foot in the door. That's all."

"I'm going to tell you a secret. Sewing isn't a fallback skill. Just keep doing what you love. If it's acting then maybe you're on the right path. Passion gets you noticed, and then you won't need Andrew to make connections for you."

Viv shoved her hands in her pockets. "It's not like that with him. Andrew's a nice guy."

Jenny hoped Viv meant that.

She had seen people get taken advantage of. Jenny had been that person once. "Karah Stewart was in the same department, wasn't she?"

Vivian's eyes dimmed. "Karah? She quit after Eleanor died."

"I'm trying to help Andrew and Stella find out what happened to their sister. Karah told a story about an argument with Eleanor."

"That doesn't make any sense." Viv shook her head. "She was in charge of the extras and supporting cast. Karah never worked with Eleanor, at all." She glanced down the hall nervously and started to pull the door closed.

"Wait." Jenny stepped forward. "Karah wasn't the one arguing with her. But where were you? Did Andrew ever make any connections with you and Eleanor?"

Viv kept her smile casual and held the door for Jenny. "Why don't you come in?"

"Thank you." She went in, followed by Viv.

The room was a simple compartment, similar to Jenny and Ron's, except that it had an extra door behind the chair under the luggage rack. Probably adjoining the neighbor's room. The bathroom door was open and empty. Andrew wasn't there.

Vivian offered the only chair in the room. Purple fabric draped over the tufted back, a stripe of silver tucked in the folds and a sewing kit beside it. Jenny picked up the slip of silver. The belt Viv had worn the previous day.

The smooth finish slid over her fingers. It was made of overlapping metallic rings, like stacking cups or scales that moved together over a vaguely elastic core. The clasp had snapped on one side with a bend in one of the scales. It could have wrapped around Stella's neck, several times if necessary, burning lines into her skin and keeping Vivian well out of the way.

"Sorry about the mess." Vivian snatched the belt and dress, putting the used clothing in the armoire.

"Oh, it's nothing," Jenny said politely. "I noticed that belt yesterday. It's too bad it broke. It's cute." She perched on the edge of the chair, her bag at her feet, while Viv sat on the thin bed.

"Thanks. It's vintage, which in this case just means that it's been through a lot." Viv crossed her legs and propped her hand against the bed. "I'm trying to fix it. So, what do you want to know about Eleanor?"

Jenny took a breath and jumped right in. "How did Andrew feel about you two fighting?"

"We weren't fighting. We were friends." She looked up with big eyes.

"Karah heard you yelling outside the fitting tent." Jenny prodded.

"We weren't yelling." Vivian looked away briefly. "We were friends. Besides, I thought she didn't know I was there."

"She didn't. I do now. You were the costume girl trying to make it big as an actress, and Eleanor Grace was your big-name connection. Only she didn't help you. What happened?"

Viv opened her mouth and closed it with a sharp breath. "We had a disagreement, but that was it. It doesn't mean I killed her, or even that I was upset with her."

"No one said you did. I'm just curious what Karah heard, and it seems like you might know." Jenny waited for Vivian to share her side of the story.

Viv stood and started pacing. She did a full turn to the window and back to the bed, then leaned against the upper bunk. "Everybody argues. This is not a big deal. I liked Eleanor. As long as Thomas wasn't around, anyway."

"You didn't get along with Thomas?"

"No one does." Viv looked away, examining the wall. "But that wasn't the argument."

"So, what happened?" she asked, and Vivian hesitated.

"It was a big misunderstanding. I accused her of ruining my career." She turned to the window and crossed her arms. Her hair fell dramatically across her shoulder. "Everyone knew Eleanor had been handed her fame on a silver platter paid for by Thomas Quinn. I just wanted my shot. Every time I went after a role, she magically ended up being cast. She knew I was being dramatic. I mean, hello, actress." Viv pointed to herself.

"How many roles have you auditioned for?" Jenny asked.

"Hundreds. It's what you do. Until you get your break, and usually even after. You audition, over and over."

"And how many roles did you go up against Eleanor?"

"Just a handful. Maybe six."

"And how many of those did you get?"

"None."

"How many did she get?"

"All of them."

"I bet that was hard for you. Did Andrew know about Eleanor stealing those roles away?"

"She didn't steal them. It was a misunderstanding. Like I said. She didn't decide who the casting directors chose."

"No, but it didn't really matter how well you did, or how perfect you were for the role if Eleanor Grace came in. You knew they would choose her."

Vivian glared like she could melt the bones in Jenny's body.

Jenny just waited. "Did you point it out to Andrew? Or did he see on his own how she was hurting you? Did you ask him to take sides?"

"I didn't have to ask Andrew to do anything."

"He was already there." Jenny leaned her elbow against the arm of the chair, keeping her eye on Viv. "It's nice to have someone choose you, isn't it?"

"Plenty of people have chosen me." Her voice took on a bitter edge.

"Just not the studios."

Vivian crossed her arms and narrowed her eyes at Jenny. "So?"

"Nothing." Jenny sat back. "It would just be sad if you let a misunderstanding turn into murder."

"I think you should go." Vivian grimaced at Jenny in a vague attempt at a smile.

Jenny stood, picking up her bag.

Voices on the other side of the wall suddenly started shouting. "I can't believe you! Why would I do that?"

"My sentiments exactly." Vivian's smile turned sickly sweet, and she held a hand up to the door. "After you, Mrs. Doan."

15

JENNY'S STAKEOUT WAS short lived. The window in the vestibule door didn't afford much of a viewing. With even less from the angle Jenny had forced herself in to stay hidden.

Viv reappeared in mustard yellow slacks, a white top, and giant sunglasses. The new outfit belonged on the streets of an Italian beach town, while her huffy expression could have sold her to any producer as the villain of a romantic teen drama. Death threats and all.

The fuming actress-hopeful sent Jenny's heart into mini palpations, when she turned toward Jenny instead of the dining car. Jumping back, Jenny leaned briefly against the wall of the vestibule but without movie magic this would not be a good place to hide.

In the next car Jenny checked several compartment doors until she found one unlocked and slid inside.

In the dark entry of the cabin Jenny congratulated herself. It hadn't been perfect, but that had gone as smoothly as she could have expected.

Behind her someone cleared their throat, and Jenny whirled around.

A woman in pajama's sat with a blanket wrapped around her on the edge of the bunk. While a man wearing only a towel leaned around the corner from the bathroom.

"Did you need something?"

"No!" Jenny's hand came up to her mouth and right back down to rest on her hip. Her plan hadn't gone quite as smoothly as she'd thought. "Well, it's funny actually. Or maybe not so much. I'm just checking to make sure everybody is being taken care of, which it looks like you guys are doing a good job of. The crew would love a good rating for your trip. Also, I don't have to tell you, but I will, the lemonade and chicken fettuccine are excellent. Let the waiter know that Je—ssica . . . Cherry sent you."

"I thought your name was Jenny." The woman looked even more confused.

Jenny laughed, brightly. "Jenny, right." She smiled for several seconds and gave up. "Hi I'm Jenny from the Missouri Star Quilt Company. Do either of you happen to quilt? Would you like a signed MSQC magazine? Or a free quilt pattern?"

She really should have done some scouting before jumping into this new plan.

The door to the hall was cracked open and Jenny reached for it, hesitating as footsteps sounded on the other side. She couldn't leave until Vivian was gone.

Jenny turned back to the couple. "You know—" She gestured to the woman's pajama set. "Have you ever considered making matching quilted pajamas? It's a very unique way to say, I love you."

The young woman squeaked, bouncing back on the bed as if Jenny had attacked her. Jenny glanced from the young woman to the man who both bore shocked and confused expressions.

Jenny waved a hand between them. "Or, if you're not there yet, personalized pillowcases are an excellent option for a sentimental gift."

A door closed in the hallway and Jenny turned.

Behind her someone cleared their throat again and the man's voice sounded. "Right then, Ms. Jessica Cherry. I think we're all right. Thanks for coming by. Have a nice day."

She hadn't fully processed what he was saying until he reached past, opened the door, and gave her a push into the hallway.

Jenny stumbled into the empty corridor. Viv was gone and a head of dark hair walked away through the distorted glass of the door.

"Now we see if the rest of the plan goes any smoother." Jenny turned back toward Vivian's room. She walked through the doors and stood in front of door number twenty-three. Jenny crossed her fingers and pulled at the compartment door.

It stayed latched.

It wasn't a very good plan.

Next time she visited Andrew, she would need him to teach her to pick locks, before she asked if he'd murdered his sister.

Beside her, Carey's door burst open, the vague scent of smoke returned to the hallway. Bonnie stormed out with it. "You can't blame me, too. I just followed your lead."

Jenny assumed Carey was at the other end of the argument and stepped aside, letting Bonnie pass.

"Of course, I can blame you." Carey appeared in the door frame. He looked at Jenny, recognition masking his expression with brief insecurity.

He turned back to Bonnie. "No one else had control of that party. We all know who's responsible."

"I thought you were on my side." A hint of tears trembled in Bonnie's voice. She sucked down a huge breath somewhat upset but before Jenny could confirm the starlet had any real emotions, she'd thrown her shoulders back, glaring at Carey. From three doors away, she pointed her finger like she could jab him in the chest. "You told me I could always count on you. You're worse than Eleanor, and I hope whoever's killing people off gets you next."

In a whirl of shiny pink fabric, Bonnie spun around and headed to the end of the train.

"Sometimes it's just easier if she goes back where she came from." Carey stared at the closed vestibule door where Bonnie had disappeared.

Jenny furrowed her brow. She'd never had a major issue with Carey, but she didn't trust Bonnie and the two of them had been inseparable. Which only made Jenny want to know what they'd been arguing about even more. "Things don't seem to be going particularly well. I heard a little of your argument earlier too. Is everything all right?"

Carey inhaled slowly, not taking his eyes off Bonnie's departed frame. It was several seconds before he nodded and sent a quick look to Jenny.

"I think so." Carey considered her and stepped back, Holding the door open. "I heard a little of your argument as well. Do you want to come inside?"

Jenny almost accepted, taking a step forward before she paused. The gun weighed heavy on her shoulder. She was supposed to be hiding the dangerous bag away but instead she'd been in and out of cabins like she was room service for half an hour.

Talking with Carey was not a necessity. Aside from this argument with Bonnie, Carey had been fairly neutral in his relationships with the actors and actresses causing all the drama. But that was the job of an agent.

Attempting to stay focused Jenny pulled together her resolve. "I really shouldn't. I'm headed to meet Ron after I put this away." Jenny squeezed the handle of her bag in theatrical concern. "Nobody likes a heavy bag."

He smiled and started to close the door. "I totally understand. Maybe we can talk later."

A rush of panic overtook Jenny, and her hand flew up blocking the door. That had been too simple. He was supposed to deflect at least once. "Or I can take a minute now."

"Oh." Carey glanced into the hallway and shrugged. "Okay, come on in." He pulled the door open and pointed to the room behind them. "Why don't you take the chair over there."

Jenny walked into the room, chastising herself with every step. What was she thinking? Letting her curiosity lead her around like a poodle failing obedience school. She did not need to be here.

She glanced nervously, something was out of place. It took her too long to realize it was the stench of melted chemicals. She'd been holding the scent in her memory as part of the gunshot in Eleanor's appearance.

The rancid smoke lingered near a metal trash can with a tiny smoldering pile in the bottom. With the sudden context of smoke and the fancy coated paper, she felt silly for having thought it was a gunshot at all.

But where there's smoke there's fire.

At least she hoped so. In a not too dangerous way. Besides, it justified her being there to ask about the argument.

"What's burning? I don't think the conductor will be very excited about that." Jenny raised her eyebrows, indicating the trash can.

"That? Bonnie's sense of humor." Carey's casual tone piqued her curiosity.

Jenny chuckled when she failed to keep a straight face. "No loss there I suppose." A tiny pot of forget-me-nots sat on the end table over a decorative riser. "This is sweet. They're Eleanor's favorite, right?"

Carey grinned and pointed away from the table. "Yeah, would you mind sitting over there? I like to be here. I brought them for her. There's been a lot of memorializing, and this is my chance to be where she was so, I thought I'd try to remember her the way she would have wanted. With beauty and grace." He slid in front of her and sat in the chair by the table.

"Oh." Jenny blinked. And turned to the other chair. "Sure, sorry." She was sitting beside the bathroom and had to lean forward to see Carey.

"No problem at all." Carey waived a hand in dismissal. "What about you? You've been all over this train today. I really did only hear a little of your argument, but Andrew seemed pretty concerned about Stella. I haven't seen her, is she still sick?"

His question caught her attention. She had expected him to ask about her visit with Vivian, assuming they had been loud enough to hear through the wall as she had heard him and Bonnie.

"We're a little concerned." Jenny hedged not wanting to reveal everything she suspected just yet. "Nobody has seen her since last night. At least as far as we know. You haven't seen her, have you?"

Regret painted his features as he shook his head slowly. "I haven't. I wish I could give you a better answer. I remember noticing that she was not at the mine though."

"With the way Thomas was growling about it, I think everybody noticed she wasn't there." Jenny tucked the negative response away and turned her attention back to the present. "I overheard just a little of your argument earlier as well. Can I ask what Bonnie is getting blamed for that is so bad she wished you dead?"

Carey sighed. His gaze fell to the waste basket and his lip curled in disgust. "Someone has been leaving note cards in my room from the dinner party."

"The ones that say, I killed Eleanor?"

Fear glazed his eyes and his breath shuddered. After holding it for several seconds all he managed to do was nod.

"That's awful." Had felt similarly when she found the stray card in Stella's room.

Carey shrugged, shaking his head. "It's just a stupid prank." He watched her, waiting as if he wanted her to confirm his nonchalance. "Anyway, I thought we picked up all those little papers, before they locked us out of the room."

Jenny couldn't imagine Bonnie doing that when she could have asked one of the waiters to do it. "Bonnie helped?"

Carey's lip twitched with a reluctant laugh. "Fine. Bonnie asked me to pick them up. She didn't want to give people a reminder of . . . what happened."

"But she wouldn't go passing them out if she was that worried about it." Jenny tried to come up with a way to make sense of it. "That's why you got all weird when I found one in the hall earlier."

"Weird?" Carey asked. "I didn't get—okay, yeah, I was weird. But I didn't know what was happening. It didn't take much to figure out that Bonnie is the only one who could have more of those cards." He leaned forward, dropping his elbows to his knees, and his head leaning toward the ground.

"Why?" Surprise pushed her question out quickly. "I thought Bonnie said it wasn't her. You don't believe her?"

"No." Carey's head lifted. "You're giving her too much credit. Bonnie thrives on attention. She wants 'em talking about her. Especially when they're talking about Eleanor instead."

"So, why does that mean it's her?"

Carey met her gaze and looked down at his clasped hands. "I saw a stack of the cards in her room. Maybe she thought she could scare people enough they'd quit talking about her."

"It doesn't usually work like that." Jenny said skeptically.

"You don't have to tell me," Carey muttered.

Jenny frowned and moved back to the trash. The smoke had dissipated but she could still see the ashen impression of a thin card embossed in gold. "It seems like Bonnie would go to some pretty serious lengths to make sure Eleanor wasn't stealing her spotlight."

"She wouldn't have hurt her, if that's what you're thinking." Carey Garrettwatched Jenny's progress around the room from the side of the bed. "Bonnie's a snob but she's a good actress and frankly, too worried about what people would think, to do something as frowned upon as killing someone." He stood up moving to the trash when Jenny walked away and picked it up. "It'd ruin her reputation."

With the trash can in hand he crossed the room again, his foot catching the corner of Jenny's bag where she'd left it. It tipped and the blue corduroy pants tumbled out.

"Oh, I'm sorry." Carey dropped to pick them up at the same time Jenny did, hitting her in the head with the trash can.

"Ow," Jenny rubbed the sore spot on her head as ash danced through the air. "Goodness."

"I'm so sorry." Carey dropped the trash can, trying again to be helpful. "Here, let me."

"No, it's fine, really." Jenny lunged forward. Determined to get them first, she caught a corner of the blue fabric as Carey grabbed the bundle from the other side. The entire thing flipped, end over end, tumbling out of its wrapping as Jenny held the hem of the pants she'd used.

"Oh," Carey looked down at the floor. "That's not what I expected."

In the pile of dark blue corduroy lay a black gun. "We should probably have been more careful with that."

"I can explain." Jenny said, dropping quickly and picking up the gun.

"Jenny!" Carey threw his hands up backing away, as if she'd threatened him.

She froze halfway up. Pointing it to the ground. "I'm not doing anything." Jenny held her hand up in a flat, hopefully calming motion. "I found this earlier. Thomas stole it." She opened her mouth to tell him more about Stella's situation and Thomas but his eyes were wide with worry and fixated on the gun in her hand. "I'm not going to do anything. I'm trying to return it to Chris, but the keys to the safe are missing, so he can't exactly secure it."

"The keys are . . . missing? The keys that kept the gun locked up." Carey finally looked at her. "Do you have them?"

"No." Jenny's eye roll took in the entire room, with its level of exasperation. "I told you Thomas stole it. I guess they were fighting about it in Denning. Thomas wanted it back, so he stole it. And probably the keys to get it."

"Can you steal it if it belongs to you?"

"If people are at risk of being shot, I think yes." Jenny hovered the gun over the pants trying to figure out where the end was so she could wrap it up again.

"You're just going to keep it in a pair of pants?" Carey's lip curled and his brow pinched in a cross of confusion and disgust. He shook his head. "No. Jenny, I'm sorry, but no."

She looked up and Carey jumped. "Watch out, with that."

"My goodness, Carey." Jenny held the gun to the side. "The safety's on and I've handled guns before. Please, stop acting like I'm going to shoot you."

He narrowed his eyes, lowering his hands. "Okay. I guess, I thought I'd got it wrong, and you really were out to kill Eleanor's *misprotectors*." He kept an eye on the gun until Jenny set it on the table. "What are you going to do with it? If they can't keep it in the safe anymore?"

"I haven't figured that out yet." She'd spent so much time back and forth across the train like Carey said that she hadn't figured out any other options. "I was just going to take it back to my room for now."

Carey lifted one eyebrow, keeping his eye on the gun and his lips in a tight line. "At least you'd know where it is." He narrowed his eyes and looked up to Jenny. "What if I had somewhere we could hide it? It's not a safe but there's a hidden compartment behind the stairs. It might feel safer if it was hidden."

"The stairs in the dining room? That seems pretty public."

He shook his head. "Not at all. There's a door at the back of the coat closet. Only about a foot across and a few inches deep with a simple lock. It would be perfect for something like this."

Not having it attached to her shoulder every time she turned around sounded better than anything else. She nodded and Carey grinned. "Good. I don't like the idea of this walking around the train. Can you come tonight? I'll show you where to put it."

"Can we do it sooner?" Jenny looked at her watch. "It's almost eight. The dining car should be empty, except for Ron. Unless he took dinner back to our room. I'm a little late."

Carey looked over his shoulder as if he'd be able to see the dining car. After a moment's hesitation he agreed, "We can try and if it's too busy, we'll meet later?"

"Sounds good." Jenny laid the pants out and set the gun on the end before Carey stopped her.

"Don't wrap it this time." He picked up the gun and set it on the table stuffing the pants in the bag and then setting the gun in the center of the pile. "It won't fit in the hidden compartment if it's wrapped, and I don't want to unwrap it out there, like we did in here."

Jenny chuckled. "That could be awkward."

Carey handed her the bag. "I'll meet you there in five minutes. Hang the bag on one of the hooks in the closet. When I get there, we'll see if we can hide it."

16

"CAN WE TRUST HIM?" Ron shifted closer, leaning as far across the table as he could.

"I don't know." Jenny inhaled deeply and held it, considering what she knew about Carey. The biggest selling point was his honesty and that Eleanor trusted him with her secrets. "He feels safer than Thomas. And we have a plan." The door at the end of the car opened as she said his name, and Thomas came in. "Speak of the devil."

"Shh." Ron stroked his thumb over her knuckles.

Jenny grinned and let the sensation of his touch soothe her from the inside out. "You're trying to distract me."

"Why, yes I am." Ron's blue eyes danced with as much excitement as when they were young. "Is it working?"

"I'm not sure yet," she chuckled. "Do it again."

Ron laughed and lifted her hand to his lips giving her a kiss as Thomas leaned up against the table.

"Jenny," Thomas said loudly, pulling their immediate attention.

"Thomas." She shot Ron a glance, before turning a perfect smile up to Thomas. "What are you doing here?"

"Not much. Done any sneaking around lately?"

Jenny laughed weakly her hand dropping to the bag. The need to keep it safe sent her pulse racing. She turned to Ron, sending him a silent plea for help, and he took the hint.

"Good evening, Thomas. I haven't seen you much since Denning. How's your day been?"

Ron rarely struck up conversations with suspected psychopaths.

Jenny could have kissed him.

Thomas didn't respond right away, just looked them over and pushed away from the table. "It's a good day, Ron." He looked at Jenny while he spoke, his hands at his hips, coat pushed back. "I've spent most of it in the lounge, watching your wife walk back and forth from one end of the train to the other."

"I do like to get my steps in." Jenny smiled.

"Hm." Thomas' smile soured. "Funny thing, when I came back to my room, a couple items seemed to be missing."

Jenny's attention couldn't have been pulled away with a commercial sewing machine. She knew exactly what he was missing, and she hoped he'd say it. She wanted to hear that he'd stolen the gun back, the conductor's keys, and then she wanted to hear him say he knew where Stella was. She was no longer sure if he'd taken her, but she wanted to hear it anyway. She wanted to find her.

He didn't say any of it.

Ron looked between Jenny and Thomas. "Oh, I hope you find them."

"Thanks, Ron." Thomas grinned. "I think I will."

He made her skin crawl.

Without putting her hand on the bag, or even looking at it, Jenny smiled at Thomas. "Good luck."

"Mr. Quinn." The kitchen manager came into the dining room with arms extended. "We've reworked the menu as you've requested. Come see what I have for you—"

The two men disappeared into the kitchen leaving only one other couple in the dining room. They had been pinned to their seats since Jenny had arrived, engrossed in their own captivating dialogue.

Jenny squeezed Ron's hand. "I'll be right back."

She picked up her bag and slipped over to the closet, glancing nervously at the kitchen door. If Thomas came out—

"Jenny?"

Carey's voice startled her, and in her surprise she backed into the wall.

"Oops." He didn't laugh, but his smile widened enough to see he was entertained.

Carey reached for the bag and split the coats and excess uniforms apart, revealing the wood panels at the back of the closet. The wall looked perfectly average. Running his hand along the seam, Carey revealed a hidden notch and his smile finally relaxed.

The board lifted away from the wall, revealing a metal door with a keyhole along the side. "I had a couple files I wanted to keep safe on our last trip. And for obvious reasons, I didn't want to hand them over to the conductor. So, the owner of the Summit Group told me about this compartment and gave me a key."

Her lips pushed up into a slightly puckered frown. "And you're the only one that has a copy?"

"I'm sure he does. But Todd's not on the train." Carey winked and checked the safety on the gun, then put the weapon inside the thin metal container.

Jenny's breathing sped up as she tried to understand how this made them safer. "So, how is it that you have a key, but Thomas doesn't?"

"I told you the owner of the Summit Group owns both Quilter's Square and the train?" Carey locked the metal door in place as she nodded at the vague memory. "He's a family friend. It comes with its perks." He replaced the board and shut the closet door. Then, in an abrupt change of tone, Carey pushed past Jenny and growled at her. "Bonnie isn't interested in your excuses, Jenny. She just wants you to stay out of her business."

"Um." Jenny's instinct did a one-eighty at his cruel tone. This could have been a very big mistake.

Carey sent a sharp glance over his shoulder, and Jenny heard the footsteps before she saw the reason for Carey's quick personality shift.

Thomas had emerged from the kitchen.

"I wouldn't have to be in it, if she'd be a little more forthcoming." Jenny fell into character quickly, calling on her old acting skills.

"Well, that's not her problem, is it?" Carey turned away, and Jenny caught the hint of a smile as he went.

When she turned back, Thomas sent her one of his poisoned glares. How did he know it was her that was in his room, anyway? Andrew was the only one with her and—and she hadn't seen him since then.

"I'm meeting with someone shortly, Mrs. Doan but I know what you took, and I want it back." He leaned forward, falling nose to nose with her, and lowered his voice. "The camera and the gun."

"I DON'T KNOW what you're expecting to find on there." Ron watched as Jenny flipped through images of the party on Stella's camera.

"I don't know either," Jenny said. "But if he wants it back, it means there's something he doesn't want me to see and I don't want to miss it."

"Well, you're not going to miss her." Ron pointed as another image popped up with Bonnie's face on the screen.

"Yeah." Jenny flipped through several more pictures on the camera. "I think she's in all of them." There weren't that many photos to begin with. Jenny wasn't a photographer. The camera had been purely to get her into the party.

She paused on the one of Thomas kissing Bonnie's hand. He hadn't deleted it. Probably because you couldn't see his face. Jenny scanned the photo Bonnie had been so upset about.

She looked great. There'd been no reason for her to— Jenny accidentally flipped the screen to the next photo and stopped.

She had taken two photos in a row as Bonnie got upset with her. And something changed in them. She went back an image to the one with Thomas. The way he was holding her hand . . . When he'd kissed Cherry's hand at the premiere, he'd barely touched her fingers.

With Bonnie, he was clasping her hand in both of his like he didn't want to let go. A large yellow gemstone graced her hand, rising to his lips for a kiss.

Jenny clicked to the next screen. Bonnie alone glared at the camera. Her anger had required all of Jenny's attention at the time, and she only now noticed that the large ring on Bonnie's hand had disappeared. Jenny flipped back to the previous image to confirm her suspicion. There was no question.

Bonnie's ring was missing.

METALLIC PINK PANTS gave way to a cream-colored sheer robe, edged in feathers. Bonnie's "between outfits robe" was little more than a negligee. "Not that it's any of your business, but I'm meeting Warren for a date, at nine."

Jenny had to keep her eyes leveled on Bonnie's face to avoid seeing things she wouldn't be able to unsee.

Over Bonnie's shoulder Jenny tried to scout out the room. It was trimmed in white and gold with a chandelier almost as large as the one in the parlor. Her room was by far the fanciest of the compartments Jenny had seen. There was even a marble goddess statue standing just past the entry with a familiar trench coat hanging on its arm.

All the glitz made the worn coat look even more out of place. It was standard khaki material, though the fabric over the elbows had paled with wear. Its most identifying feature was a leather strap edged in thick red zigzag stitching, that hung useless off the upper arm.

"Your room is beautiful." Jenny said still mulling over where she'd seen the coat before. "Would it be all right if I came in?"

"I really don't have time to give you a tour," Bonnie complained. "You can see it from here. Isn't that enough?"

Isn't that enough? The conversation Jenny had overheard when she'd first gotten on the train rushed back to her.

I told you I'd find the killer. Isn't that enough?

The person who'd left through the dining room had been wearing the trench coat hanging in Bonnie's room. She looked at the starlet tapping her finger on the door. Jenny finally had a clue to who had been in the dining room before the party, even if she didn't know why . . . yet.

"Of course. I don't want to be a bother." Jenny looked over Bonnie's shoulder. "It's got to be hard being so perfect. What do you do when you're having a rough day?"

"I don't have those."

"Come on, we all have those. Days where you wake up and you just don't feel right. You don't have time to do a full makeover on the puffy skin or fried hair. Those are the days you just wanna put on a trench coat and a pair of sunglasses and hide in plain sight. Am I right?"

Bonnie didn't do a full turn, but you could almost hear her hair snap as she whiplashed a glance at the trench coat-wearing goddess behind her. "That's not mine. I'm holding it for a friend." The door slid closed in a crack against the doorframe.

Jenny pounded against the dark wood. "I saw you in the trench coat, Bonnie. What's the big deal? Who were you meeting?"

"That didn't take nearly as long as I thought it would." Ron raised an eyebrow from his place against the wall. "Should I be proud of that interrogation? I think I'm proud."

As soon as Bonnie had appeared in her barely there clothing, Ron had disappeared. He had turned away, watching the windows on the opposite side of the corridor.

"Quiet." Jenny half-smiled and half-rolled her eyes. There was truth behind her husband's teasing. "Thanks for your help, by the way. This is some real quality time we're spending together."

"Next time you interrogate a fully dressed suspect, I will be right there to support you." Ron put an arm around Jenny's shoulder in a show of support. "Remember, this was your call on what to do tonight. I voted for streaming a movie. Or I would have if you'd asked."

"Okay, what should we do tonight? Watch a movie, or find a killer so we don't get murdered in our sleep?"

Ron's teasing smile disappeared, and Jenny harrumphed, content with having disrupted his triumphant attitude.

He stopped in the middle of the corridor. "If you aren't done talking to Bonnie, why are we leaving?"

Jenny frowned. "She doesn't want to talk to us and I can't make her. What would you do?"

"She's got a date at nine, correct? So, she'll be headed there soon." Ron looked around, found nothing but the hallway, and shrugged. "We find somewhere to wait her out. Then we talk to her on the way, when she can't get rid of us."

"She's probably lying." Jenny didn't want to look on the bright side. "She said she had a date with Warren, but Warren isn't dating Bonnie. Trust me."

Jenny knew she sounded grumpy.

She was grumpy.

She'd come looking to find out if Bonnie had switched the cards at the party, to confirm Bonnie's alibi, to see if Bonnie was acting suspicious about Stella. Jenny'd come to find out many things, and all she got was that Bonnie wouldn't admit to even owning a less-than-perfect clothing item that Jenny had seen her wearing while having suspicious conversations.

Ron leaned against the corridor wall. "Lying or not, we can wait here and find out."

"We can't wait here?" Jenny let out a breath. "That's so suspicious. She'll never talk to us if we interrogate her and then wait outside her door to do it again.

Ron's expression hardened. "Come on, Jenny. Tell me where you would hide then. If you weren't in a terrible mood, where would you wait for Bonnie when there's nowhere to hide?"

Jenny glanced at the vestibule. "There are places to hide. But that's not the point." She looked over her shoulder and back. "If there's nowhere then you don't hide."

Ron dipped one eyebrow low and lifted the other. "But you just told me waiting here was a terrible idea."

"It still is." Jenny's lips twitched up, and she turned away. "Follow me."

They walked down the hall and into the first-class lounge.

"Have a seat." Jenny gestured to the wide arrangement of seating areas in the excessively fancy room. "Just make sure one of us is facing the hall."

Ron turned to the hall and then back to the lounge with a smile. "I knew that."

Jenny chuckled and followed Ron past the large round coffee table, inlaid with marble and translucent stone. He sat in an intimate placement of only two chairs. Jenny joined him, appreciating the large Ficus tree that blocked the view, more for the passersby than them.

Ron picked up her hand without a word, running his fingertips over her knuckles from joint to fingernail and back.

"You're doing it again," Jenny whispered.

He stopped, looking up at Jenny. "What?"

"Distracting me."

Ron chuckled, and he started brushing his fingers over her skin again. "Is it working?"

She let him run his fingertips over the back of her hand. He'd been distracting her since she'd screwed up her interview with Bonnie. With a sigh, she leaned back in her chair and closed her eyes. "I don't know yet," she whispered. "You might need to try again."

Ron stopped moving, and Jenny's eyes opened. "I meant it as a compliment. I like when you do that."

Ron squeezed her hand. "Thanks. But quiet. She's over there."

"Already?" Jenny twisted to see Bonnie crossing the room in heels and a silver dress.

"Shall we?" Ron asked, adjusting his grip so Jenny's hand lay on top of his.

"Not yet." Jenny leaned around the Ficus. "If we find Chris, do you think he could get us in a locked room?"

"I don't know. We could ask."

Jenny sat quietly as Bonnie passed them by, letting her go all the way to the vestibule on the other side of the train car.

Ron cleared his throat. "So, you don't want to talk to Bonnie."

Jenny stood, waiting for him to follow. "There's not much I could say right now that would get her to talk to me. And since I know she's leaving . . . I thought I'd check her room first."

Jenny led the way back down the hall and pulled against Bonnie's door. It jostled and clicked but didn't move.

"Careful, Jenny." Ron watched beside her. "Those can break."

"Really?" Jenny turned to Ron hopefully.

He frowned. "That's not a good thing."

Jenny turned back to the door, her face pinching in concentration. "Actually, it might be," she muttered. Turning to Ron, Jenny cradled his jaw with her hands. "Thank you. For always trusting me," she said and turned to the door. "Now we have to try and break the lock."

Setting his hands on her shoulders, Ron sighed. "Oh, Jenny."

"What?" she asked as he moved her to the side. "You don't think I could break it?"

"Oh no, you absolutely could break it. In fact, I think you're going to."

Jenny watched in confusion as Ron knelt in front of the door and examined the slide and latch. "You're going to pick the lock? You didn't tell me you could pick locks."

"Because I can't. It's not so much picking locks as understanding how they work."

His admission did little to deter Jenny. She leaned in close, watching him work. By the time he waved her away, her chin was practically on his shoulder.

"It's not that impressive, I promise. And it would probably be impossible on a normal door. You're just lucky these old pocket doors aren't terribly secure. And that you're trying to get into the room of a killer." Ron's brow furrowed, and he looked at Jenny. "That didn't sound the same out loud as it did in my head."

Jenny chuckled. "I'm quite grateful you're helping me get into the room of a killer."

Ron held up a finger like he wanted to dispute what she'd said, but then changed his mind. "Forget it and watch the hallway. This is neither impressive or discreet."

Pulling out a pocketknife, Ron slipped it behind the thin curved trim that blocked the edge of the door. With a slight twist, the trim board curved outward. He moved down a few inches and pulled out a little more.

The trim couldn't be more than half an inch thick. When he'd raised enough of a gap that he could slide his blade between the door and the frame, he did. He arched the blade upward, and the blade connected with the lock in a metallic clink of metal.

"Shoot," he whispered and glanced at Jenny, trying the same motion again. "It's stubborn. Probably a tight lock."

"Can I help?" Jenny wasn't watching the hall at all. Her attention was trained on Ron's method of bypassing the lock.

"Just give me a second. I can't get my knife in far enough." He pulled his lower lip between his teeth and focused on the door. The trim bent away from the frame, and Ron slid the blade farther down the gap, pressing the thin board out. With a crack, the lower half of the trim board popped off the doorframe.

"That's what I was afraid of." Ron pulled the thin trim away and released it, letting it wobble from the point where it was still attached to the wall. "I guess I have enough room."

He smiled and took a breath.

"Is everything okay?" Jenny asked.

"Of course." He slid the knife between the door and frame again, coming up with the same clink. "Actually, can you pull the door toward the frame? Like you're trying to close it tightly?"

"Won't that pinch the blade?"

"Yeah." Ron nodded, slipping the knife into place and gesturing to Jenny. "It should also create enough room for the latch to release, if this is the kind of lock I think it is."

Jenny gripped the handle.

"Ready?" he asked.

"Ready." She pushed toward the doorframe, and Ron chuckled.

"Let's not go crazy. Just a light push. I can't move the knife."

"Oh." Jenny relaxed her pressure. "Better?"

Ron nodded. "Okay, on three." He met her eye, and she nodded. "One."

She braced herself, body against the door, and Ron positioning the knife.

"Two."

He took a sharp breath and Jenny held hers, pressing the door gently to the frame.

"Three."

17

A LUMP FORMED where Ron's head collided with the door frame.

After Jenny landed on him.

They successfully bypassed the latch mechanism in the door to Bonnie's room, she'd slipped and knocked his sweet bald head right into the corner of the frame.

"Do you think she has a first aid kit?" Jenny didn't bother with admiring the décor. She went straight to the bathroom sink.

"It's just a bump," Ron said from the main area of the compartment. "I told you it wouldn't be discreet."

"But I'm not supposed to injure you when you're helping me." Jenny groaned, digging through empty bathroom cabinets.

In the space of six drawers and two full-size cabinets, there was a stash of toilet paper, two drawers of makeup, and one full of prescription medications. None of which were made out to Bonnie Beale.

"So, Bonnie never gets hurt." Jenny huffed and stepped back from the cabinets. "But she takes a lot of medicine."

There on the counter was a jewelry tray. Jenny scanned the pieces until she found the large ring Bonnie had worn at the dinner party. "She got it back," Jenny muttered, picking up the stone. It was lighter than she'd anticipated. The gold band was solid, with wide prongs holding the stone in place.

"Jenny? What are we looking for in here?"

"Shoot." Jenny dropped the ring. "Just a second." She scrambled after it, returning it to the jewelry tray, and then she paused.

She picked it back up, noticing a thin crack around the stone. Jenny lifted the top half of the stone away and found a lovely, pill-sized opening in the stone.

"Jenny? I think you should see this." Ron's voice came again.

She slid the fake rock on her finger and waltzed out with her arm extended. "Look what I found."

"The stolen ring?" Ron didn't have to ask twice.

With a grin, she reached out and popped the stone open. "I think I know how Garrett was poisoned."

"I think you might be right, my dear." Ron took her hand and kissed her fingers, slipping the ring away. "It's big, a simple exchange, and perfect for any high class drug dealer."

Jenny put the ring back on. "It doesn't look fake. She must have had this specially made."

"Look at this." Ron glanced at her from beside the large bed. "I found this under the edge of the bed."

"That's a terrible hiding place," Jenny said, sidling up to Ron and looking over his shoulder.

He nodded at the ring. "I think she's an 'in plain sight' kind of girl." Ron opened the folder. Right on top was a picture of Eleanor. "So, it's suspicious, right? That she has a folder full of details about a dead woman."

"Yeah, it's suspicious. And stupid." Jenny examined the picture, barely believing she was looking at it. A black and white of Eleanor Grace. Her hair blew across her face. She wasn't smiling, but she looked peaceful, relaxed. Shadows played over her cheeks, long lashes framing pale eyes.

It wasn't at all how Jenny was used to seeing her, dressed in the 1940s clothing she'd died in.

Jenny flipped the image over. Behind it was a list of appointments, covering approximately a week before Eleanor died. Another page had what looked like bank account numbers, phone numbers, and contact names. Doctor's names followed by patient notes. Page after page of information about Eleanor's life filled the folder.

Jenny shook her head. "No. This is too much. If it's real, why would she still have it?"

Ron held out a page. It was an order form with a sample stapled in the corner. *I killed Eleanor Grace* printed in gold, on white linen cardstock. Bonnie Beale was signed at the bottom for proof approval.

"She really did it." Jenny flipped quickly through the pages again. "She did the whole thing."

There was so much information about Eleanor, and then in the last several pages were lists of names. Warren, Vivian, Carey, Stella, Garrett, Mia, everyone who had been at the party.

"Why is your name in there?" Ron asked, pointing to the bottom corner of the next page.

Jenny flipped it over and found a seating chart with a large X through it.

"I was there. This is from the dinner party she threw." Jenny scanned the chart past her own name and pointed to Warren's. Bonnie had circled it in red. "This is where Garrett ended up sitting. Warren traded him seats."

She had scribbled and marked across the page, but Jenny could still see it clearly. Apparently, Bonnie hadn't been happy about it.

Still, when she looked back at the list of names on the front Garrett's was crossed off, along with Stella's.

Jenny couldn't breathe. The yellow ring glittered on her hand. Bonnie had used it to kill a man with Thomas' help.

Jenny shook it off, dropping it on the bedspread.

The list made it look like Stella was already gone. Jenny'd been banking on the fact that whoever had taken Stella had taken Eleanor's quilt as well. That they wanted them together to solve the mystery.

Stella couldn't be gone.

"Ron? We need to find Stella's quilt. I don't know if it's here, but I hope it is. It could mean she's still alive."

"But now?" Ron looked from her back to the folder. "Are you sure? It's almost nine."

Jenny shook her head. "I don't know what you mean." She pointed to the closet. "Check there first. There's a large shelf at the top. At least, there is if it's like Stella's room."

"What about Warren and Vivian?" Ron put his finger at the bottom of the page.

A connecting bar had been drawn between Warren and Vivian's names with the words '*Day Two – Dinner Audition. Nine PM.*

Warren's name had been heavily circled again.

"Bonnie's going to dinner with Warren at nine." Jenny was grasping at straws, but she needed those straws. She needed this difference to mean something. "She's not gonna kill him if it doesn't match the schedule. She's supposed to do Vivian and Warren together."

"Unless something changed. You said Warren traded names with Garrett at the dinner party and Garrett died. Maybe Warren and Vivian already had a date planned, and Bonnie is trading names again." Ron shook his head. "If it's her game, she can do what she wants. But we need to stop her."

She couldn't see much except Ron's eyes staring into hers as she nodded her agreement. "You're right. You're right. Warren's room is right next door. We should check and see if he's left already."

"Good." Ron squeezed her shoulders, and she inhaled like it was a command. She hadn't even realized he'd been holding her.

Taking her hand, Ron moved her quickly out of the room. "Good. Let's go."

"Wait. I need to put the folder back. We can't take it. She'll know we were here."

Ron didn't stop moving. "If we stop a murder tonight, she'll know we know. And if she knows what we know, I want to know what she knows." Ron flinched, as if he wasn't even sure he knew what he knew. "Never mind, just keep the folder." In the hallway, he paused. "Which one is Warren's room?

"There." The movement was helping, getting her blood flowing and her adrenaline pumping.

Ron pounded on Warren's door, but no one answered. He checked his watch and growled. "We've only got a few minutes. He's already gone."

Jenny grabbed the door handle as Ron started down the hall. "It's open," Jenny shouted. "I'm just gonna scan it."

Ron stopped and turned around. "Jenny, no. There's no time."

"Keep going," she told him. "I'll catch up!"

"Who's there?" Warren groaned sluggishly within the room, as if something was caught in his throat. "What's going on?"

"Warren? Where are you meeting Vivian? For Bonnie . . ." She wasn't sure who he would be expecting.

"What?" He groaned again. "Ugh, what did you do to me?" Warren stumbled to the corner of the entry and looked at Jenny.

"It wasn't me. Where were you going to dinner tonight?"

"You mean the audition? Thomas canceled that. I got a note from some guy in a trench coat."

"A trench coat? He brought you a note from Thomas?" Jenny asked, distracted, and then she immediately felt frustrated at being distracted.

"And a drink." Warren shrugged and cringed, leaning away from the door. "It must have been strong, though, cause my head is killing me."

"A drink." She looked at him and shook her head. Bonnie had drugged him. "Where was the dinner? Uh, I mean, the audition?"

"It wasn't a big deal. Auditions get canceled sometimes."

"Warren!" Jenny yelled, trying to get him to focus. "Where?"

"Geez!" Warren's hand flew to his head like he was protecting it from the sound. "He said to meet in the empty baggage room. Said it would be quieter. He doesn't know what he's talking about, though, that's at the front of the train. It's so noisy up there."

"The baggage room. Thank you!" Jenny hurried out of the room, calling back, "stay there."

A SHOT EXPLODED in the distance, the blast ringing through the air. Jenny and Ron had barely passed the dining room on their way to the meeting place.

But they were too late.

Only one train car away, and they were too late.

Time slowed and the room fell dark, dimming as it had before Eleanor's visit in the corridor. Sound waves pulsed around them in the gut-wrenching rhythm of a gunshot.

"It's gone. Help me."

Jenny struggled for breath as the familiar words flew through her body on a gust of wind.

Eleanor's urgency pushed Jenny forward, as if she'd physically shoved Jenny in her non-corporeal form. Jenny caught herself against Ron's shoulder, spilling forget-me-not petals to the floor as the lights returned to normal.

Jenny was left gasping, her body sucked dry by Eleanor's spirit.

"What happened?" Ron asked. "Jenny, are you all right?"

Her breathing wasn't quite steady yet, but Jenny nodded and waved him forward. Petals drifted down from her hands, dancing across the floor as she did. "Keep going," she said. "We have to stop Bonnie. We have to tell them what we know."

Voices picked up around her, the staff of the kitchen spilling out the single file door. Jenny and Ron pushed through, into the second dining car where a handful of people stood huddled around the vestibule door.

"What happened?" someone behind her asked. "There's a gun!" another person yelled. And then there were whispers. "Did you see that?", along with, "It's her."

Jenny pushed forward with Ron at her heels. Voices surrounded her, but Jenny didn't have time to listen. "Who's in there? We need to help them." Jenny twisted the door handle and squeezed through the door to find the second vestibule door locked. "I need a screwdriver," she called to the packed room. "Or a blade, something. The door's locked."

Moments later a man ran from the kitchen holding out a thin old skeleton key.

"For the door!" he yelled, handing the key forward through the group.

When she finally got the door open, there was no question. The woman in the baggage car was dead.

"She's gone."

Jenny whirled around at the whispered statement. It had sounded like Eleanor. But the words were floating through the crowd. And there was nothing ghostly about it. Jenny put her hands up, trying to keep people back. "Please, everybody stay back. Ron? We need Chris or the other conductor."

She looked behind her to where the employee quarters were. Why hadn't any of them appeared?

She took a step closer to the body. Jenny couldn't tell who it was. The costume and makeup made the whole scene that much more confusing.

She was dressed like Eleanor, in a purple suit and pillbox hat. Her hair was blonde instead of brown, and her face was turned to the back wall at a harsh angle.

She knew too soon who she was looking at, but it didn't make sense.

None of this made sense.

The blonde hair and delicate features of the woman lying there belonged to the woman Jenny had thought was a killer.

Blood pooled around her figure, spilling from the gunshot wound in her chest. Above the wound, where Eleanor's jeweled brooch would have been, a tiny forget-me-not bloom lay over Bonnie's dead heart.

18

THE ROOM GREW crowded very quickly. As passengers and employees found themselves in various stages of shock and panic.

Jenny pressed herself to the back of the car. It had been completely empty aside from Bonnie's dead body. Her killer had vanished leaving a locked door. While the crowd filled in waiting for someone to tell them what to do, her gaze went to the back of the baggage car and the only other exit.

Movement flashed through the vestibule window, light reflecting off what looked like glasses. Someone was watching them. Jenny moved quickly, pouncing on the door handle, and pulling it open.

No one was there.

The empty vestibule led to the employee car. Whoever had done this would have had to leave on that side of the train. Jenny stepped slowly into the passageway and crept across to the toward the door.

The employee car was still and quiet, aside from the snoring of men who were in between shifts. Jenny scanned the car, searching for movement or an exit. The train jostled, and the door on the far wall bounced, unlatched.

Her eyes hadn't quite adjusted to the dim light as she crossed the room. Her foot hit the open door of the safe, and pain wrapped around the lower part of her leg.

"Who's there?" Someone jerked upright in their bunk, cracking his head against the roof.

Jenny hurried past without responding.

"Mills? Who was that?" another worker said as she slipped out.

Jenny pulled the door open at the end of the hall and rushed into an even darker corridor. The hiss and rattle of the chugging steam engine raged in her ears.

Slowly, Jenny put her hand out finding the wall closer than she'd expected. The spacious cars had vanished into a black hallway, closing in around her.

"Is anyone here?" she said.

No movement or sound answered, above that of the train. Even her breathing disappeared in the clanking resonance of the rolling iron gears and breath of the steam engine.

She had to cross or go back.

Fingers brushing the walls, Jenny walked blindly through the corridor, shuffling forward an inch at a time. Grit crunched under her feet as darkness breathed dust into the air. She must be in the tender.

The darkness tightened heavy hands over her lungs. Something rattled behind Jenny, and she spun around, facing the solid night. She debated calling out until more shuddering sounds turned her around again to face back in the direction she'd been going before. Her hand struck the wall, and Jenny yelped as the door swung open.

Orange light burst into the corridor, flames in the coal box blazing as one of the men shoveled more coal inside.

Darren, the other conductor held the door open. "You're not supposed to be here."

She hadn't seen him since the night Garrett died. His angular face was thinner than Chris's and his tone harsher, but from the way the other men circled around him, she could tell he was in charge.

"Sorry," Jenny said. "Did someone else come through here?"

"Besides you? No. Now turn around."

"No one?" Jenny asked. "I followed someone back here."

"No one should be here. This is not a place for passengers. Do you need me to walk you back up front?"

"But what happened to them?" she tried to look past him into the room. It looked like the engine room, and based on this man's reaction, she wouldn't find whoever it was in there.

"I don't know. But I'm taking you back to the passenger cars. Someone could get hurt." The conductor took her arm and turned her back to the corridor.

The golden glow from the firebox lit the corridor for just a second before Darren shut the door behind them. It was enough to see a figure slide into the vestibule door in front of them.

"Someone is dead." Jenny tried to move forward, toward the door and the escaping person, but Darren's grip on her arm stopped her. "Don't hold me so tight." She pulled away and he let go, but he narrowed his eyes.

"Is that supposed to shock me?" He started down the hall. "I was there."

They entered the employee car and Jenny didn't answer, trying to stay quiet as she followed him through.

When they reached the baggage car, where Bonnie lay dead, Darren stopped cold. The room had largely emptied. Only two men remained. Thomas and a porter, in a burgundy and gold uniform, stood talking to a member of the staff next to Bonnie's body.

The angry conductor stepped forward as if pulling rank on the porter talking to Thomas. "Someone better explain this."

"Darren." Thomas broke off his conversation to talk with Jenny's captor.

"Thomas? You better tell me what's going on. Why is someone else dead?"

Jenny stepped away, grateful he wasn't paying attention to her anymore and circled toward the door.

"We may not know what happened, but we know who did it." Thomas glanced at Jenny and she slowed waiting to hear what he'd discovered. "Darren. I need you to arrest Jenny Doan."

Jenny shook her head as shock erupted in waves through her body.

"You know I can't do that. Where would I put her?" Darren glared at her.

Thomas got into his face, confronting him. "Well, unless you've seen Chris recently, you're the only authority left on this train. And Jenny has been working on this murder and others for weeks. I have proof."

To Jenny's dismay, Thomas held up the thick brown folder she'd been holding all the way up until finding Bonnie.

"I DIDN'T DO ANYTHING!" Jenny yelled as the lock to her own compartment clicked shut.

The surprise was less that Thomas had accused Jenny of being a killer, and more that everyone had agreed with his conclusions. By the time the conductor and Thomas joined forces to lock her in her away, the shock had diminished to indignant outrage.

"I'm not saying I agree," Ron said beside her. "But his reasoning was pretty sound. You start poking into all of their business just as someone starts threatening them. You've broken into rooms—"

"We," Jenny corrected with her hands on her hips. "We broke into Bonnie's room."

"—You got very close to Stella before she disappeared. You and Bonnie didn't get along and now she's dead. You stole his gun." Ron could have been counting things off on his fingers as he went through his list.

"I was trying to protect people." Jenny looked through the peephole. All she could see was the back of a dark head standing guard in the hall. "I was trying to solve a murder."

"Not anymore." Ron rattled the door handle and let out a huff beside her. "Be careful what you wish for, I guess."

"We're under house arrest." Jenny leaned back against the wall. She couldn't just sit here. "You wished for this?"

Ron shrugged, and Jenny's brow pinched in confusion.

"Not this specifically. Just more time with you." Ron sighed. "I guess you can't control how that turns out."

"Ron, I love you. But I don't know if time is the problem. We spend a lot of time together. So much so that I feel guilty when I'm not spending time with you." Jenny set her hands in his.

He squeezed her hands. "That's a lot of guilt."

"I know." Jenny walked to the back window and shoved the curtain aside. Trees and mountainside rolled past, but it didn't matter, she and Ron weren't going anywhere. And even if they did get out, what would they do?

"If it's not time, maybe it's recognition." Ron's soft voice turned Jenny around.

"You think I don't recognize you?" Jenny asked.

He shrugged again. "I know you're doing a lot. But everyone gets a piece of you. You give yourself to them and make them feel valued. I miss that. I miss being seen by you. Having you find interest in what I love. I don't want you to feel guilty, I just want you to love all of me, not just the side of me that's there for you."

"But I do." Jenny defended herself. "I love that you're interested in different things than I am. We're different people and that's okay."

"I know you love me, Jen. I love you too." Ron's smile was sad as he looked away.

Jenny stopped. She wasn't saying the right things. She circled around him till she could see his face and put her hands on his cheeks. "I love that everything you do comes from your heart. Whether it's racing, or engines, or embroidery. You do so much for me, but everything you do teaches me about you. I wouldn't be me if I lost you. I don't ever want you to feel unseen, because everywhere you go, I see you. I feel you. You are my person."

"I know." Ron laid his hands over hers and soaked in her features as Jenny did the same.

"How did we get here?" Jenny broke away. "We were vacationing and celebrating and now, we're locked in our room, accused of murder, and struggling to understand each other."

Ron walked around the room, skirting Jenny. "All I know is, I don't want you going to prison for something you didn't do. Jenny Doan, jailbird, doesn't sound nearly as nice as Jenny Doan, quilter extraordinaire."

"I'm partial to the second version myself." Jenny laughed. "Though I wasn't consulted for either of them. It would be a lot easier if we knew who did it."

"I wish we knew who you'd seen in the baggage car." Ron muttered.

She'd tried to explain what had happened after Thomas accused her, but it was likely Ron was the only person who'd heard what she was saying.

"Then we'll have to find the real killer," Jenny said.

Ron groaned. "How do we do that while we're here?"

"Well, at worst, the killer will strike again, and they'll know it's not us."

"And at best?" Ron asked, not commenting on the fact that she'd claimed Ron as an accomplice.

"At best we get out and find the killer before they hurt anyone else." Jenny turned to look over the room. "Thomas didn't go through our room did he?"

"No." Ron looked around the room himself, a quizzical tilt to his brow.

"Good," Jenny said. "Can you unlock the door?"

"Of course. It's not even supposed to lock from that side." He pulled out his pocketknife. "They would have had to tie it up or wedge something in the lock."

"Okay, you work on that and I'm going to look through the camera again."

"Is something on there?" Ron paused in the center of the room.

"I don't know." Jenny took it and picked a place on the edge of the bed, powering up the device. "I'm going to look though. It's one of the last times we saw Stella."

Jenny began flipping through images. They'd arrived from the kitchen stairwell, and the first image was of Stella smiling in front of the large windows with Bonnie in the background. Then Bonnie kissing Warren on the cheek. Vivian didn't show up until several photos in, and Jenny paused on an image that caught the side profile of a waiter who looked a lot like Andrew.

Jenny hesitated. If Andrew was there, maybe Bonnie hadn't poisoned Garrett. Maybe it was Andrew. It didn't fit his story, but he could've been lying.

The pictures scrolled by until they started over. Thomas was barely in there because he'd deleted almost all of his images. It was very suspicious. Even Mia had a couple appearances. The only person Jenny didn't see was Carey.

Jenny got to the image of Thomas kissing Bonnie's hand and flipped past slowly. Several images later, Jenny stopped and stared. There was another image of Thomas.

She hadn't seen it before, because the picture was actually of Stella standing in front of the viewing window. Thomas was reflected in the glass, having an intense conversation with a familiar waiter.

"Thomas and Andrew." *Andrew had been at the dinner.* Jenny set the camera down and looked at Ron. "Stella chased Andrew off the train, and no one saw him until after the dinner where someone attempted to poison Warren and killed Garrett."

Ron had moved to the door and nodded to the corner. "If you say so."

"I think he was talking with Bonnie before the dinner too. And he's missing again, right after finding Eleanor's journal." Would he kill to find his sister's treasure?

Jenny let the facts play in her mind. She glanced at the murder quilt in the dim lighting. It hung colorfully against the wall. She still didn't know who the competing studio was that Thomas had been meeting with. The affair had been bogus, but the pregnancy . . . In a way, Eleanor's death had helped Thomas. With Stella and Andrew gone no one was looking into the murder. Now Thomas had sent the authorities after her too.

She glanced at the camera and the picture of Thomas and Andrew. They weren't talking, Thomas had a glass in his hand. "Thomas doesn't know the affair is fake." Jenny realized looking at the producer's image. "Now Warren's in his room sick, he could have been poisoned."

"And his alibi is a lie. He could have killed Eleanor. No wonder he didn't push the investigation." Jenny stood. "We need to get out of here."

"Almost there," Ron said to the wall as he worked. "They must have done something outside the lock."

"Let me help." Jenny walked over to the door and knocked. There was no answer. She pressed herself up to the corner of the door and called out. "Excuse me. Whoever's there, we need some water in here."

"You have a bathroom," the man said.

Jenny rolled her eyes and smiled, glancing at Ron.

"He's talking." She whispered, then raising her voice she turned back to the door. "It's not working, and my husband has medication."

Ron pulled back, looking offended that he was being made into the problem. Jenny raised an eyebrow and tipped her head to the side with a shrug.

"That's convenient," the man said. "Just a minute."

Footsteps walked away, and Jenny turned to Ron. "Are you ready?"

"Do you want me to fight him when he opens the door?" He grimaced as he rubbed his arm and stretched his fingers. "I'm not sure that's a good idea.

"I don't want you to fight him." Jenny shook her head. "Just finish. You said you were almost done. Lets get out before he comes back."

"Oh. Sure." He stuck his knife in the gap of the door frame. "Okay, help me press the lock." He edged to the side and Jenny leaned in.

Ron tipped his head to meet Jenny's gaze and started counting. "One. Two. Three."

Jenny pressed and Ron shifted the mechanism with a click, but it wouldn't open.

"Try again." Ron knelt, inching closer to the door. "One. Two. Three—"

Before they finished, a hand smacked on the door as footsteps ran down the hall.

"What are you doing?" a woman's voice called out.

Jenny froze with Ron, no breath and no movement coming from their side of the door.

"They needed water." The footsteps slowed as the door's surveillance spoke.

"They didn't need water. They're trying to escape."

"They're old people. Are we really worried about them escaping?"

"Old?" Jenny mouthed to Ron. Her offense at the verbal attack was nearly as high as her fear of discovery.

"They're killers," the woman snapped. "Go tell Thomas you almost let this couple escape." There was a pause, and she reiterated herself. "Go! Thomas should know what a terrible job you did. Tell him I'm taking over."

Jenny bit her lip and stood as a set of footsteps walked away. She and Ron watched each other, listening and waiting to understand what was happening.

Something in the hall snapped.

And the door slid open.

19

VIV STOOD OUTSIDE the door, a broken board lay at her feet and a thin gold key was gripped in her fingers. "Welcome to your escape."

Ron laughed and clapped a hand on her back. "I don't even remember your name."

"Vivian." She turned to Jenny. "Is there anything in there you need?"

Stunned to see her standing there, Jenny took a quick mental inventory and shook her head. Her last conversation with Viv had ended with Jenny suggesting Viv wanted Andrew to murder his sister for her ego . . . or something along those lines.

Viv leaned past them after they'd exited the room and locked the door again, hiding half the board inside and shoving the other half into the pocket side of the door as a wedge.

Her broken silver belt was wrapped loosely through the belt loops of Viv's mustard yellow pants. She tried not to think about the belt or Stella's neck. But she couldn't hold back her questions. "Where did you get the key?"

"Thomas," Viv said softly. "He just doesn't know it yet."

"What are you doing here?"

Viv ignored Jenny's question and beckoned them out of the room. "Good. We're going to lock this door and see if we can fool them for a little while." She locked the door and turned the opposite direction, toward her room.

It wasn't where Jenny had planned to go. She hesitated. "We can't just go walking around. What if someone sees us?"

"Then you hide." Vivian's sharp enunciation was a cold-water reminder of the stakes. "Which you can't do standing around."

Jenny blinked and nodded. Safety first, then find Thomas. "Right, let's go."

Viv started down the hall again. And after checking the vestibule led them inside and into the next car. They made it all the way to Viv's room before they heard movement behind them. The door at the end of the car pulled open, and Viv shoved them into her room.

"Bathroom!" she hissed and pulled the door shut.

"What are you doing?" a man asked, his footsteps slowed as he passed their door. "Everyone's supposed to be in their rooms."

Jenny's mouth dropped open in an "oh" as she realized why the halls had been so empty.

"Just getting antsy. Do you know what Thomas is going to do about Jenny?"

"Beats me. I still can't believe it's her."

Vivian laughed. "I'm not convinced he's right. I think he just wants it to be."

"Huh," the other person said. "I thought it made sense. The plans in that folder were pretty specific."

Viv made a "hmm" sound and the door shifted like one of them had leaned against it. "How better to make her look guilty?"

There was a beat of silence, and the inquisitor mumbled something noncommittal, and footsteps walked away.

Viv came back in, rolling her eyes when she found Jenny and Ron in the hall. "I told you to hide in the bathroom." She walked past the pair and flopped onto her bed. "What if he'd tried to come in? You should hide in here until we get to Quilter's Square."

"Thank you," Jenny said. "But why do this for us? I treated you like a suspect and Andrew disappeared?"

"That's actually why I trust you." Vivian rolled onto her side, propping her head up with her hand. "You were honest. Andrew told me everything you were doing, everything you were checking. I didn't like that the suspicion fell on me, but it was honest . . . and you asked more questions than anyone else, the police included."

"Well, thank you for your trust." Jenny walked past Ron, circling the room without touching anything. "But we need to find the real killer. Things aren't going to change because we get off the train."

"Everyone is talking about you. Thomas has convinced them all you're guilty. You can't go out there."

Jenny shook her head. "I can't just sit here and wait for Thomas to give the police some skewed version of reality. And I don't want to get you mixed up in this. I need to find Thomas."

Vivian sat up, staring at Jenny. "You don't want to do that. I left him in the dining room where he was monologuing about how many terrible things you've done."

"That's ridiculous," Jenny said. Ron watched her from the corner, his arms folded across his chest.

"I believe you." Vivian gripped the edge of the bed and looked over her shoulder, as if organizing her thoughts or gathering courage. When she looked back, she was focused. "But you can't confront Thomas. He has gone so far as to speculate that you were working with someone to kill Eleanor in the first place. All to get a mythical treasure."

The treasure. The quilt. Stella. "I won't go looking for him—yet. But there are still so many questions."

"Yet?" Ron asked. "Vivian's right. We shouldn't go confronting a killer. We should wait here."

"We can't." Jenny didn't have time to explain this again. "Trust me. Thomas has too many connections and too many people on his side. We have to find who did this."

"I agree." Viv stepped between them. "But let me ask the questions. No one saw where you went."

"I said I wouldn't go looking for Thomas. But Stella's still missing. Finding her could give us just as many answers without having to confront a killer."

Viv paced to the door, stubbing her toe and heaving a breath as she steadied herself. "Have you checked the back of the parlor?"

"The parlor?" Jenny asked, trying to picture it. "What's in the back?"

"Supposedly, it's got a secret room." Viv closed her eyes and took a breath. "Stella could be there."

Jenny threw her hands up in the air. "Why didn't anyone mention this before?"

"Because Andrew was taking care of it. He told me today. Then he went AWOL, and I kept hoping he'd show up. And before Bonnie stole my audition and got shot, I thought I had time to figure it out."

"Stella is missing! He's missing!" Jenny started to the door. "I can't believe Andrew knew about this and didn't say anything."

Vivian blocked her path. "No, I can't let you wander around the train and get caught."

"I'm not going to get caught," Jenny said.

Viv shook her head. "I already failed Andrew's family once. I'm not doing it again."

"You haven't—"

"Just wait here." Vivian put her hand on the door. "I'll be right back. If anyone comes by, hide in the bathroom." She paused and looked back at them. "But actually hide this time."

"Thanks," Jenny said unenthusiastically. "We'll be invisible in there."

After Viv left, Jenny looked at Ron. "We escaped one prison for another?"

He took her hand and led her to a chair. "At least it's one that's not guarded."

"So, we wait? What about helping Eleanor and Stella? They deserve to be free. Stella could still be alive." Jenny steeled herself for resistance. Ron would have to listen.

Her phone dinged. Jenny checked her pockets and looked up. "That's not mine. I haven't had my phone in days."

Ron patted down his own pockets and shook his head.

The phone pinged again. On the nightstand, a light flashed, and Jenny picked it up. "It's Vivian's."

> —*It's me. S is upstairs. Key in the drawe Rjn star*
> *well don't response*

She read it twice, and Ron leaned over her shoulder. "What is it?"

Jenny turned to his voice and looked back at the phone. "I don't know. They seem to know Viv, but it's an unknown number . . . it doesn't make much sense."

"Huh," Ron took the phone. "Wasn't Eleanor's quilt supposed to be a key?"

Jenny furrowed her brow. "You don't think—the quilt? Could S be Stella?"

"Have you checked the upstairs dining room?"

"Well, no. It's a locked crime scene." Jenny heaved a sigh. "Which is probably a perfect place to hide someone. But it's too easy. We just randomly get a text that tells us where she is?"

"I don't know about easy." Ron put the phone down. The message had vanished from the screen. "I don't know Rj or what star well is."

"Rj . . . Ron and Jenny? Ron and Jenny star well . . . don't response . . ." Jenny looked up and frowned. "They probably just mistyped. The R could easily be attached to drawe—drawer, but then what's jn star well?"

"I don't know." Ron picked up the phone again. "Jn star well . . . the j is close to the o and the i. If they mistyped, it could just be in or on star well. Not that it's helpful."

"On star well, in star well—" Jenny closed her eyes with a sigh. "Oh, my goodness." It was painfully obvious. "He missed the 'i'. It's supposed to say, in stairwell. The key is in the stairwell." Jenny started for the door.

"The key or the quilt?" Ron followed Jenny. "Wait, are we leaving now?"

"Why not?" Jenny stood still, listening. "No one is out after Bonnie's murder. This is the perfect time to check."

Ron grumbled as Jenny slid the door open and followed her staying close to the wall all the way to the end of the corridor. She gestured for Ron to duck and peeked through the window of the vestibule door.

They still had several more sleepers to go without much of a hiding place. Then Jenny saw the shadow of an approaching person. She found an abandoned room that didn't hold any surprise guests, and shoved Ron inside. They waited for their footsteps to pass.

Jenny slid the compartment door open, continuing on their way. When they made it to the last vestibule before the dining room she was almost giddy. All they had to do was get up the stairs to dining room and the key.

She peeked through the window.

They'd also have to pass a room full of people.

Jenny's good feelings diminished as she watched the people milling around the room. She could see the stairs and the closet that held the gun, but she didn't know how they'd get there.

"How are we going to get past all those people?" Jenny whispered.

Ron peeked through the window after she stepped away. "I have an idea," he said, taking a wide step across the vestibule. "Hang on."

"It's all right. I'm working on it." Jenny's brain circled the problem while she tugged at the corner of her sweater. "Just give me a second." She'd figure it out . . . eventually.

Ron took her by the shoulders and looked at her. "See me, Jenny," Ron whispered. "I want to help you save this girl. I have an idea. I'm trusting you. Trust me."

His eyes darted to the little window, and when he looked back, Jenny met his gaze.

"All right," she said. "What are you thinking?"

"Every car has a fire alarm. We just need to pull the one in there and everyone will scatter."

Jenny's lips parted in surprise, then slowly lifted into a grin. "I've never been more grateful that you love this train so much."

"It's just a fire alarm."

"And it never occurred to me. Take the thank you." She squeezed his arm, and a grin appeared on his lips.

"Where's the alarm?" Jenny asked, peeking in the window again.

"It's on the far side of the car."

She heard the words and recognized their problem, but she'd just seen Thomas. Vivian had left him in the dining car, and he'd never left. And that made the problem even worse.

"Thomas is in there. If I go in, he'll lock us up again or worse. He may have the gun again."

"He probably does," Ron said in a matter-of-fact tone. "He came out of the kitchen as you and Carey hid the gun."

Jenny blanched and looked through the window.

"Don't worry." Ron leaned close to her ear to whisper. "I'm going to get past the dining cars. I'll set off the fire alarm, and as people rush out, you go in."

"How are you going to get past the dining room without being seen?"

"Trust me. I have a plan. Wait here for the fire alarm." Ron pulled open the back vestibule door.

"Wait, Ron?" Jenny leaned forward, a sense of foreboding settling over her heart. She kissed him and looked into his pale blue eyes. "You're not doing anything crazy, are you?"

Ron grinned. "Maybe a little, but I've always wanted to do it, and this is the perfect chance."

Jenny's forehead squeezed tight, wrinkles forming over a headache that had no business being there. "Be careful."

"Of course." He kissed her back and let the vestibule door click shut behind him.

Her skin grew clammy in the tiny, dark passageway. Her heartbeat fast and out of control.

The people in the dining car rotated around Thomas. His expression shifted between snarling and bitter laughter. It wasn't much of a change. The main difference was he stopped talking when he was laughing.

Jenny checked her watch. Five minutes. She didn't want to know what Ron was doing. There was only one way to the other side, and that was through this car. Unless you went around it.

Jenny's lungs stopped working.

He wouldn't.

Ron was strong, but he was in his sixties. His late sixties.

She opened the vestibule door on the sleeper side. The door that led outside was closed. Jenny's lungs pumped a double breath, and she hiccuped. The door was closed. That wasn't his plan.

Then a thump landed on the roof near the dining car. Her heart took off again, racing at breakneck speeds. "No."

She stared at the ceiling and stepped into the vestibule, trying to follow the sound. It went quiet.

She grabbed the door handle in front of her and paused. She wanted to run through and find some way to stop him. But it wouldn't help, and it would ruin Ron's chance of succeeding. She waited, holding herself back like she was strapped into a catapult.

Inside, Thomas was still ranting.

People glanced at the ceiling randomly. Jenny forced herself to swallow.

She hiccupped again and flinched.

That wasn't good.

She tried to breathe slowly. Taking in deep, even breaths—*hiccup*.

Jenny growled at the painful bubble in her chest. Then something crashed above her, and Jenny screamed and threw open the door to the dining car.

No one noticed. Even Thomas was looking at the ceiling. Jenny didn't know if this was part of the plan or not, but the fire alarm was on the back wall, and she hurried across the carpeted floor and yanked the handle down, then bolted beneath a table.

Bells rang through the car and people yelled, looking around the room and finally scattering as planned. They went in both directions, some toward the baggage car and some toward the rest of the train.

Maybe people were looking for the conductor.

Jenny waited until everyone was gone. She'd missed seeing where Thomas went, but she crept first to the closet and pulled it open. She didn't want the gun, but needed to know—

The cabinet door was open, and the gun was missing.

"So, Thomas was right?"

She whirled around. Carey stood behind her.

20

CAREY'S EYES DARTED to the gun cabinet and back to Jenny.

"You know I defended you?" He gripped the side of the door with a tight fist.

"I didn't take the gun." Jenny threw her hands up in defense, and Carey grabbed her bicep. "I was checking to be sure it was still there. After Bonnie got shot, I was afraid—and I was right."

"I can't believe I trusted you." Carey pulled her away from the closet. "I should just leave you here to get burned up by whatever fire set off the alarm."

"I set off the alarm." She pulled back, but he held on like she was nothing." There isn't any fire. I did it."

Above them, Ron moaned loudly.

"Carey, let me get Ron." She couldn't take her eyes off the ceiling. "Please, come with me if that's what you want, but I need to go to Ron. He's hurt. I've got to help him."

"I don't think so. I'll come back for Ron. But right now, I'm taking you somewhere safe."

He dragged her across the floor, barely slowing when she stumbled.

"Carey? Don't do this. I don't know everything Thomas is saying, but let me defend myself."

He pulled her through the vestibule. "Explain the folder."

"Thomas planted it," Jenny said quickly. Carey laughed, and she realized it was probably too quick.

"That's convenient." He bit the words out. "Eleanor deserves better than this, you know. You said you were helping, that you were a friend, but all you've done is hurt people."

"I'm sorry." Jenny kept looking behind her, trying to will herself back to Ron. "I didn't want to hurt anyone."

He pushed through another car, pausing at the doors. As he pulled the second set of doors open, she took a wide step, pulling around and tripping him.

"Hey!" he yelled and caught himself as he stumbled.

Jenny turned around, grabbed the door behind them, and yanked it open.

Carey's hand closed around her arm again. He stood there breathing hard and holding her so tight she knew she was going to bruise.

"I'm really sorry, Jenny." Carey dropped his voice till it was almost tender, and when she looked up at him, his eyes were wet. "I'm really sorry. You have to see how this looks. You came in out of nowhere and people started dying. You told me you broke into Thomas' room and stole his gun. I helped you hide it. But if you're here because you killed Eleanor, just tell me why. Tell me what happened. I can protect you. Or I'll try."

Jenny shook her head in disbelief. "Is that what Thomas is saying? You can't really believe that. I didn't kill Eleanor, or anyone else."

"Then where's Stella? Or Andrew? You were the last one to see either of them." He waited, but Jenny didn't have an answer, and it tore at her like fabric ripped to rags.

"I wish I knew." She examined the floor, not able to meet his eye.

His grip held, and Jenny followed when he tugged on her, guilt pulling her after him. "I didn't want to hurt anyone."

"We never do."

The words were a strange comfort. The hallway was cool, and Jenny wasn't surprised when Eleanor's blue petals danced over the floor. Carey walked right over them.

As he passed his own compartment, he paused. "Come this way. Maybe I can help."

Jenny frowned. "What do you mean?"

"I mean, Bonnie was in here before she died. She was asking about Viv's audition. She had a paper, and she left it. I want to see what it said. Maybe it says something that can clear you." Carey looked at her. "What do you want me to do?"

"Go get it," Jenny said. "I haven't done anything."

Carey paused, looking her in the eye, a muscle at the side of his eye twitching as if trying to control his emotions.

We did well for a couple of high school sweethearts. "You really loved her, didn't you?" she said.

"Always have, always will." He nodded. "So, you know why I have to check?"

She didn't respond as he opened the door and pulled her in with him. Something about his answer unsettled her. He latched the door behind them and guided her into the main area.

"Stay here, please?" He started by the chair, bending over the trashcan and moving to the little table with the flowers.

He looked behind the chair and shoved it aside when he found nothing. The little pot of forget-me-nots tipped over the table, spilling purple flowers and dirt.

Jenny walked up behind him to fix it. Beside the flowers, the lid of the wooden box had slid off. Blue and white diamonds sparkled in the familiar shape of a flower. Eleanor's brooch lay inside. A jeweled forget-me-not, next to the fresh ones tumbling across the antique wood.

Jenny picked it up. In the corner of the box lay a thin gold band with a tiny diamond pressed into the center. She knew the engraving without having to look.

Always have. Always will.

Thomas had deleted himself from the photos of Bonnie's party, but Carey had been missing, at least until dinner. Plenty of time to switch the cards. She took a step back. There was nothing in Bonnie's folder about Carey except his dental surgery, that he'd mentioned himself.

He reached into the corner, adjusted his glasses, and dug through the box.

The same glasses Jenny had seen in Stella's room the night she was strangled and Thomas was shot.

"Where's the gun, Carey?" Jenny took another step back, placing the discarded chair squarely between them.

"What are you talking about?" He stood, stretching his shoulders and looking at Jenny. She could almost see the glare from his glasses as he watched her being accused by Thomas.

"It was you, outside the window of the baggage car when Bonnie died. You killed her." A breeze blew through the room. Eleanor was there, but Jenny didn't mind; her heart was racing again.

She backed away, going for the door, but not fast enough.

Carey grabbed her and reached into his pocket with the other hand. "I told you to stay where you were. I even asked nicely." He pulled a small ring of keys from his pocket and let them dangle in front of her for a second. A thin gold one, several standard brass keys, and one long thin one. He snatched them back into his grip and replaced them in his pocket. "I locked us in. You're not going anywhere till I find what I'm looking for."

"You don't need a key to get out of a room."

Carey let her go and returned to his search. "You do in my room."

Jenny spun around and stopped. She didn't know how she'd missed it before, but there was a padlock installed on his door. Not particularly high, so when he was latching the door, he'd simply locked the padlock as well. Jenny scanned the room for a duplicate key, remembering the odd way he'd insisted she sit on the far side of the room.

Her hand fisted around the brooch. She needed to get the keys while Carey was still busy. Just a distraction. She was good at distractions.

She took a step to the side and popped the clasp on the pin.

"Got it." Carey stood, catching the tiny motion of her hand as he did. At first his eyes widened, then his lips curled into a smile. "You found her pin. Good. We're almost done here." Carey pulled a rope and a tangle of notecards from the box.

Three tiny papers tumbled onto the tabletop. Gold embossed lettering read, *In honor of Eleanor Grace*, exactly as Bonnie had said they were supposed to.

"Oops." Carey picked up the stray cards and tossed them in the trash bin. "I guess I missed a couple."

Jenny stumbled back a step, the room growing smaller by the second. "You're not here to clear anyone's name."

Carey smoothed the rope in his hand. His smile trembled as a soft laugh came out.

She didn't wait for him to explain what he wanted. He stepped toward her, and she jabbed the open pin into his arm.

He yelped and grabbed her wrist, shoving her back. The pin dangled from his bicep, and he pulled it out, glaring at her. With a burst of adrenaline, she shoved the chair between them into his shins.

He folded forward with a groan over a hopefully painful injury. His head hit the wooden trim of the chair as he went down.

She hated the guilt she felt, but all she saw was the ring of keys protruding from his pocket. She lunged for them and looped the ring around her finger. Carey swiped at her. He missed, and she turned to the entry, careening down the short hall and into the door. With a tiny prayer in her heart, Jenny took one of the brass keys and shoved it into the lock. It twisted and the lock popped as a body slammed into her. Icy air billowed under the doorway, and Jenny cried out, sliding to the floor.

Carey stood over her, blood trickling from his forehead.

THE TRAIN PICKED up speed as Carey led Jenny to the kitchen stairwell. She hit the wall several times as the fire alarm rang below, her sluggish footsteps carrying her up the narrow stairs.

When they reached the top, Carey stopped at a small sideboard and retrieved a key from a drawer. Just as the text had said.

— *Key in the drawe Rjn star well*

If she used her imagination, anyway. All the while he told her how silly it had been for her to even try to find Eleanor's killer.

He stopped talking as the door opened to the upper dining room, his expression morphing into shock to match her own.

Wind whipped through the room, blowing against dangling panes of shattered glass. A large hole in the curved ceiling of the panoramic windows left the room open to the night air. She'd admired the dramatic wall of glass that curved all the way overhead on her first day there.

The statement wall had been reduced to a bed of tiny crystal-shards scattered among large chunks of the window pane, like a glass mine field across the floor.

The glass debris was all in one section, below the broken window. Something—or someone—had fallen through.

Jenny didn't like to think about the most likely possibility. Remnants of blood stained the nearby furniture. Stella sat in the corner, her head down, tied to a chair, a smear of blood on her arm.

Who Jenny didn't see was Ron.

Carey cursed, looking up at the broken glass. "How did he survive that?"

"He's tall."

Jenny's flippant answer earned her an expected jerk as Carey pulled her to the table below the destroyed window.

Jenny's wrists burned under the ropes Carey had tied around her. Jenny fought as he shoved her into a chair until he gripped her by the shoulders and glared at her.

"I have things to do," he said. "Now you're going to sit here, or every piece of glass I find large enough to hold in my hand is going to be used to hurt your husband when I find him." He waited as Jenny's eyes went wide. "Do you want that?"

She shook her head.

"Good. Now open." He held a cloth napkin bundled in his fist in front of her mouth.

There was no way to get out of this. Not if it meant Ron got hurt. She whimpered and let him stuff her mouth with the wadded-up fabric.

Stella hadn't acknowledged her, sitting vacantly on the other side of the room. She hadn't even made eye contact.

Carey shoved the cloth in her mouth and tied her wrists to her ankles behind the chair. It was a long leash between them, but not so much that she could move her feet without tugging her arms and shoulders backward.

When he was done, Carey looked at the two of them with pride. "If nothing else, I've saved the train from the vicious killer, Jenny Doan. But we've still got half a day tomorrow. I might still be able to finish." He winked and pulled the main door shut completely. "Off to find Ron and Warren. I've got to keep Thomas and the rest of them thinking you're the killer as long as possible."

He moved to the service entrance and turned back. "Oh, and thanks for keeping Chris company."

He gestured to the corner behind her. There, leaning against the glass, was Chris Wiley with a knife lodged in his chest.

Jenny's muffled screams were nothing on the rolling and puffing train. Her outcry had as much to do with the shock of seeing Chris dead as her pain and fear all coming to a head.

Her cry turned to gasping tears, choking around the fabric in her mouth as Carey chuckled.

"You would never have the fortitude to do what I'm doing for her. It's all right. We'll all see Eleanor again."

Jenny's sobs slowed as his words found purchase in her mind.

It wasn't over yet.

His grin cooled, and he shot an icy glare over the room. "I'll let you know if I find Ron. It would be unfortunate if he just disappeared."

If it were possible, Jenny's eyes must have widened again. She shook her head and started yelling. She bounced in her chair, making as much noise as possible.

Disdain bled from Carey's sneer. "Make as much noise as you want. I told them yesterday that to preserve the crime scene, we put an air conditioner up here. It was in the baggage area, leftover from production, but it's broken and noisy." He glanced up at the window. "And now with that new damage, it's bound to be worse."

Jenny only stopped long enough to feel the desperation of what he said. No one was coming.

Except for Ron. He would come.

She yelled and clunked her chair against the floor. It was harder than it looked, and she was tired before Carey turned away.

"I'll be back. Alone if things go well." Frustration pooled in his clipped phrases. "With friends if they don't. Behave."

She yelled louder just to spite him, though it made little difference through her newly installed muffler.

The door closed behind Carey, and Jenny quieted, staring at the corner behind the door. The lock clicked, and she shook her head.

Ron stood behind the door, hidden when Carey came in and opened it, tied her up, and left. He was amazing.

"Ron." She tried to speak, but she could barely move her tongue or close her mouth.

He didn't respond. Not really. He wavered, took a single step forward and nodded to her, but his movements didn't seem intentional.

Her brow tightened, and she called him again. Her muffled cry was more desperate. "Ron!"

It didn't sound like his name, and she knew it. She couldn't shape consonants around the cloth napkin in her mouth, and the noise did little more than pull his gaze in her direction as it drifted away.

The haze of triumph faded as she took in Ron's condition. Blood dripped from various wounds. A gash on his cheek cut into his beard. The carefully trimmed white hair had been stained red on one side. But he was standing.

His eyes focused on her, and in a slow gesture, he raised a finger to his lips.

Help me.

Not now, Eleanor! Jenny wanted to shout at the ghost.

Ron didn't seem phased. He didn't seem conscious of much that was happening except when she held his gaze.

Jenny hopped her chair closer by inches. Her breathing turned shallow.

Ron frowned. His eyelids dropped out of sync, in a slow blink. When his focus returned, he smiled weakly, and her breath caught altogether.

He took a step forward, wavered again, and collapsed to the glass-covered floor.

Her heart raced like someone had pushed the pedal on her chest. It beat like a sewing machine at full speed. Her breathing sped up, and the chair pressed against her arms with her wrists tied behind it.

It didn't matter that she was tied to her chair or that her mouth was stuffed with fabric. She cried out as if she could turn back time with her voice.

"Ron!"

21

JENNY DIDN'T BREATHE until Ron did.

He groaned and rocked to the side, and she pulled forward to follow him. With her hands still tied behind her back, she couldn't go far. scraping her arms as she felt his pain and ignored her own.

"I didn't get to the alarm for you." Regret wove through his words as Ron pushed up to see her and dropped to the ground again.

"Ih oh-A—" Jenny wanted to tell him everything would be fine, that she'd gotten the alarm for him, but when she tried, her napkin-filled mouth only produced garbled sounds.

The tones bore no resemblance to the words, *it's okay*.

"I'm sorry." Ron squinted up at her from the glitter of glass on the floor before he closed his eyes as if it was too hard to keep them open.

He rolled back, cringing as glass crackled beneath the weight of his body.

His eyes stayed closed.

"Own uve." Again, her muffled voice failed to form the correct words. *Don't move.* The rag in her mouth was a solid, dry obstacle she had to get out. Jenny pushed with her tongue till she could spit the napkin into her lap.

She started looking around the room. There had to be a way out of this. Broken glass, table, chairs, silverware, there wasn't much that could help.

Silverware.

Jenny hopped her four-legged prison over to the table in a slow process. With her back to the table, she reached for knives, forks, anything that could loosen or cut the knots on her wrists. She didn't know if it would work, but it didn't matter. She couldn't reach them. Whether he'd meant to or not, the ropes Carey had tied around her wrists held her hands too low.

Jenny pushed back against her chair, bumping into the table in frustration. The table settings moved. Dishes clinked and danced as she did it again, and the settings moved farther. A knife on the other side of the table hung off the edge.

"It won't work."

Stella's voice was unexpected. With Jenny's worry over Ron, she'd almost forgotten the girl was in the room.

Stella looked at Jenny for the first time since she'd come through the door.

"Why not?" Jenny pushed the table again, the knife teetering on the edge.

Stella sighed. "Because you can't reach the top."

"I don't have to reach the top if I knock the silverware off."

"How would you pick them up?"

"Fall on them?" Jenny looked at the ground, wondering what would happen if she fell, really fell, from this height. She wasn't as young as she used to be, and she knew from experience that her bones didn't like to be broken. "Or you could." Jenny looked at Stella hopefully.

The younger woman flattened her lips into a straight line, letting out a breath through her nose. "You'd have better luck than I would." Stella hopped her chair to the side and her arms stayed hooked on one of the built-in buffet tables. "I can't get close enough."

Jenny looked from the teetering knife to the ground. "Maybe there's another option."

She scanned the room again. Her resources consisted of a well-set table that was unreachable until she was free. The broken window glass littering the floor was too low and would probably cut her as soon as she put enough pressure on the ropes anyway. Ron was passed out. Stella looked drugged. And Chris Wiley was dead with a knife in his chest.

A knife she could probably reach if she could get close enough.

He leaned upright against the window as if watching the evening landscape pass by. If it wasn't for the knife and bloody clothing, Jenny would have guessed he was sleeping.

Of course, she couldn't just go and pull the knife from his body. Even if it wasn't entirely disrespectful, putting her fingerprints all over it would set herself up to look even more guilty than Thomas had painted her. Plus, there was the matter of *pulling a knife from a dead man's body*. Even without the other problems, the task sounded impossible.

She couldn't do it.

Jenny shifted away from Chris, scooting her chair back to face the door. Ron lay in front of her again, his body sprawled across broken glass.

"What other option do we have?" Stella asked.

Jenny looked at Stella and around the room, landing again on Chris.

"Only one," Jenny replied. She closed her eyes and shifted her chair backward, scooting and hopping through the mess of the broken window.

The staff door stayed closed as she reached Chris' corner, the chair thumping into his stiff body like she'd hit a board. He'd been dead a while.

"Do you remember when Chris got here?" Jenny asked. "I'm assuming Carey did this?"

"I don't know for sure, but he brought him in with that other conductor. Carey told him to keep it quiet, or he'd tell the police how the conductor really died."

Jenny glanced over her shoulder apologetically and looked away, watching the wall behind Stella. For the first time, she was grateful her hands were tied behind her back and she had her face away from him. She wouldn't have to look at the dead man while she tried to save herself.

"How did he die?" she asked.

Stella shrugged. "I don't know. They didn't say."

Jenny paused, turning to Stella briefly. "Well, that's not terrifying, is it?"

Stella laughed humorlessly and closed her eyes, her body pulling against her ropes as the fight left her.

Jenny fumbled for the murder weapon, finding the cold body of the conductor against her hands after several attempts.

She pulled away and looked behind her again. The blade was right there . . . she kept the position in her mind as she moved her hands in reverse to find it.

Only a few inches back and left. She tried not to see Chris' bloodied uniform or unmoving body in her mind, focusing on the handle of the knife instead.

When her fingers found the grip, she almost cheered.

"Almost there," Jenny encouraged herself. Gripping the handle tightly, she pulled, but nothing moved. With her hands behind her back, the effort it took to get the knife from his stiffened body was more than she'd anticipated.

Stella peeked at her, tipping her head to the side.

Jenny wasn't ready to fail again.

She did it anyway. Pitting the weight of her body against the strength of her grip, Jenny leaned forward, wiggling the knife until, in a miraculous flash of effort, the knife pulled free. But every step forward came with a price, and the momentum of the knife's release shot Jenny forward.

She pushed back against her fall, as the momentum was too great. All she managed was to angle the chair so she didn't land on her knee. Instead, she hit her arm, pinching it between the chair back and the floor as she slammed against solid wood.

Stella's gaze shot from Jenny to the door. Jenny watched with her, frozen, waiting to hear someone coming to investigate. The chair lay on her arm, blocking the blood flow, but no footsteps pounded up the stairs, no door clicked, and nobody entered the room.

"Carey does have a list of people left to *take care of* still." Jenny adjusted her position, working off the floor.

She found the sharp edge of the blood-soaked blade by her hand. Flipping the knife upward, she went to work.

With minimal range of motion, Jenny held the blade against her bindings and sawed at the fibers of the rope. She focused more on not nicking her arms with the bloody knife than how quickly she made it through the rope.

After several minutes of exertion and focus, Jenny's arms drooped. She was breathing hard, and she hadn't cut through enough of the rope to even get more range of motion.

"I'm so sorry," Stella said. "I didn't know it was him until too late."

Jenny lifted her head. "Me too. If I'd realized sooner, I wouldn't be here."

The room fell quiet. Or as quiet as it could get in what had become an open-air train car. The vintage iron machine rumbled over the tracks, hissing steam into the night. Jenny took a breath and gripped the knife tighter, setting the blade to the rope. She started cutting again, her arms aching from elbow to wrist from the repeated motion.

A rope split, and Jenny's wrists wiggled slightly apart. Not far enough to escape, but far enough to make her job easier.

"He came in my room after Andrew left." Stella started talking as Jenny cut.

It took her a second to realize Stella was talking about the night Thomas was shot. "Who came in?"

Stella glanced at Jenny. "Carey," she said. "I think he thought I was sleeping. When I caught him trying to take Eleanor's quilt, I got up and stopped him. Or tried to. He made up some story about Eleanor and that he wanted to find the treasure for me and Andrew, like he was doing us a favor."

"He just snuck in after everyone left?" Jenny's cutting slowed as Stella's story spilled out. "So he didn't shoot Thomas?"

Stella furrowed her brow. "I don't think so. I didn't see him until late last night."

"But he did steal the quilt?" Jenny asked.

Stella swallowed hard and looked down at her lap. "Not exactly. He told me he was trying to find the treasure for Eleanor. I told him no thank you and tried to take the quilt back. I just wanted him to leave. But he wouldn't. He started talking about the day she died. How she was going to meet up with him before they got back to Quilter's Square so she could leave Thomas. How she should have married him, but she died. He got all kinds of crazy, and I took the quilt back. It made him really angry.

"But out of nowhere he apologized and told me he had a confession and he wanted to show me something. We came here. Garrett was still lying on the floor. He started talking about how poison was such a terrible way to die, and he looked at me and said he needed to know what Eleanor's secrets were. He said we both knew she didn't have any treasure and asked what she was hiding. When I couldn't tell him, he drugged me and knocked me out. I woke up tied to the chair." Stella lifted her head to meet Jenny's gaze. "I can't be here when he comes back. Please, I can't be here."

"It's okay." Jenny looked at Ron. "I don't intend to be. We're going to get out of here."

Jenny's hands had completely stopped cutting while Stella spoke, and she quickly restarted her sawing motion.

The rope frayed audibly as she pressed the blade against it, praying she didn't catch her skin. When the next rope broke, Jenny's wrists pulled free. She collapsed to the floor with a gasp, then let go of her claw-grip on the knife.

"Help me, please?" Stella's voice sounded just like Eleanor's and the words brought on a familiar chill.

Jenny nodded and pulled her arm out from beneath the chair, the pain of the blood returning releasing a flood of feeling into her cold limbs.

"I'm coming." Jenny pushed the chair aside, pulling herself up.

The blade lay in the corner of the abandoned chair. She picked it up and almost dropped it when she saw what she'd been holding. A hunting knife with large, serrated peaks on one edge and a long, curved blade on the other. She glanced at Chris, sorrow for what happened to him gripping her chest, like the bones of her rib cage had shrunk, holding her insides too tightly together.

Jenny forced herself to breathe through her nose and dropped her gaze. The ropes from her wrist lay in a pile, the fraying edges stained red from Chris' blood.

"Hurry," Stella's voice hissed. "I need your help."

Jenny looked at Stella and nodded. "Just a second."

With quick resolve, she took the offensive blade to the ropes on her ankles. When she was free, she cut Stella's ropes and moved straight to Ron.

Rolling him back, Jenny shook her husband. "I need you to wake up. Ron?"

He blinked awake, and Jenny sighed her relief.

"We have to go," Stella said. "Carey's going to be back soon."

"Maybe," Jenny muttered, sliding her arm under Ron's back and helping him sit up.

"What do you mean, maybe?" Stella's breath came quickly. "He's trying to find the treasure before we get back to the station. When he gets stuck, he'll be back to get information I don't have. 'We only have one more day."

"Yes, but that's not his only agenda. He has a list of people and how they're going to die. He's not finished."

22

THE TINY FLOWER lay emblazoned on Bonnie's chest, a beacon to Carey's guilt and the truth Jenny should have seen sooner. All she'd been able to think of was Eleanor.

Ron leaned on Jenny's shoulder as she helped him into the baggage car across from Bonnie's body. Stella followed, growing more anxious about Ron's injuries as they went.

"I wish Andrew was here." Stella sat beside Ron, worry in her eyes. "He's so much better than I am with injuries like this. We need to clean this up. Do you mind if I . . ?" Stella hovered her hand over the bloody side of Ron's beard.

He pulled back, his brow pinched in question. He looked from Stella to Jenny.

"It's fine," Jenny said, nodding to her and Ron both.

Ron relaxed, and Stella began the careful work of clearing shards of broken glass from his wounds.

"Can you help him?" Jenny asked.

Stella glanced over and back to Ron. "I don't have the same training as Andrew, but I know how to clean a wound. Our mother was a nurse. That's what Eleanor was supposed to be, until Thomas. Anyway, she taught us a few things before she passed." Stella wiped her hands and carefully pulled the fabric away from one of Ron's more serious wounds. "Do you think we could get some water?"

"Of course, I'll go." Jenny didn't need any further prodding to hurry off on her mission. The kitchen was unusually empty. "No wonder it didn't bother anyone when I crashed and bashed all over the floor up there."

She dug through the cupboards to turn up a pitcher that she filled with water, grabbed a rag, and returned to the baggage car.

"I've got it." Jenny slid the vestibule door open to find Thomas on the bench where Ron had been.

"You're a slippery one, aren't you? I've been looking everywhere for you. And now I find you've been hiding Stella along with everything else you've done."

Jenny set the water down and turned to Thomas, not breaking eye contact. "Where are they?"

"Ron and Stella are fine. Now Vivian . . . that's another story. I'll deal with her later." Thomas took a step toward Jenny.

She took a step back. "What did you do?"

"Nothing compared to what you've done." Thomas raised an eyebrow. "Relax, they're safe."

"Then why steal them away? Ron is hurt." Jenny looked around as if she might see them hiding. "I was helping them."

"I feel like we've had this conversation before. Stop where you are." Thomas took a deep breath, his nostrils flaring as Jenny moved toward the back door of the baggage car. "I placed you under house arrest once, and I plan to do it again."

She stopped moving and glared at him. "Why? I didn't do anything wrong?"

"A woman is dead!"

"I didn't kill her. Carey's the one you should be looking for." She tried to remember what he'd actually confessed to, but in this moment it didn't matter. "He killed Eleanor."

"Don't pull her into this. I won't let you make her a tool of your convenience."

"Trust me, she's anything but convenient." Jenny had been confronted by her ghost all over the train, regularly being made to look or at least feel crazy because of it.

"That's enough." Thomas stomped his foot and held the door open for Jenny. "Follow me."

"Where is my husband?" she demanded.

Thomas frowned. "Carey has them. Him and Stella both. They're fine. See?"

Jenny's jaw dropped open. "And you just let him have them?"

"He was worried about them." Thomas glared. "We were coming to talk about talent for my upcoming films. He about lost it when he saw what had happened to them."

"Because he did it." She wanted to shake Thomas and make him see what he was missing. "Look at Bonnie," Jenny yelled. "Whoever killed her set a forget-me-not on her chest."

"So? They didn't have her pin." Thomas was busy justifying his truth against anything she said.

"Carey is the only one I know of that has a pot of live forget-me-not flowers blooming on this train."

Thomas shook his head. "No. Stop that. Jenny, you're coming with me." He walked over and pulled her hands behind her back. "And I want my gun back."

"I don't have it."

"You took it. After I was shot at, I set up a camera in my room. I know you took it."

"Carey has it. He helped me hide it to keep it safe, and now it's gone again." She talked over her shoulder as he pushed her through the dining car.

Thomas scoffed. She tried to stall him as they passed the closet, but he wouldn't have it.

"It was right there," she said. "How did you get your gun back to begin with? Was Chris already dead, or did you kill him and Carey just found him?"

"I don't know what you're talking about. Chris isn't dead. He gave me my gun back. It was my gun."

"But he is dead. And you don't have your gun anymore, do you?" Jenny let out a breath, and Thomas' step slowed. it seemed her words were finally getting through to him. "Neither do I, so . . . who has it, if not the killer?"

Thomas moved her through the dining cars and toward the sleeper cars. "I'm taking you to my room this time So I can be sure you stay put."

It's gone.

The fierce need in Eleanor's voice sent a familiar shiver down Jenny's spine. She kept walking.

Thomas slowed, looking around the corridor. "What was that?"

"Eleanor," Jenny said without thinking.

Thomas' gaze shot to Jenny before doing a full circle in the corridor. Ice peeled its way across the windows, painting frost flowers over the glass panes. Blue flower petals danced across the floor. But he didn't seem to see any of that.

Eleanor's voice whispered in the distance as the room cooled until even Thomas' breath showed in the air.

"We need to talk. This isn't what I wanted for my life." She paused as if someone was responding, and her body coalesced in the hall. *"I know you need this. It's the only reason I've kept doing it, but I want to be a nurse. I can still do that. And I want a family."* She paused again, and her hand fell to her stomach. Her gaze followed, her head bowed in reverence. *"It's too late for that. We're going to be a family whether we're ready or not."*

Jenny jumped when Eleanor's head snapped up. Her eyes were wild and focused beyond Jenny and Thomas.

"Thomas, no!" Her shout cracked through the fabric of reality.

Thomas gasped, taking a step forward. He didn't take his eyes off his wife. "I'm sorry," he whispered. "I shouldn't have said it."

Eleanor lurched to the side as if she'd been slapped, and Thomas cringed.

"I wouldn't do that." Tears streaked Eleanor's face, leaving shimmery trails around her fingers as she held a hand against her pale cheek. *"This is supposed to be a good thing. It should be. Please, Thomas. It's all I ever wanted."*

She paused, and Thomas filled in the narrative as if he knew the conversation by heart. "You never wanted the jewels and fame. Everything I could give you."

"You have so much more to give than that. There's more to you. I knew it the first time you took my hand. You helped me find myself again. Let me show you who we can be . . . together. You'll be a wonderful father." Then she flew backward through the wall of the train, grasping at the paneling as if she could stop herself.

Jenny reached out instinctively to catch her as she fell, their hands crossing before she was gone, and Eleanor's face changed. Her eyes turned black, her skin stretched, pulling away from her features, blending into something more ghostly and terrifying than Jenny had ever seen.

An intense cold spread through Jenny's body as Eleanor vanished.

"*It hurts. Help me, Thomas! Help me!*" Eleanor's scream accented the abdominal cramping Jenny was feeling for Eleanor.

Before Jenny's first child, she'd miscarried many times and knew too well the harbinger of painful change that foretold the death of your unborn child.

"*Carey? Carey, it's gone. Can you meet me? —No, I have to go to wardrobe. —Okay, then. Three-thirty. Thank you.*"

The final whispered words were pinpointed with footsteps and tears.

Her body hung doubled over, remembering the ache and emotion of Eleanor's reality. The pain slowly faded as the echo of footsteps did the same. The absence of pain allowed her to straighten. Emotions flooded through her, knowing what that loss must have been and to be alone in that emotion.

It was several seconds before Jenny registered the quiet in the corridor. Thomas wasn't there. He'd left with the footsteps of Eleanor's memory.

Before he changed his mind, Jenny fled the corridor, only to turn around and go back to Vivian's apartment. It was empty. The door that adjoined the neighboring room hung open.

She didn't have time to wonder what Vivian had been doing in Carey's room or the other way around. She scanned the room quickly. She'd seen a sewing kit in there on one of her visits. She found it tucked into the chair under the muted purple tunic she'd worn the first night.

"Perfect." Or almost.

Jenny picked up both the dress and the sewing kit and paused at the open door adjoining Carey's room. There was a second locked door barring her from crossing through. She suspected that was an upgrade from the vintage train design. Normally she would have appreciated it, but she needed a few things he was hiding and would have to find a new way in.

With nothing else to be done, she took the dress and kit and moved into the hall. Carey's door was only feet away. Walking in on him would be a death trap, and she couldn't get caught again.

Taking a deep breath, Jenny knocked and slid back to Vivian's door and hid inside the room. Then she waited to see if anyone would answer. The door stayed closed.

Jenny tried the handle with no better luck. She could get in easily enough with the right tool. She thought about Ron's pocketknife and lamented not having her own, until she remembered the sewing kit. She didn't know if scissors would be thin enough but unzipped the bag anyway. Right on top sat a six-inch, metal measuring stick—a seam allowance ruler. She moved the plastic slider back and slipped the thin metal between the door and the frame.

In one swift arch, Jenny released the latch and let herself into Carey's room. The flowers had been shoved back into their pot and set on the table, but the jewelry box was gone.

The armoire held nothing but shoes and button-up shirts. The suitcases were empty. The bathroom appeared empty until she checked the drawer. The wooden box sat under a pile of pill bottles, cologne, razors, and other various bathroom products.

The little box opened easily with an inset lid. She pulled the wooden cap off only to find the box empty as well. She turned back to the room and shook her head. Everything was empty. It was like he'd tried to expunge anything beyond "average traveler" from his room.

It didn't matter, not really. They'd find Eleanor's things eventually. Her gaze lingered on the chair in the corner. It was pushed out from the wall where it sat in Jenny and Ron's room.

She'd forgotten about the box Carey had kept behind it. The box Carey had pulled the rope from. Jenny pulled the chair out and slid the box into the center of the room.

It was filled with wires and compactly wrapped cylinders and black boxes, lots of electrical equipment Jenny didn't recognize. But tucked against the side of it all, a brooch made of blue and white gemstones sparkled against the wall of the brown cardboard.

So simple.

The thin metal tangled with the wire when she tried to pull it out. She took an even breath to try again, stopping short when footsteps stopped outside the door.

A key scraped in the door. Jenny's head spun with fear that Carey had returned, along with the fear that it might not be Carey and whoever was looking for him would find her there.

Jenny picked up the entire box, grabbing the pot of forget-me-nots almost as an afterthought, and pulled the door adjoining Vivian's room open with the click of a lock. She crossed through before Carey's door opened, closing the door silently behind her.

Movement brushed through the hall in Carey's room. Gentle whispers told her whoever was in there wasn't alone. No one had reason to feel safe on this train yet.

It only took a moment longer to disentangle the brooch. She slid the box onto Vivian's table and gave it a wary glance. An ominous feeling accompanied the mess of wires. Jenny had been in a lot of film studios, and she'd never seen anything like this. If anything, it looked like the bombs made by subway bombers or disgruntled postal employees in the movies.

Jenny reached toward the box and pulled back. If it was Carey's, it would be a touch safer now, and the voices on the other side of the wall wouldn't be able to find it either. Still she didn't want to leave it out.

She glanced around the room and shoved the box under the lower bunk on the side of the room. The bedding hung over the side and when Jenny lifted it she paused. The standard blanket covered a beautiful quilt of stars made of bright colored fabrics on a white background.

Whether it was Andrew or Viv that had taken it she didn't know. But she pulled it off the bed and wrapped it up with the brooch and flowers.

Jenny plunged into the hallway, turning to the baggage cars and took off in the direction of the last place she'd seen Ron. In a slight detour, Jenny climbed the steps to the upper dining room. The key to the locked room was right where Carey had left it before. Inside, the broken windows gave a full view of the starry sky. It was a beautiful night, aside from the broken glass and dead body.

Jenny tucked the quilt in the corner of the room and pulled the tablecloth off the table and laid it over Chris' still form, then set to work pulling scissors and thread from the sewing kit.

In minutes, the dress was cut to shreds and Jenny had begun stitching the ribbons of fabric together, gathering

255

them around the pole of a beaded floor lamp. It looked a bit like the Mardi Gras version of cousin it. But it was the best Jenny could do.

Finished with the brooch, Jenny loosely stitched it to the pole inside the new fabric dressing. Leaving the thread long enough to reach the staff entrance, Jenny left the entire spool in the corner at the top of the enclosed stairwell, next to the flowers.

It wasn't terrible. With the light on, the fabric glowed. The broken window created a constant breeze, fluttering the fabric around the lamp.

She didn't know if it would work or even if she'd get to attempt it, but Eleanor was the only lure Jenny knew of that would bring Carey to a specific place.

Now she just had to wait.

23

"THIS WAS A TERRIBLE IDEA." Jenny had succeeded in finding a fan in the kitchen below to aid the ghostly appearance of her fluttering purple lamp costume. With the extension cord, she would be able to plug the whole thing in from her hiding place in the stairwell.

She'd left the main door open slightly to lure Carey, hoping his curiosity would take over when his secret prison became not so secret. Forget-me-not petals were scattered down the stairs, and she'd left the brooch just inside the door. The only thing she hadn't done was trail blood down the stairs.

Maybe she should have done that.

Jenny had gotten pretty good at not noticing Chris lying across the room. But that didn't mean she could forget he was there.

She sent him her first intentional glance since she'd gotten in the room. The knife she'd pulled from his body had been bloody, but Chris hadn't bled . . . If she was going to leave blood on the stairs, it would have to be her own.

The bloody knife lay on the ground. her only other option was Eleanor's brooch. Even the knives from the table had disappeared. Which was just as well, since she didn't want them around if she tried to trap Carey inside.

She picked up the brooch. She didn't have to leave a lot of blood, it was a trail, after all, a border thread, not a whole quilt in glowing neon color. The point pressed to her finger without drawing blood. She wasn't very good at hurting herself.

Closing her eyes, she tried not to feel the sharpness of the needlepoint against her skin and pressed harder. Pain emanated from the thin point of the tiny metal dagger, and she opened her eyes.

She hadn't even stabbed herself yet.

With a deep breath Jenny pressed again, this time with her eyes open, determined to finish—

Footsteps pounded up the stairs and slammed against the open door. Jenny jumped as the door swung in, and her finger throbbed with pain. Deep red blood rose around the needle hanging from her skin. She'd pressed further than she'd intended.

Andrew and Thomas stormed into the room.

"Eleanor!" Andrew called with wide eyes.

The fact that he thought he'd seen her was a good sign for Jenny's plan. "She's not here." Jenny gathered herself, hiding her bloody finger. "Where have you been?"

"I was, well—Thomas—" Andrew stopped himself several times before Thomas stepped in.

"I locked him up in my bathroom." Thomas' blunt answer was more direct honesty than Jenny had gotten in a long while.

"The bathroom?" Jenny asked. "I heard you had a secret room in the parlor."

"That's my fault. I heard someone mention it before. They were talking about the train owners having secret hideaways." Andrew raised his eyebrows.

"And you told Viv about the parlor?" Jenny could see where this was going.

"Yeah, how'd you know?" Andrew only hesitated a second before shaking it off. "Anyway, he found me there and knew we'd been working together."

"He told me you were investigating everyone," Thomas said. "I thought that connected you closer to the murder. I told him I'd help and locked him in the closet. Then when Bonnie died, I was sure it was you, until we saw Eleanor."

"I can't believe you saw her." Andrew swallowed and looked away as if trying to hide his emotion. He looked right Chris' body and got a queasy look on his face.

"Carey has been busy," Jenny said.

Andrew looked back at Jenny. "We were coming to help, and saw all the forget-me-not flowers. Thomas thought—" He looked around the room and shook his head. "I got my hopes up, is all. What are you doing here? Why the petals?"

"I was assuming Carey would come back for me. Only he's probably waiting on me, since he has Ron." Jenny paced the floor. "He's right, I should be looking. Ron fell through the roof, he needs medical help."

"What happened?" Andrew's focus tuned into Jenny. "Why does he need medical help?"

"See that?" Jenny pointed to the broken glass. "He fell."

Andrew looked up at the ceiling, speechless. "That would hurt."

"And then Thomas let Carey take him and Stella away." Jenny turned to Thomas.

"I thought I was protecting them." Thomas' eyes shifted across the room.

"Maybe, but I only know one person who would know if there really were a secret room in the parlor." Jenny straightened her shoulders and tried to find her confidence. "Carey. He knows the owner of the train and knew about a secret compartment where he first hid and then stole your gun."

"So, he may not have had Stella there before, but he could have her there now?" Andrew asked.

"And Ron." Jenny affirmed Andrew's thought. Her trust had been stretched beyond capacity, and before the night was through, it would be as thin as webbed iron on adhesive. "You should look for them, please, and meet me back here. I'll be waiting."

WAITING WAS NOT at the top of Jenny's skill set. She hated to waste time and that's all waiting felt like.

Andrew and Thomas had been gone for twenty minutes. Twenty minutes in which Jenny had dripped blood down the stairs, repositioned the brooch and ghost replica for Carey to find, and hid across from Chris' body.

At twenty-one minutes, Jenny abandoned it all.

With Eleanor's quilt in hand, she descended the steps into the kitchen and stood in the doorway to the dining room. The entire car was still. The staff and guests gone, hiding away. It was like watching Main Street of an Old West town at high noon. Tumble weeds would have blown through if they'd been filming the right movie. She hadn't found the gun yet, but Jenny had prepared for a shootout.

She'd sent Thomas and Andrew to the parlor so Jenny turned toward the front of the train and the baggage car.

Bonnie's body lay in the same place, finally covered with a large white tablecloth or sheet. Her nerves lit up, tingling over her skin when she saw herself reflected in the light of the window at the back of the car. It was an impractical bodily response, as it made it as uncomfortable to move as it did to stand still.

She passed through the second baggage car and called out for Carey with no answer.

The quilt was thick and hot on her arm. She hadn't really expected to find him this quickly but disappointment still hung in her sigh.

Jenny stopped herself as she came to the next car, the staff quarters. The whole room was unnaturally dark. There was no sound, no chatting, or snoring men. Jenny squinted into the low visibility. Running a hand beside the door, she flipped on the light switch.

No light reflected off the windows. She touched the blackened glass, her finger coming away coated in coal dust. Someone had blacked out the windows.

"Hello? Carey? I have something you want."

There was no answer. The room was full of empty beds and discarded belongings. Belts, and hats lay on the beds, playing cards were discarded on the corner table. Jenny tried to ignore the barren room as she crossed to the vestibule door and pushed. It was locked.

She reached for the lock with shaking hands. Her heartbeat thrummed through her body, from her overactive pulse to the electricity humming under her skin. The illogic of what she was seeing left too many unanswered questions.

"You're not supposed to go in there."

Jenny spun halfway around to find Carey standing behind her in the center of the car. His foot was propped on the open safe door, swinging it slightly before he stepped off, walking toward her. "That's only for my special guests."

"Like my husband?" Jenny spat. Her fingers gripped the latch, unlocking it.

"I wouldn't do that." He pulled the gun from behind his back, and she froze.

"Oh, good." He grinned and took a step forward as Jenny took a step back. "You do know when to stop. I shouldn't be surprised. You're familiar with this gun, after all. Only two shots have been fired from it so far, which means I've got six left, and you know I'm not afraid to use another one. So," Carey gestured to the quilt she had gripped to her body. "Tell me about that? Have you found her treasure, her secrets?"

Jenny looked down at the quilt in her arms. A trail of red spots ran over the point of a turquoise star. She lifted her finger up and found another spot. Blood. The red soaked into the corner of the bright blue fabric, highlighting the smeared ink of a capital letter E. *The key to her treasure is with her favorite star.* She hadn't noticed the tiny letter before. "The key—"

"Louder, Jenny," Carey drolled. "I'm up here. What was Eleanor hiding from the people she loved most?"

"The key—" She looked up quickly, pressing her finger on top of the bloody letter. "It's gone. Stella looked for it with Andrew and it wasn't there. All that quilt and treasure business was a waste of time."

Carey's gaze faltered. He glanced at the door behind Jenny and back to the quilt, and Jenny knew what she needed to do.

With a step back, she bumped into the wall. "They kept looking, of course, but it's gone. That's what her ghost told me, anyway."

"Her ghost?" Carey laughed. "I almost believed you for a second. I guess Thomas was right. He suspected you were a little crazy. I mean, you'd have to be to plan such a big murder over a woman you only knew from the movies. But you're also an opportunist, and thanks to your little friends, opportunity struck here, didn't it?"

"You can't think those kinds of accusations would hurt when we both know you're the one killing them."

"They should. Because that's what the world is going to hear and remember about you. The secret life of Jenny Doan. Quilter by day, but she'd kill for a little fame."

"No one will believe that."

"They will. It's my job to make people see you the way I want them to. I'm a talent agent. I can spin truth into gold, or in your case iron bars, or bullets, if you prefer." He waved the gun between them for effect and narrowed his eyes at her. "So, tell me what you know about Eleanor's final secrets."

"I know she shared secrets with you and got killed for it," Jenny snarled and stepped to the side, her hip bumping the door handle.

"That's not what happened." Carey kept the gun steady as he shook his head. "You don't know what the treasure is, do you?"

"Does that matter? If she left something behind, you don't have any claim to it." Jenny dropped her arm behind her as if bracing herself against the wall.

Carey's eyes followed the movement before darting back to Jenny's face. "She loved me. She would have been with me if Mr. I-Can-Buy-Your-Love hadn't swooped in. She knew it too. She was leaving him, and we were going to be together."

"Always have, always will, right?" Jenny slowly let her hand drop as she stepped to the side again, in front of the door handle.

Carey inhaled, nostrils flaring when she quoted the engraving on the ring. "Don't say that like you know what it means. I stood by her for years. I was so mad when she married Thomas, but I stood by her, like a good friend should. She thought she was in love, but I knew better, and when things started to go downhill, I was still there. I would do anything for her." He shook his head and aimed the gun at Jenny, catching the quilt as she side-stepped.

The gun went off, hitting the wall behind Jenny. A scream echoed inside the vestibule, followed by pounding and muffled voices. Jenny grabbed the doorknob and twisted, pulling it out and sliding into the vestibule. She pulled the door shut, ready to hold it, and only narrowly missed being shot when another bullet cleared the wood of the thin door panel.

"That's four shots left," Jenny called. She ducked and swiveled away, praying he wouldn't find her from the sound of her voice. "Don't waste them."

Instead of a gunshot, a lock clicked. "Good call," Carey said through the wall.

Something tapped the door, and Jenny stepped back. She looked to the side and saw Stella, gagged and tied to the rail on the wall. Ron had been tied up similarly, on the opposite side of the vestibule.

"But you don't need to worry," Carey continued, his voice crooning in the small quarters. "I know where the treasure is. I just needed to know that you didn't. You've been stepping on my toes since you got here."

"I'm not done yet." Jenny spoke softly, but Ron stomped, and her gaze snapped to his.

He shook his head violently, and she bit her tongue.

"All I wanted was to be with Eleanor." Carey tugged on the door handle, and the knob jostled in front of Jenny. "And finally, I'll get to. We'll all get to, in just a few minutes."

Her skin went cold, and she grabbed the door handle.

"What's in a few minutes?" She yanked on the door. "What are you talking about?"

"I'm sorry you won't get to see it in life. In about fifteen minutes, we'll be in the same place we were when Eleanor died. A beautiful green countryside, next to an expansive desert." He sighed and his footsteps carried him several paces away.

"Now, stay there this time, okay, Jenny? I'm going to collect the treasure and make sure I'm ready to return it to my love before everything blows up."

"Before it—" Jenny hadn't wanted to believe it when she'd seen the box. "It's really a bomb."

She grabbed the door handle and yanked again as he left. She tugged at the door and yelled until she lost her grip and stumbled backward into the door on the opposite side of the vestibule.

"Of course," she muttered. She tugged at that door. It opened into the blackness of the coal car.

She moved over to Ron and pulled the gag from his mouth.

"Jenny, this is too dangerous." Ron immediately began pleading with her. "You can't do this. Please, we need to get help."

"Ron, it's okay." She put a hand to his cheek. She wanted to calm him, but he cringed at her touch. "You don't need to worry. That's what I'm doing. I'm going to get help."

She stepped around the door and pulled Stella's gag out. "I'll be right back."

"Okay." Stella nodded.

Ron thunked his head back against the wall. "Be careful. I mean it." His voice became urgent as she grabbed the door handle to the coal car. "Jenny! No. They're not going to help."

"I have to find someone." She stepped through the door, and something grabbed her shoe, tugging. With a gasp, she pulled away.

"I'm serious!" Ron hissed. "Jenny!"

She stumbled back into the vestibule, her heart racing. "What was that?" she sputtered. "What's in there?"

Ron took a deep breath. "Carey's paying the other conductor," Ron said. "He killed Chris. All Chris's guys are locked up in the tunnel through the coal car. They can't help you even if they want to."

"Okay." Jenny shut the door on her hopes and changed direction. She felt for the edge of the frame and dug in her pockets for something she could use to flip the lock.

"You're still going for the door?" Ron asked.

"I'm sorry." Jenny didn't look over. "We have to get out of here. I don't know how long we have."

"I dropped my pocketknife when I was trying to escape." He paused and Jenny grasped at the thin hope.

"But it's here?" She looked at the floor like it was a black hole. "Give me a second." She knelt beside him, holding his legs for support.

"You won't be able to open that lock as easily as the other ones. It's an outdoor lock."

Against the creak and hiss of the steam engine, she almost didn't hear Ron's voice. "Can you open it?"

"I'll try."

Jenny's hand closed around the cool cylinder of the knife, and she carefully opened the blade.

"Hold very still," she said, feeling her way to the wall and the knots tying Ron in place. He pulled to the side, trying to give her as much room as possible, and in a few seconds, she'd cut the knots free and released him.

He immediately went to work on the lock while Jenny tapped her foot and tugged at stray threads. Her eyes had begun to adjust to the dark, but with the blacked-out windows, there was very little light for her eyes to work with.

Ron pulled back from the handle, and Jenny leaned forward.

"Is it working?" she asked.

"I don't know." The sound of metal on metal tapped and clicked again as Ron returned to the lock. "A light would be nice. Do you have your phone?"

Jenny patted her hips, though she knew it wasn't there. "I haven't had it all night."

"Me neither," he said. "I figured Carey took it."

"The conductor has a key," Stella said from her place against the wall. "He came out once and used it to go through."

Ron turned to Stella. "He'd never give it to us."

"But he has one?" Jenny asked.

Stella nodded. The movement was hard to make out, but Jenny caught it and turned to the opposite door, gripping the handle.

"No. I'm getting it. Jenny, don't confront him. He killed a man."

"We will die too if we stay here." Jenny held the door handle. "You heard Carey. We may already be too late."

"I know." Ron closed his eyes and stood. "Let me go talk to him."

"No." Jenny put her hand out, stopping him. "You need to keep working on this. If I can't get it, we'll need another option."

Ron pulled Jenny into a hug. "I know you can do this. But—" He leaned close, his good cheek pressing to hers. He kissed the side of her forehead. "Be careful."

"I will. If he knows Carey's plan, maybe he'll help us." Jenny kissed him back. "Even if he's getting paid, he can't spend it if he's dead."

24

THE PASSAGEWAY THROUGH the coal car was as black as its cargo. Even with her eyes adjusted to the lack of light, Jenny could only just make out shapes.

Bodies lined the side of the corridor. They hung from a railing, their arms tied up and over a long pole. She looked back for Ron, but she'd shut the door to the vestibule so that if things went poorly, Ron and Stella would stay undiscovered. Finding people in the coal car didn't constitute going poorly, yet.

She made out three bodies hanging from the rail. Her first thought was that they were dead, but a head lifted, and like before, a hand grasped her ankle.

Jenny didn't startle this time, but pulled back sharply, breaking the grip.

"Help me." The man's voice crackled weakly against the noise of the train.

Jenny looked more closely at the man hidden in the dark corridor. She thought she could place him as the large man she'd met in the staff quarters, the one who'd been kind enough to answer her questions.

"What happened?" Jenny asked.

He reached for her again, and she stepped back. She couldn't escape the fear that seemed to hang in the air with the fine mist of coal. Pieces of rope clung to his wrist, scratching her as he attempted to get to her.

Jenny sucked in a breath and took a step along the corridor. "You're not tied up." The engine room waited at the far end of the corrido. She matched his lowered volume against the rattling steam engine. "Why haven't you left?"

"He broke my leg." His voice hitched as someone shoved him.

"Quiet," they said softly. "He'll come back."

Suddenly the gruesome picture of these men's cruel attacker fell into place, and Jenny stared hard at the far door. She would have to face him to get the key.

The man on the ground inched closer. "Please, help me. Help us."

"I'm trying," Jenny said softly. "I'm locked in with a couple others. We need a key. Do you know where Darren keeps it?"

"What key?" someone said, and the second man's voice shushed them both.

"I'm not getting beaten again," the second man said.

"If I don't find the key to the vestibule door, we're all going to die. Darren's working with someone who's got a bomb on the train. We will all die before we get back to Quilter's Square if we don't stop them."

The voices stopped for several seconds before the same doubtful voice spoke up again.

"Are you going to stop a bomb? I don't think so," he hissed. "Our only chance is making it back to the station."

"Don't be stupid." The third man wasn't angry or pleading. "Bobby might already be dead. We have to get out. I don't know where the keys are. He probably wears them, keeps them in a pocket or something."

"By the door," the man at Jenny's feet croaked. She couldn't see what had happened to him, but from the sound of his voice, he'd been hurt badly.

A noise scraped the door in the engine room. "Quiet in there."

Everyone hushed until the sound of movement picked up again.

"Who's in there?" Jenny asked softly.

"Darren, and the guys who didn't fight back." The man closest to her gave the only answer. Everyone else had taken the hint.

"Check the wall by the door," he said. "On the left. I don't know for sure, but he hits that wall every time he leaves."

Jenny moved to the door, brushing lightly against the dusty surface. The clink of cold metal hit her fingers, and Jenny's heart leapt. "Thank you," she whispered. "I'll be back—"

Golden light poured into the hall, blinding her as a voice at the other end of the hall swore. "I told you to be quiet!"

Jenny could only see his silhouette, but she pulled the door open as he roared something about her being where she shouldn't.

She glanced to the men on the walls. Bruises covered their limbs and faces. The dark bruise on one man's face swelled from his eye to his jawline. She slammed the door shut as the figure at the end of the hall barreled toward her.

"Help me, Ron." She pressed her shoulder to the door.

Ron was already beside her, leaning into the blockade. Jenny pressed a key into the door lock, but it didn't turn. The door pulsed outward as she tried again. She shoved the second key in, twisted it, and the lock clicked.

"It worked, but it won't stay," she huffed as the man on the other side pounded.

"You're right. We need to tie it off." Ron moved between Jenny and the door, pulled his belt off, and looped it around the handle. He stretched it to the rail beside Stella. It was inches away, but still too short. He looked back at Jenny as the key turned in the lock.

Ron threw himself against the door, and it became a battle of wills. "Go!" he shouted. "Go! Now!"

Jenny pulled the key out of the lock and rushed to unlock the opposite door, her heart racing at Ron's insistence. She let herself and Stella into the staff quarters. A belt hung off one of the beds, and Jenny grabbed it.

"Here!" She pulled Ron's belt up to attach the two. "I can make it longer."

"Go!" Ron bellowed as the door thumped.

"Okay!" Jenny stammered, dropping the belts. She rarely heard Ron yell, and the look on his face frightened her more than the conductor barreling down the corridor had.

Stella was already halfway through the staff's sleeping car when Jenny followed, moving to avoid the door of the safe, but for the first time, it was closed. Stella ran ahead and held the door for Jenny, following as they passed through the next car.

"Where are we going?" Stella panted as she hurried alongside Jenny's long stride.

"For help. Andrew and Thomas are looking for Carey." Jenny grabbed the next door for Stella. "We need to find them before Carey does."

Stella rushed through the door and screamed, dodging a wooden pole. Carey appeared at the other end. It looked like he had torn a piece of trim from the door frame to attack anyone who entered. He swung again and clipped the back of Stella's head.

"Run!" Jenny shouted as Stella stumbled.

For a moment, Carey was torn between which of the two women he should chase. Jenny took advantage of his indecision. She pulled the sheet from Bonnie's body and hurried into the dining room.

Stella screamed behind her, followed by a heavy thud. Jenny's pulse increased.

She was next.

Carey appeared, breathing heavily, he leaned against the far doorframe.

She used the full length of her stride hurrying to the stairs as Carey spotted her. He growled and lifted the dark wood trim over his shoulder.

By some miracle, Jenny made it to the top of the short flight of stairs before he did. She flew through the door, grabbing the tablecloth from Chris' body as well. With moments to spare, she hid herself in the staff stairwell on the opposite side of the room.

Carey's footsteps tapped lightly across the starlit room on the other side of the door. She almost tripped on an extension cord. She kicked the small pot of flowers she'd left in the corner. She plugged in the lights and across the room, the fan began to blow.

The door crashed open, and Carey stumbled into the stairwell. Pale purple fabric danced in the corner, glowing with ghostly light from the lamp below. The chill of the open window aided the ethereal feel.

Through the gap in the doorway, Jenny only had a limited view of the room. Carey stared, jaw hanging open, chest heaving.

She crouched outside the door with the large sheet in her arms. As he turned in a slow circle, Jenny suspected she just might have done it. She'd have to lock both doors in order to trap him.

Only now did she realize how hard that was going to be.

When his back turned to her, Jenny ran out and threw the sheet over him. His arms flailed, and Jenny slipped the latch outside the door and hurried down the stairs into the kitchen, taking the stairwell that led to the opposite side of the room.

Carey growled above her. She was only halfway up when Carey appeared at the top of the stairs.

"How many times do I have to lock you up?" He came down the steps as Jenny back tracked, but he caught her before she'd gone very far. "I didn't want to waste time killing people not on my list, but you ruining everything."

He pulled her up the stairs and into the dining room. "You've done a great job setting up this little prison. Is that supposed to be a ghost?" He pointed to the lamp and laughed. Jenny wilted. "Did you want to scare me?"

Jenny shook her head. "I don't care if you're scared." She let him drag her across the room where he picked up the pieces of her rope, tsking at them.

Eleanor's brooch was in his front pocket.

While he lamented the lost rope, Jenny reached up and snatched the brooch away. Pulling the pin out, she jabbed his arm with the sharp point.

He howled. Jenny couldn't tell if the sound was in pain or anger, but he let her go.

She dashed away, circling the table to stay out of his range, and froze on the opposite side of the table from Carey.

"Get back here, old woman. You will not beat me," he growled.

"You say 'old woman' like it's a bad thing." Jenny inched left and then right as he circled after her. "Old just means I know better than to listen to you. I don't have to beat you. I don't even *want* to beat you."

The door was a quarter of the way around the table, and based on how Carey mirrored her every move, she'd have to run to get there.

Run, she told herself.

She didn't. Her body didn't cooperate with the command. She walked as fast as many people jogged but running . . . There had to be another way.

He'd dropped the trim board at some point, but that didn't make him any less dangerous. "Then just come here and do what you're told."

"I rarely do as I'm told." It was Jenny's turn to laugh at him. "I'm bringing justice to the woman you killed."

Carey lunged, and Jenny gasped, cutting off her speech. He threw a plate across the table like he was playing table hockey.

"—To the women you've killed." Jenny corrected herself. "And the man! How could you think you'd get away with this?" Jenny sent a plate flying back, followed by a glass.

Carey dodged and lunged for her again. "I'm not trying to get away with anything. I just wanted them to regret her death as much as I do."

As much as I do.

His words chilled the air, resonating in Jenny's soul, taking on a deeper meaning.

He regretted her death because— "You killed her."

"Shut up!" Carey said. "It was their fault."

Jenny pressed her hands into the table. "No one has as much regret as you."

"They made me!" Carey shouted. "Warren was always telling her how much better he was than me. Bonnie used me to make her jealous . . . and Stella, she was so needy. And Andrew . . . No one was ever good enough for her, me especially." Carey's eyes lost focus as he looked through Jenny. "I really wanted to kill Andrew." He shook his head circling closer to Jenny. He kept talking like it made him feel better. "Then she married Thomas! When she was finally leaving Thomas I thought I had my chance. I met her in the caboose and told her I'd take care of her. I proposed and she laughed. She thought it was a joke. She was the one with the gun. She dropped it and I picked it up. I didn't want to kill her. It was the rest of them. No one thought I could or should be with her. So I took her away, to a better place."

"Killing someone is not better." Jenny echoed Carey's movements keeping an eye on the door. She wasn't close enough yet.

"But it's so effective." Carey followed her and she retreated. "And I still want to kill her brother. It would be so right. And Thomas. He really should have been first."

"Aren't you, though? Or is the bomb a ruse?" Jenny inched toward the door. Just a little closer, and she could trap him here. "Did you just want to scare me?" She threw Carey's words back at him with as much mocking as she could muster while fighting for her life.

"You weren't the one I wanted to scare." He refocused on her and let a lazy smile curl his lips. Jenny's blood turned cold. "But sure, a little fear would be nice, before we all meet up with Eleanor."

Ice spidered up the windows, and Jenny pulled back. Maybe it wasn't only Carey's cruel demeanor that made her anxious. She rubbed her arms as they both began exhaling frosted air.

"Eleanor," she whispered.

Carey narrowed his eyes at her, and she scoffed.

Jenny pointed to the windows. "You see all that ice?"

"It's getting cold." Carey looked back and hesitated seeing the patterns on the glass.

Jenny scoffed. "Look closer. You wanted to see Eleanor again?" Flower petals blew across the ground, impervious to the direction of the fan Jenny had set up in the corner. "She's here . . . for you."

Jenny took a step toward the stairwell as Eleanor appeared below the open window. Carey stared, his jaw hanging open. He was seeing his love appear for the first time since he'd shot her.

She was more beautiful than Jenny had ever seen her. Moonlight spilled over her ghostly form, slowly brightening as she absorbed the cold light. Her presence reflected a supernatural luminescence on the broken glass dangling over her head. The delicate shards became an organic chandelier, sparkling like the stars.

Eleanor stared at Carey, blue flowers rising up in a cyclone around her.

Carey never broke his gaze. "Ellie?"

Eleanor shook her head. *"It's gone. Carey, it's gone. You have to help me."*

25

"I'M SCARED. I can't wait till the movie wraps." Eleanor's ghostly face glowed as Carey held her gaze.

He didn't respond like Thomas had, filling in the conversation. He just watched, mouth open, like he didn't know she was just a memory, a ghost loop.

"No, I need to go now. I'll cover the losses. I'm sure I have enough by now, I just have to go." Eleanor shook her head furiously, her hand going to her stomach in between sobs.

"You don't understand. I know it's early, but I could feel it. I'm afraid to tell Thomas." She paused and looked into the distance. "No, I can't go home. We were going to be a family. I ruined it. Help me, please. I'll hurt him so much if he knows I lost our baby. I have to go away forever, or he'll find me. I can't go back to him."

Eleanor sniffled and shook her head. Her arms crossed over her chest as she shook her head more adamantly. "No! Carey. I'm not staying. They'll be fine. I've left them a treasure anyway. They'll know how I feel."

She dropped her head to her hands briefly, wiped away a tear, and laughed. "Oh, Carey. Be serious. You don't have to *marry me. It's not really the fifties. I know how to be single . . . I've been doing it for years."*

Jenny looked at Carey. His brow furrowed, and every few seconds he shook his head. "No, Ellie. I can't do it again."

She looked at him like she saw him. *"Please, I'm not going to marry you. Get up. What if someone comes in?"* Her brow pinched to match Carey's. *"Carey, listen to me. I don't love you like that. And you don't love me. Come on, we can't—I would never do that to Thomas or Bonnie. Where did you get that? We're friends. We've always been. Always have, always will."* Her eyes went wide and her hands came up. She backed away as she talked to the memory of the man in front of her. *"Don't be like this. You know I love you."*

"Ellie. That's enough." Carey rubbed his forehead. "Make it stop, Jenny! I don't know what you're doing, but—"

"I never meant to make you feel like that. I don't want to lose you."

Carey turned to Jenny and shouted. "I said that's enough!"

Eleanor continued paying Carey's regret no heed. "You have to believe me. I'm sorry. Wait! I could try. I do love you. Really. Carey!"

Then the too-familiar gunshot sounded, but the pain didn't hit Jenny this time.

This experience was meant for Carey.

Eleanor fell backward through the glass pane window and into the night. As her glowing form disappeared, Carey ran after her.

While he was chasing her ghost, Jenny hurried to the staff stairs. She pulled the door closed.

Except it didn't close. It was stuck on the thick electrical cord she'd used for the fan and light.

She unplugged it and pulled the cord in. quickly wrapping it together so she could get it out of the way and lock the door.

"Jenny!" Carey called. "You see? You see how Eleanor made me do it? You're going to pay for putting me through that again!"

"Oh shoot." She breathed the words lightly. The extension cord tangled over her feet and hands as she tried to shove it inside the room.

Carey grabbed the door and swung it open, and Jenny threw the tangled cords in his face. He didn't even flinch. He swiped them to the side, grabbing her arm as he did.

"You're not leaving, are you?" He pulled her back into the room, and she stumbled after him. "You've had so many questions about Eleanor. I think we should talk."

"I didn't make that happen. I didn't even know any of that. Well, most of it." Jenny tripped over her words.

"I don't believe you." Carey threw her into a chair.

"What do you want me to say?" Her nerves on high alert, goosebumps flaring with a rush of fear on the back of her neck. Jenny tried to get up, and Carey pushed her down. She whimpered.

"Don't go weak on me now, Jenny. You've been so formidable." Carey's lip hitched up in a snarl. "Is it just that you can't handle being face to face?" He lifted her from the chair by one arm. Holding the pin up to her face and flipped open the sharp needle on the back.

Jenny reached up, squeezing Carey's arm where she could still see blood from when she'd jabbed him with Eleanor's brooch. She knew how badly a needle point injury could hurt, especially when jabbed straight into a muscle like she'd done. It would be fine, but it would take days to heal.

In the meantime, Carey cried out, releasing her. She bolted for the open door.

"No!" he roared. "Don't even think about it!"

He hauled Jenny from the doorway by the arm and pushed her against the wall. In one swift motion, he slashed at her cheek with the pin back. Pain razed the side of her face, and she stumbled away when his grip slacked.

Carey tossed the bloody brooch in her lap like it was nothing. "There you go. Thought I'd return the favor."

Jenny touched her cheek. Pain seared below her fingers with the barest touch. Her stomach turned when they came away red.

"Maybe now you'll remember to do what you're told." He kept his hand on the door, staring down at her.

As she pushed herself up, Jenny clenched the last tablecloth in her fist. As Carey turned, she billowed it over his head and wrapped her arms around him, locking the tablecloth around him.

"What are you doing?" Carey yelled.

Jenny sucked in a breath. "Yeah, about that 'do what you're told' thing." Jenny shook her head and held tight. "Never have. never will."

His arms pressed against Jenny, trying to battle his way into freedom. And they stumbled into the dining room.

The flowerpot landed with a crack on Carey's head and Jenny pulled away. Dirt dusted over Jenny as Carey's body relaxed and he crumpled to the floor. A broken pot of forget-me-nots on the floor by Ron's feet.

She didn't question his presence. There was no time for that. "Thank you!" she said running into his arms. Then she moved to the doorway, pulling him with her.

"Where are you going?"

"We have to hurry. The bomb. I think it's in Vivian's room. I moved it when I thought it was just wires and mess."

They only made it halfway down the stairs before an explosion louder than dozens of gunshots and the screech of iron pistons and brakes reverberated through the night.

THE SUN ROSE on the grand devastation of a pristinely derailed steam engine beside a brand-new crater. A prime example of the bang being worse than the bite, Jenny had never been more grateful to be dealing with an amateur criminal.

The dining cars and several of the standard sleeper cars had jumped the line and now sat on the side of the rails. While no accident was "pretty," this one had no major injuries. The car with the bomb was damaged badly, but no one had been in it thanks to so many leaving early.

Only a handful of sleeper cars had tipped, and even then, they were only leaning off the tracks.

"How long before help gets here?" Stella asked.

She and Jenny strolled along the corridor of the first-class train cars toward the lounge, avoiding the influx of passengers in the only remaining "safe" cars still securely on the tracks.

"Thomas said they'd be here by noon. Then it will be half a day before they can get us all back to Quilter's Square." Jenny stopped at the door to the vestibule. "I need to go check on Ron. Do you mind if we go out?"

"Not at all." Stella followed Jenny outdoors. "I like it out here. Besides, there's a little too much gossip circling the lounge area for me."

The train wasn't excessively long, somewhere between fifteen and twenty cars. They walked past the central cars of the train that had been blocked off to the guests and reentered the train on the derailed and still upright baggage cars.

Thomas and Ron stood watch over a bound Carey and Darren, the conductor, while the engine crew had been removed from their captivity and Andrew was checking their injuries.

Jenny met Ron with a renewed affection since the start of their train adventure. She kissed his cheek and stood by him while he kept one eye on their prisoners. "Every time I'm away I miss you."

"I can tell." Ron happily returned her kiss and settled back into his work.

Stella didn't stick around. Giving the two men plenty of berth, she made her way to the next car to check on her brother.

"He hasn't said anything about where the quilt is, has he?" Jenny asked, watching Carey.

Ron shook his head. "He's not said a word. Not even to request food."

She hadn't seen it since he'd taken it from her before getting locked in the vestibule. Now that she had seen letters on the block corners, she wanted to look for more. And her pictures weren't cutting it.

"Well, the treasure may really be lost this time." Jenny tried to inject the statement with an element of teasing or pleasantry, but it was more sad than anything else.

Ron sighed and Jenny squeezed his hand. "I'm going to go see if Andrew needs help."

She skirted the captives similarly as Stella had, giving them plenty of space.

She walked into the staff quarters and saw Stella and Andrew visiting with another man. Stella pointed at Jenny and whispered something to him.

"It's her!" the man said and began applauding. The other men joined him. "You did it! Thank you! You saved us."

Only five of the six beds in the staff quarters were occupied. One of the men had died, probably before Jenny had found them, which brought the train ride's fatalities up to a total of three.

The gratitude of this limited crowd was overwhelming. She blinked back tears and gave herself permission not to reply until she'd gotten closer so she could speak without crying. "I wasn't alone. You have eight heroes in the room today. I can't believe what you went through. Thank you for what you sacrificed."

Stella and Andrew echoed her, and the group settled into rounds of checking patients and resting.

Jenny crossed the car and looked through the previously coal-blackened window. The belt still hung from the door, and Jenny backed away, anxiety over what they'd done rolling around inside her like mud over a new quilt. She'd left those men who cheered her as a hero in a room with their attacker.

She hadn't had another option, but as she smiled and wished them well, she felt sick.

"I'm doing another search for the quilt," she said, backing out of the car. "Let me know if anyone remembers hearing anything about it."

"Of course." Stella straightened a blanket from a starry-eyed man sporting a scraggly gray beard.

Stella caught her before she left. "Andrew and I are both really grateful for what you've done. You know that, right?"

The sludge dredged up inside her again. "I feel like I may have done more damage than good this time."

Stella shook her head. "You saved my life several times over. You made hard decisions, and in the end, we were able to find my sister's killer and save the lives of everyone still on the train. Don't forget that."

"Thank you." Jenny smiled. "You're an excellent cheerleader."

Stella hugged her and went back to help her brother.

Jenny stood next to the safe. It had been closed up after Carey left her in the vestibule. Right after he stole the quilt.

She looked at the safe curiously. It was on the small side, but large enough to put a quilt in if it were alone. "I'll be right back."

She retrieved several sets of keys before returning. One of them was Carey's, one Darren's, and one had come from Chris, though those ones looked more like tiny locker keys and old skeleton-type keys.

The safe required two keys. She started with Carey's and found the first. A long fat brass key slid into the first lock perfectly. Jenny went through nearly every other key before trying one of the tiny locker-looking keys. She almost laughed when it twisted and the second lock clicked.

She looked at the key ring. There were at least a dozen of the tiny keys, and they all looked identical.

Stella leaned over her shoulder as Jenny giggled. "What?" Stella asked.

Jenny lifted the key ring. "He really was paranoid about losing his keys. He had a dozen of these, and it was the other one that got stolen." She pulled the thick door open, and Stella gave a sobbing laugh.

The quilt lay in the safe, folded and waiting.

"It's here." Stella pulled it out and dropped to the floor, holding it. "Andrew! We found her quilt."

When he was there, Jenny leaned in close. "I think I know what the key is too."

Both their heads lifted to look at Jenny.

"What is it?" Andrew asked.

Jenny glanced to the men in their beds. They appeared to be resting. Jenny looked for the blood she'd left on the turquoise quilt and in the process spotted another letter. "Look at this." She pointed to the blood-spotted letter. "They just looked like random marks on some of the blocks. But the blood highlighted letters. What do you think?"

Stella and Andrew opened the quilt by a couple of folds, excitement dancing in their eyes.

"That is totally something Elle would do," Andrew murmured his nose to the blocks. "It looks like all of them have letters. Maybe it's a word-search kind of puzzle."

"Not all of them have letters." Stella pointed to a string of three stars that had no letter on the corner of the blocks. "Where should we open the quilt up?"

"Probably not here." Andrew picked up the quilt. "I'll get Viv to watch out for these guys for a bit and we can meet up in Stelle's room. Sound good?"

Stella narrowed her eyes at Andrew. "You're not going to run off with it, are you? Maybe I should take it, since I can go straight to my room."

Andrew hesitated. "I'm not going to run off with it." He let out a breath and handed it to Stella. "It's just hard to let go of it now that there's a real clue. Keep it safe. I'll meet you there."

26

"THERE ARE NEARLY a hundred letters in here. That's too many." Stella's complaint wasn't unfounded. They'd settled in her room with the quilt spread out on the large bed and confusion on their faces.

Looking down at her list of possible clue words, Jenny started throwing out ideas. "I found flannel, bread, and newsquack-L-er," Jenny chuckled at her fake word. "That last one is a compound word for 'quilting updates' from our duck mascot, Chuck—Minus the 'l', it's news-quacker . . . Huh," Jenny hesitated. "Maybe quackler sounds better."

Andrew tossed his paper on the bed and dropped into a chair. "Elle didn't leave us a note about your quilting updates. It's not like a secret decoder, telling us to drink our Ovaltine. This is Elle. She's trying to talk to us."

"She's trying to talk to *you*." Jenny tapped her pen on the paper and stood. The whole quilt had to make a different picture. "What did she say to you before? What was her first clue?"

Andrew didn't even have to think about it. "*The key to the treasure is with her favorite star.* Stella and the quilt."

"Okay. The key to her treasure is with her favorite star." Jenny tipped her chin to the side and looked at the brightly colored stars. "What was Stella's favorite color?"

"Purple," they both said in unison.

Jenny raised her eyebrows. "Well, that was easy." Jenny pointed at the nearest purple star. "Find all the letters on the purple blocks."

"Of course!" Stella stepped back and started scanning for blocks. She pointed to one and shook her head, then started again with the next. "This isn't right."

"I know." Jenny had a whole list of blank purple squares.

"There's no letters on the purple ones." Andrew raised an eyebrow at them. "Care to try again?"

Jenny took a deep breath, scanning the quilt. "*The key . . . is with her favorite star.*" She frowned and tried to make sense of the chaos. "You sure her favorite star is only a reference to Stella? Maybe she had a favorite constellation or her astrology sign? When was her birthday?"

"No." Andrew shook his head. "It's Stella. She's been 'our favorite star' since she started film school."

Jenny wasn't sure, but it seemed like there was a touch of bitterness as he said it.

Stella smiled weakly. "He's right. Every time I came home, she'd greet me with 'There's my favorite star!' like I was twelve. I never grew out of it, and she never got tired of it. It was embarrassing."

Jenny sat up. "Our favorite star, my favorite star, but the clue says *her* favorite star." She looked at Stella. "What's your favorite color?"

Stella looked surprised. "I don't have one."

Jenny's excitement died as Andrew laughed.

"Sorry," Stella said. "I've never had a favorite color. Elle knew—" Stella cut herself off, a thoughtful expression crossing her face, and Jenny and Andrew looked at her.

"What is it?" Andrew leaned forward, his attention fully on his sister.

Stella shook her head. "Do you remember when we were little how Mom got us those glow in the dark stars for our bedroom? Mine were pink and yours were blue."

"Kind of." Andrew furrowed his brow in thought. "I remember you were never happy with yours... And we fought over the ones that fell, because Mom told us they were—"

"Wishing stars. Yeah, but that's not why we fought over them." Stella's smile had spread, but her eyes were unfocused. "I liked yours better, but you'd never let me have them."

"Oh geez, I remember that." Andrew laughed. "You were so stubborn."

"Well, I needed one of your wishes." She punched her brother lightly and dropped her eyes, nostalgia clouding her vision. "Because all my little six-year-old heart wanted was to be just like you."

"You're lying." Andrew shifted his jaw and glared at her. "You just wanted what you couldn't have."

Stella shook her head. "Elle snuck me one of your stars the next time they fell. I kept that blue plastic wishing star for years."

"Her favorite star." Andrew's glare softened. "So, I was your favorite star?"

Stella grinned. "I guess so."

"Okay, so, blue?" Jenny asked, and Stella nodded.

This time they came up with a list of fourteen letters.
GRELNROESEFTE

"Greln Rosefte." Stella looked at the letters. "That mean anything to you?"

"Ha, ha." Andrew fake laughed and looked down at his paper. "Maybe I'm not your favorite star after all."

Stella shook her head. "No. That was it. I'm sure. And it's just like Eleanor to make clues out of memories."

"You're right." Andrew smiled at Stella. "Okay, what words can we make here?"

"I see stronger—treefrog—" Stella didn't sound very confident.

"Engrose reel." Jenny gave a flourish as she produced another nonsense word.

"We have to use all the letters." Andrew rolled his eyes. "Greenest role . . . f. Shoot, so close. Frole?"

"This is stupid." Stella frowned. "It's still too many letters."

"You're right." Jenny said. "Look at this, though. There's one blue star in each row. We found them at random. What if we do it in order?"

Both siblings nodded and began putting the stars in order.

"Green Ro Self-T," Stella pronounced. "Is that like a kind of selfie? Are we looking for a picture?"

"I don't think so," Andrew muttered, staring at the letters. "What about Green Rose Left?"

"Where are we supposed to find the left green rose? That doesn't make any sense. They don't even make green roses unless it's Saint Patrick's Day."

"They're right here." Jenny pointed to the ground.

The floral rugs in Stella's bedroom had large corner bouquets, each one featuring a green rose.

Stella went to each of her roses. "Okay, so where's the treasure?"

They scanned the room.

"Well, if you're standing in the doorway, this is left." Jenny pointed, and Stella shook her head.

"Except that my room was adjoining hers. She always came in that door." Stella turned as if coming into the room through the side door. "So left is there."

"So, it's this one." Andrew walked over to the corner rose and looked between them. "It's the overlapping left if you use both directions."

"That's got to be it." Jenny followed him. "Green rose left." She looked at it, circling the hooked floral design. It had several loose threads but no directions.

She walked around the room and did a quick examination of the other florals. The only difference was that Eleanor's Left Rose was more worn.

"Can we move the dresser?" Andrew asked.

"Why?" Jenny didn't know what he was getting at, but moving the dresser would need more muscle than they had.

"Maybe it's underneath that corner of the rug?"

He was just guessing but it gave Jenny an idea. She hurried back to the rug and pulled at the loose strings. Nothing happened, but as she looked at the rose, she noticed all the loose threads were around the border of the rose.

"Help me," Jenny said and a slight chill cooled her skin. Jenny smiled.

Eleanor was excited too.

With all three of them tugging at the edges, they managed to lift the rose out of the carpet. A thin gold key lay beneath.

Andrew whooped, and Stella frowned, crossing her arms.

"Great," she said. "What does it go to?"

Jenny pulled a small note from the underside of the carpet. It had sticky glue lines over the letters, but the words were clear.

> —*I love you both. You are the stars of my sky. Use this key to find what Thomas will have hidden. In the journal with the green rose.*

"The green rose, again. You think it's the one from Thomas' room?" Andrew sounded nervous. "The green journal?"

"Don't you?" Jenny asked.

He sat down on the bed. "If it is, then it's over. Eleanor's last treasure hunt is gone. And I found the treasure before we even finished."

Jenny shook her head. "Not quite. The treasure is what's in the book and that's what this—" she picked up the key and put it in Stella's hand. "—will give you."

THE VINTAGE TRAIN limped into Quilter's Square with a partial crew, broken and blacked out windows, and a full array of terrified passengers. The sound system crackled on with Thomas' voice as the brakes screeched and pistons hitched.

"Ladies and gentlemen. We want to apologize for the distress and challenges of this trip. Our condolences and prayers go out to the families of Bonnie Beal, Garrett Brandt, Chris Wiley, and Robert Johns."

Camera crews huddled close on the vacant platform. Word of the deaths and drama had somehow reached the media. Cherry waved her arm as high as she could, her citrus orange pants standing out from the crowd. Her excitement cooled as she took in the state of the train.

Jenny and Ron zipped up their luggage and made their way to the lounge. Scanning the crowd, she saw a brunette she hoped was Stella. "I'll be right back." She moved through the crowd, leaving Ron with the luggage. "Stella?"

Jenny turned to the crowd. Stella wasn't anywhere but a few moments later Andrew appeared.

"Hey Jenny, I wanted to thank you again for all your help. This journal is gonna open doors for Stelle and me."

"Really?" Jenny glanced over his shoulder. She still hadn't seen Stella. "Is it more than a journal, or is she really insightful?"

Andrew laughed and patted a thick rectangle in his pocket. "Both. We learned a lot in here. Including how much we'd misjudged some people. Elle had a talent for loving people."

"Which I'll miss everyday." The salt-and-pepper haired man came to stand beside them.

Jenny flinched and looked toward the engine. "Weren't you just on the PA? You must have been running."

"Pre-recorded." Thomas waved her question away. "I didn't want to forget anyone, so I did it this morning while we were waiting on the train rescue."

"I see Stella over there. I have to go. Bye Jenny, Thomas." Andrew's grip tightened around the journal, and Jenny watched as he walked away.

"Jenny." Thomas' voice called her back with his confident charm that wouldn't be ignored. "I want to know if you'd be interested in consulting on another film. Depending on how this one does, of course. I might be doing a follow up. 'Quilted Medal of Honor.' It would be set after the war, and the soldier's girl, the quilter, she becomes a spy, and they send messages behind enemy lines with their quilts and fabric supplies, while she falls in love with another spy and has to choose, either her first soldier, the disabled medal of honor winner, or the handsome—"

"I'm not interested." Jenny waved her hand, cutting him off.

"Does it make a difference if she stays with the first guy?" Thomas hunched into the intensity of his stare, waiting for her to fall in line.

"I'm not sure I can handle another of your films. The adventure and risk get a little too true to life."

"What if Stella comes back as Madeline, our beautiful and brave quilting spy?"

"I hope she does. She would do an excellent job." Jenny patted Thomas' arm and paused. She recognized the trench coat from various clandestine meetings over the past weekend. "Would you mind signing an autograph for me? I have a friend who's a big fan."

"You turn down my offer of work, and then you ask for an autograph?" Thomas rolled his eyes, reaching for his pockets. "Yes, I'll send her an autograph. Do you have paper?"

Jenny shook her head apologetically. "Sorry. I'm sure you don't just carry around headshots."

She laughed, and Thomas swallowed an embarrassed chuckle. Jenny's laugh faded into shock.

"You carry around headshots?"

"I mean, small ones." He reached into his coat and pulled out a rolled, glossy eight-by-ten.

"Small. Because it's so challenging to keep up with the poster-sized versions."

"It really is." Thomas made a face and brushed his sleeve. "I tried a long time ago but that was just embarrassing." With a flourish of a pen he signed and handed over the picture. "Here you go." With only a slight hesitation Thomas leaned in closer. "You don't happen to have a theory about who shot me, do you?"

Jenny shook her head. "Not yet." Jenny patted his arm and smoothed the corner of his collar. "Nice coat, though." Jenny paused. "Did you find it in Bonnie's room with her drawer full of pills?"

"What drawer full of pills?" he asked, his face a mask of innocence. "You're not suggesting that Bonnie—No, that's none of my business. And anyway, it's best not to speak ill of the dead." He lifted his lips in a half smile. "Good to see you, Jenny. Let me know if you change your mind about the sequel." He reached into his coat again and pulled out a wallet-sized version of his headshot with a phone number and email on the back.

"Nice to give people options on the size of the headshot." Jenny held the card up, tipping it in an informal salute.

Thomas grinned and slid into the crowd. She tried to keep her eye on him and couldn't. The trench coat was impressive camouflage.

Jenny looked back to where she'd left Ron. He waved, and Jenny wove through the crowd to catch him.

"Let's go." She looked him over. No blood or obvious injury. "My assistant will have a lot of questions for us."

"Better get started," Ron said.

They stepped off the platform, and right away Cherry had her arms around Jenny. "I'm so glad you're home! I heard all these terrible things, but you never even called!"

"I know." Jenny returned her hug and walked away from the train with her arm over Cherry's shoulder. "It was just nonstop."

"No!" Cherry's pinched brow and dropped jaw were very gratifying. "This was supposed to be a relaxing train ride."

"You forgot." Ron was right behind them. "Jenny doesn't relax."

Cherry laughed, and Jenny rolled her eyes.

"Well, as long as neither of you were there when the giant window fell into the room, I'll be okay," Cherry said.

Jenny exchanged a glance with Ron, and she pinched her lips into a bright smile. "I'm sure it would have been terrible."

Cherry narrowed her eyes and turned her gaze from Jenny to Ron. She lifted a single eyebrow. "You should think about replacing your razor, Ron. Your cheek got all scratched up along the edge of your beard."

"You should have seen it yesterday." Jenny let out a breath and stopped. Stella and Andrew huddled together away from the crowd. Jenny started in their direction, sliding her arm off Cherry's shoulder. "I need to go say goodbye to these two. I'll be right there."

Cherry nodded and started asking Ron about the details of the train. The two of them talked train models and gears that Jenny had no desire to understand.

The Grace siblings were in deep conversation. The journal wasn't visible but, like before, Andrew patted his pocket and Stella nodded, tears flowing.

Jenny stuttered in her progress across the platform. But Stella had already seen her and ran toward her wrapping Jenny in a huge hug. "Thank you for everything! I'm so grateful for what you did and so grateful to know the truth."

Jenny let Stella pull her to be by her brother, her arm around Jenny's waist. "I feel the same way." *Grateful to be alive.* "Your family made this an unforgettable experience. I hope you got what you needed. Thomas gave you Eleanor's brooch, right?"

"He did. And we want you to have this." Andrew opened Eleanor's journal and pulled a thick string of jewels out of the back of the book. "I wanted to give it to you earlier but I had to check with Stella first."

"Is that Eleanor's necklace?" Jenny's eyes widened "It was there the whole time?"

Stella nodded. "Right under our noses."

"Or roses," Andrew teased, laughing alone at his joke.

Jenny shook her head. "I can't. It's too much. This is your sister's treasure."

"She left us more than one treasure." Stella looked at Andrew and put her arm around him too. "I have my family back."

"And the brooch." Andrew laughed.

"Right." Stella laughed softly. "And I can actually wear that. That necklace and I don't work together. I'm allergic to almost all metals. It's very difficult."

"I can imagine." Jenny looked at Andrew and he blushed handing Jenny the necklace. "I really thought Thomas had strangled you with this that first night."

"Really?" Stella's brow furrowed. "Why?"

Andrew put a hand on Stella's shoulder. "We were grasping at straws. But Thomas told Jenny he'd caught you trying it on and I let one thing lead to the next and we were banging down your door."

"They did catch me. But that was ages ago and it burned me terribly. That's how I knew I couldn't keep it." Stella gave the necklace a dangerous look. "Besides, Thomas didn't hurt me. I shot him. Luckily, someone hit me and I'm a terrible shot. I didn't know why he covered for me."

"Wow." Jenny said slowly. "I was so sure. My only other possibility was Vivian but that played out differently than I'd thought too."

"You weren't wrong." Vivian appeared beside them and Stella gasped. "I was in the room. I'd gone to check on Thomas and saw Stella with the gun. I just wanted to stop her. So I grabbed something and swung it at her, I don't even know what it was. But I was holding my belt too and it hooked her neck. When Thomas turned and she shot him I got scared and my belt got tangled. As I pulled it back she fell, and hit her head." Vivian's eyes were on the floor, her hands clasped in front of her. "I ran away when I heard Jenny calling and I didn't know what to do. I'm so sorry."

"Are you kidding?" Stella grabbed Vivian in a hug. "You were so brave! I'd hope everyone would have the courage to try and stop a shooting."

"That's not all." Vivian held out her hand. "Here's Eleanor's ring. I can't keep it. Not knowing what it means."

"I gave it to you." Andrew shook his head. "I don't want it back." He pulled Vivian fully into their circle. "I think Elle would have wanted you to have it. You were friends. Consider it good luck."

"Now we all have a piece of Eleanor." Stella smiled.

"And I like mine best." Andrew said pulling out Eleanor's journal from his pocket, a kind of reverence on his face.

"Thank you both." Vivian hugged Andrew and Stella.

"I couldn't have a better friend." Stella hugged her and waved goodbye as she left.

Andrew cleared his throat beside them. "There's an entry in Eleanor's journal I wanted to read to you, if we have time."

Jenny and Stella agreed and Andrew opened the book. "It's one of her last entry's, right next to the opening for the necklace." He flipped a few more pages and started reading.

"I think Thomas has finally come around. He asked if we could name the baby Andrew Thomas if it's a boy." Andrew paused grinning at them, then kept going. *"Of course, I agreed and if it's a girl, I want her to be called Mary Estelle. Then I'll have two favorite stars.*

"I count the days till the little life inside me is in my arms. Thomas Quinn hasn't been the man I thought he was, but if there's one thing I know, it's that he'll take care of me. And soon I'll get to take care of my loves again.

"As Momma said, beautiful things live and die in this world every day, and all we can do is help the process. Then she would ask me, 'Which do you choose? Living? Or Dying?'

"We are beautiful things and I want to live."

"She left the world too soon." Andrew closed the journal and smiled.

"But she loved us." Stella took Andrew's hand.

"And her baby," Andrew said softly.

A gentle breeze ruffled Jenny's hair, warm air dancing over her skin. Her first instinct was to search for a ghost, and Jenny laughed at herself. The warmth had never been part of Eleanor's presence. She was cold.

Blue petals danced over the platform, and Stella sucked in a breath. "Forget-me-nots."

Eleanor appeared again. Stella looked right through her, and even Andrew sighed. He bent to pick up a petal, but he couldn't see his sister.

"Thank you." Eleanor whispered.

Jenny couldn't tell which of them she was speaking to, so she smiled and took a step back. "I need to go. Have a safe trip home."

Stella nodded. "You too. I'm ready to go home."

Andrew stuck the book in his pocket. "Me too."

As they walked away, a beautiful woman in a purple suit with bright red lips, dark hair, and a pill box hat walked between them. Her hands held the three of them together.

Jenny didn't turn until Cherry slipped her arm around Jenny's waist.

"Well, I need a nap, and I've only heard the stories about the last few days. I bet you're exhausted." Cherry looked up at Jenny.

"I feel about as alive as a dress form." Jenny tried not to smile. But she couldn't help it. "Let's go home." She slid an arm around Cherry's waist and started toward the exit. When

Ron joined them, she slid an arm around his waist as well, echoing the position of Eleanor and her siblings.

"It really is gorgeous here," Cherry said. "The stonework is so beautiful . . . Not to mention the trains and the living history all over the building. Maybe we can come back some time."

"Not too soon." Ron muttered.

Jenny laughed and Ron chuckled, looking down at Jenny. It was contagious, and soon Cherry had joined them.

"Or not," Cherry said, giggling.

Jenny slowed their pace as they reached the center of the grand hall. A medallion of cream and gold marble shaped a large Lone Star block surrounded by a border of Friendship Stars.

Jenny pulled her husband and friend close. "Cherry, if it's important to you, I'll come. And Ron, the same goes for you. I'm tired of being tired and missing out on experiences because we're so busy. I want to live my life—every day. I've recently been told that beautiful things live and die in this world every day, and all we can do is help the process. We just have to choose if it's living or dying."

"There is no holding still in this life," Cherry drawled. "I know which one I choose."

"Loving, please." Ron leaned over, kissing the side of her forehead.

"You mean living." Jenny chuckled. "It's living and dying, not loving and dying."

Ron harrumphed. "That may make more sense, but I like mine better."

Ron's hand tightened around her waist, and she leaned against his shoulder, feeling safe for the first time in days.

She looked up at her husband and pulled her friend over into a spontaneous group hug.

"Me too," Jenny said as a warm breeze lifted the edge of her cardigan and pale blue petals danced across her feet. "I choose loving every day . . . it's so much better."

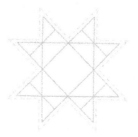

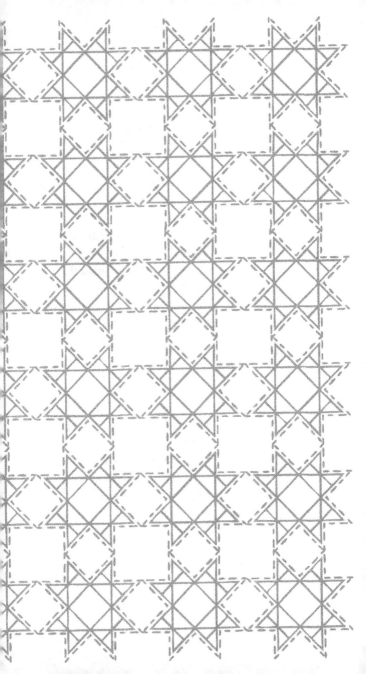

Acknowledgments

Thank you to everyone who has been so patient with me these last couple years. I could not do this without such a supportive family. As my craft grows I've found this book inparticular to have been a learning and growing experience.

I need to acknowledge my husband Q. Alex and my two dearest and best friends, Tamara Heiner and Heidi Boyd. The three of you are my angels and I literally would not have finished this without you. Thank you for saving me with words, food, tea, and love.

And thank you to you, my readers. Thank you for your patience and excitement as I've grown as an author and as my characters have grown. Jenny and Ron are largely based off my parents, but they've taken on a life of their own in these books and I've truly loved writing their stories. Jenny Doan and the Missouri Star Quilt Company have been a huge asset in that regard, and I want to thank them as well.

Here's to many more stories, and mysteries, and adventures. Happy sleuthing!

— Hillary

My name is Hillary Doan Sperry. I'm a quilter and a writer among many other things that make up me. I love steak, feta and cheesecake and the glorious smell of walking through a fabric store!

My favorite color combo is turquoise and a soft coral. And I absolutely adore dreaming up strange new things for Cherry to wear when she's hanging out with Jenny in the Missouri Star Mystery books!

If you want to read more of my books check out your favorite library or online through my website hillarysperry.com; on the MSQC website or your favorite online retailer! Thanks for reading with me!